forever,
or a
long, long
time

ALSO BY CAELA CARTER

My Life with the Liars

forever, or a long, long time

CAELA CARTER

HARPER

An Imprint of HarperCollinsPublishers

Library of Congress Control Number: 2016949993
ISBN 978-0-06-238568-0
Typography by Erin Fitzsimmons
17 18 19 20 21   PC/LSCH   10 9 8 7 6 5 4 3 2 1
❖
First Edition

For my family: G and E (and also B)

THEORY #1

We come from the ocean, my brother and me. We were rolled out of sand at the bottom of the water, in the very darkest part of the earth. Our fingers were formed first, tiny branches of sand hardening into tubes. Twenty little fingers laid on the bottom of the ocean. They swung with the waves down there. Our fingers rocked under the sharks and the stingrays, under the dolphins and the guppies, far away from the coral reefs, deep down where the sea monsters might live because it's too dark to see.

That's where we come from.

Our fingers got sick of being fingers, so they reached for more. Two fingers worked together, making a little bead of sand, until they could squish all the beads together to form hands. Four hands made four arms. Four arms made two bodies, four legs, two heads, four eyes, four feet, four ears, two brains. Two hearts.

Then we crawled on our twenty little fingers and our twenty little toes, Julian and me. We crawled and we crawled until we tumbled out of the waves and onto the shore.

We're the same. We're the Onlys. We came from the ocean.

One

FAMILIES ARE CUTE AND GROSS

I'M THE TALLEST FOURTH GRADER, WHICH means I never get to stand in front. My shoulders are squished between two of the boys and I'm on tippy-toes but I still can't see into the glass tank. The girls and boys in the front say "eww" and others say "ooh." Some say "so cute!" and some say "yuck!"

I want to know which I think, but I can only glimpse a tiny bit of Pringles's white fur. Pringles the Mouse is our class pet. It was my turn to take her home for the weekend last Friday, but Ms. K said I would have to wait because Pringles was very pregnant and Ms. K didn't want my person to have to deal with mouse babies over the weekend, in case that was when it happened.

But now it's the next Thursday. We've been waiting for the baby mice for four days already.

After a few minutes, there are more "ewws" and "yucks" than "oohs" and "cutes," so Ms. K says, "If you're in the front row sit down. Let the tall kids take the front for a few minutes."

Ms. K might be the best person ever made. She makes me feel like my heart is glowing, like it's the sun. She makes me feel like my brain is as sweet as cotton candy.

Sometimes I hate her, though. I'm bad like that.

The shorter kids sit down and I move up and press my nose against the glass of the tank. Inside, Pringles is curled up sitting on what looks like a grown-up's slimy purple thumb.

"Purple?" I say.

"Ms. K, Flora's standing too close," a boy—Brian—yells.

"Tell her to back up, Ms. K," Lisa says.

I don't know why they talk about me like that. It's almost like they think if they said "Flora, back up," it would sound like another language to me.

I back up a few inches, without Ms. K telling me to.

I can still see Pringles. She's sniffing like crazy, running her nose and whiskers all over the slimy thumb. She's using her arms to rub her own furry belly and moving her nose and arms quick-quick-quicker than she ever does.

Then there's another one. Another awful slimy purple thing being pushed and pulled from beneath her.

"Another mouse baby!" Lisa yells, and the girls who were sitting run up to try to see around the tall kids and everyone's yelling and whooping and it's all "cutes" and "yucks."

I can't decide which I think it is: cute or gross. It's sort of both, I guess.

It's very loud in the classroom until Ms. K says "shh."

We're like soldiers when she says "shh." We're quiet. We stand straight. We stop what we're doing and look at her.

"That's enough," she whispers. "If we want these babies to stay safe and turn into good mice, we have to let Pringles care for them in peace. Return to your desks and open your religion books."

It's May already. Ms. K has been training us since September to listen to her. It's like Ms. K is more interesting than purple slimy cute-and-gross mouse babies in the corner of the classroom even though we see Ms. K every day and we've never seen them before.

Ms. K is part genius because this stuff always works. We're calm. We have glossy religion books on our desks with shiny pictures of a white Jesus hugging a trillion white kids even though my person says there's no way Jesus or the kids he hugged were white.

We've almost forgotten about the mice when Ms. K says, "Are there any questions?"

Every single hand goes up. Except mine. I'm working on hand-raising. That's what my last report card said.

Flora has some excellent points but she needs to work on raising her hand.

"David?" Ms. K calls on the boy next to me.

"What will we name them?" he asks.

"Hmm, that's a good question," Ms. K says. "How about this? For your religion homework tonight, I'd like you to each write a list of four mouse names. We'll work together tomorrow to choose the best ones."

Everyone nods fast-fast. That's the best homework ever.

"Any other questions?" Ms. K says.

"Will they live in the cage with Pringles forever?" Sue asks.

Ms. K shakes her head. "Mouse mothers are different from human mothers," she says. "Human mothers like to love their babies forever. But mice have instincts, which mean they need to live on their own soon after they're born. They'll stay in the cage for four weeks, then we'll work on finding new homes for them. Some of the other teachers are interested in one of these mice as a class pet, too."

Human mothers love their babies forever.

I feel the eyes of everyone on my braids. Everyone knows my human mother situation.

I can't stand all the eyes. "What about the other mice?" I shout. I don't raise my hand.

"Which ones, Flora?" Ms. K asks. "And raise your hand."

I raise it this time but I don't wait for her to call on me before I talk. "The ones without."

Ms. K freezes, her mouth half open. I've never seen the look on her face before.

"Without what, Flora?" she asks.

I can't say it. I know the words. I know exactly what I'm trying to say. But the most important words are too heavy. They sink to the bottom of my stomach and I'll never get them out.

"What about the mice like me?" I ask, instead.

After another frozen second, Ms. K's hand lands on the top of my head. "Flora, you are our one and only," she says.

I shake my head. I'm not a one and only. I'm always forgetting how Ms. K doesn't really know Julian, so she doesn't know about me *and* Julian. And besides, there are other kids like us, in the way I'm talking about. We used to know a lot of them.

I'm sure Ms. K is going to ask me what I'm talking about. I'm sure she's going to squat by my desk and address my question in a way that makes me feel special but that the entire class can hear and be interested in. I'm sure Ms. K is the person who can tell me where mice come from if they don't have a mother.

But she doesn't.

She lets out a series of commands and before I can even think, our books are open, and she's talking about Jesus.

She didn't answer my question.

The rest of the day, I hate her.

That afternoon I sit at the kitchen island with my religion notebook in front of me. I write the date and my name at the top of the page, the way we're supposed to. Then I start chewing on the eraser of my pencil, thinking about mice names.

1. *Julian*

My brother, Julian, is behind me watching a cartoon, which he gets to do in the afternoon because third graders only get one little worksheet for homework but fourth graders get piles and piles and piles. Julian is a good name. Julian is the only person I've never hated. Sometimes I'm mad at him because he steals extra food off my plate and sneaks it into his closet and I think he should only steal food from his own plate. Sometimes he cries when I want to turn his cartoons off and watch a few minutes of a show about dancing teenagers who are real actors and not drawings, and so we argue. But I don't hate him suddenly and fiercely. I don't hate him the way I sometimes hate Ms. K and my person and Dad and all the good people.

It's because Julian is like me: mostly bad, a few dashes of good, and heaping spoonfuls of confused.

Ms. K is wrong when she says I'm a one and only. Julian and I, we're two and Onlys.

"What are you working on now?" my person asks. She's got a pot in one hand and her shoulders are crooked, which means the pot is heavy. There's steam coming off of it and fogging up her glasses, which she's wearing right now even though it's before dinner, which means she had a hard day and her eyes are tired.

"Religion," I say. "Mice names."

"Explain?" Person asks.

I stop and think about my words. I have to make sure I say all of them and that the important ones don't sneak out before they'll make sense. That's what Person means when she says "explain."

"Pringles had babies today," I say. "So we have to name

them. We all write down ideas. We vote."

"For religion homework?" Person says, shaking her head and pouring the hot water into the sink. "I'll never understand that school." She pauses. "But it could be worse, I guess."

Now it's my turn. I say, "Explain."

Person chuckles. She thinks it's cute when I say it, even though I always really mean that I want to know what she's talking about. I don't mean it to be cute. I never mean to be cute.

"I want you and Julian to go to that school because there are small class sizes and lots of individual attention and teachers who are contractually obligated to love you. But we aren't Catholic so I don't care if Ms. K makes you name mice for religion homework."

I still don't understand each and every word she says, but Person always says that the longer we all live together the more we'll understand one another without asking. So I turn back to my paper without saying anything else. I want her to feel like we've lived here longer and longer. I don't want to ask too many questions and make her think we're temporary.

I have to be a good girl. I have to try to pass fourth grade. I have to make Person happy.

Person is my mom now. My very own human mother. I call her my mom when I'm talking to her or anyone else, but in my head I call her my person because there have been too too many mommies and they all have different faces that blend together in my brain until they're one ugly face that doesn't make sense and some of them were nice but others weren't very nice and they're all gone now anyway and Person says she's here forever.

She's not. Nothing is forever. But she's been here a long, long time.

I call Dad "Dad" because he's the first we've had even though he's newest.

I write down *2*.

"Names?" I say. Then I think the question out and try again. "Do you have ideas for mice names, Mom?"

She's pulling salad bowls out of the cabinet. It's almost dinnertime, that means. This isn't my last bit of homework but I'll tell her it is because I hate when I have to do homework after dinner and I miss the time when we all four sit on the one couch and watch *Jeopardy!* and eat dessert.

"Hmm . . . ," she says. "How about Minnie?" she giggles. "Julian?" she calls.

"That's what I have," I say.

"Minnie?" she asks.

Julian appears next to me.

"No, Julian," I say.

"What?" he says.

"Mouse name," I say. "The one so far."

"What?" Julian and Person both say at the same time.

I'm being confusing again. I hate when I'm being confusing. I know exactly what I mean; I know it makes sense the way it is in my brain. But I can't get my words to work.

Then the phone rings. The one on the kitchen wall. The one that always means bad news.

"Will you set the table, J?" Person says. She moves toward the phone.

I sneak off the stool and tiptoe toward the bathroom. I'm not supposed to leave my stool until it's dinner or until my homework is done. That's one of the things Person and Ms. K and I all agreed to at our last conference. But the bathroom is the exception. I sneak in there a bunch.

"Hi, Cheryl," I hear my person sigh as I slip behind the door.

So it's Ms. K. I'm in trouble. Ms. K hasn't had to call right before dinner in a long, long time. Ms. K and Person have been telling me every day how proud they are that I'm improving so much in school. I don't want to be in trouble with her all over again. I have to stop disappointing Person so much.

Still, I'm relieved.

It's not the news everyone keeps promising us we'll never hear again.

Two

FAMILIES ARE TEMPORARY

THIS IS WHAT I REMEMBER FROM the last time we heard the Worst News.

1. The phone was purple and it was on a counter in a very small room. It rang loudly with a *BRRR*. It never got to the *innnng*.
2. The mom was loud. Gloria. I could never tell if she liked us because she was too loud and the house was too loud, too.
3. There were kids everywhere. Crawling on walls and hanging from the hooks in the ceiling. Dr. Fredrick says "That's your trauma exaggerating the memory" but this list is about what I remember. Not the truth.
4. The loud mom said "Well, Flora and Julian, aren't you lucky?" She had crooked teeth, I think. Or maybe she had braces. Or a lot of fillings. There was something

with her teeth. I remember they were very close to my face when she talked a lot of the time.

5. Or maybe a different mom had close and weird teeth.

6. We hated her loud and crowded house, but we cried. We hated moving more than we hated anyone. And we were always moving. "I wonder if we'll ever see each other again," she said.

Now I can't even see her clearly in my memory.

Three

FAMILIES KEEP SECRETS

MY PERSON IS SMILING WHEN WE sit down at the dinner table, so I guess I'm not in trouble too bad. She rubs her stomach, which she's been doing a lot, and when she sees me looking at her hand going back and forth she says, "Wow, I'm hungry."

Dad starts scooping mashed potatoes onto Julian's plate. I see Julian grab a roll and shove it in his pocket.

"Ms. K?" I ask. "Phone?"

The words fall out of me.

Other people have filters, Dr. Fredrick says. I imagine them as little metal gates in people's lungs, which they can close to catch some words before they pop into the room.

My lungs don't have those gates. He says it's one of the side effects of my trauma. He says that kids who have been through a lot, like I have, sometimes have trouble expressing themselves. Dr. Fredrick and my person and Ms. K are working on helping me build the lung gates, but I can't even feel the parts from which they'll be built yet.

"Don't know exactly why Ms. K called, Flora," Person says with a sigh. Then she forces a smile onto her lips but her eyes are so tired it's like only half her face is smiling.

I have to find a way to make the other half of her face happy.

"She says you're doing better than you've ever been. We're so proud of you."

"So proud!" Dad adds.

"She says as long as you keep up this improvement, you're bound for fifth grade!" I nod without looking at Person so she can't see that this doesn't make me happy the way it's supposed to.

"Ms. K wants to meet with us in the morning," Person says.

My fork freezes on its way to my mouth.

Person and I keep going in early to meet with Ms. K. They sit there and talk all about how I need to work on hand-raising and doing my homework and paying attention in class and how it's been almost two years we've been with Person now, so I really need to try to catch up, and how I'm already a year older than everyone in the fourth grade and it wouldn't be good if I had to do fourth grade again next year, with Julian. I'm eleven now and it wouldn't be good if I turned twelve while I was still in the fourth grade. I'm supposed to hate these meetings, and I do, but I also sort of love them. When Ms. K and Person talk like this about me, their words are like a blanket, and if these little tiny things like grades and hand-raising matter to them, then I must really matter to them.

So I love the meetings, but they still make me angry. Worried. Scared I'm not a normal kid, not the kid my person dreamed about before she met me.

At the last meeting we agreed on a homework system. I start my homework at the kitchen counter at four o'clock. I work there with Person or Dad or the babysitter until dinner at six thirty. Person or Dad or the babysitter checks my assignments. They sign off on them in my assignment notebook. And if I finish everything early, I get to watch the dancing teenagers show on TV. And if I'm still working at six thirty, Person writes a note and I don't have to do the rest of the work. But that's only if I've been working hard the whole time and not staring into space.

I do a lot of staring into space. But I don't know I'm doing it. So how do I stop that?

The homework system has mostly been working. I've even been working on hand-raising sometimes. Why does Ms. K want another meeting? Does she know I figured out the bathroom loophole?

"The bathroom?" I say.

"You need to go?" Person says. "You can be excused."

"No, does Ms. K know?"

"That you need to go to the bathroom?" Person says.

"No!" I say. This is the thing about a missing lung filter. The words that get out sometimes sound all messed up to other people so they don't know what I mean and they lose patience. Ms. K is the first teacher I've ever had who tries to understand me.

I put the words together in my mind. Then I say them. "What are we meeting with Ms. K about this time?"

Person pats my cheek. "I'm not sure, honey. She only said she wants to talk to us."

I'm staring at my plate. I'm ignoring her hand on my cheek. It's starting to feel like needles.

"Let's leave it until the morning, OK?" Person says.

Then she stares at me. Her eyes scratch my face. Her forced smile weighs on my heart. I want the attention. I need the attention. I hate the attention.

"Julian has a roll," I say.

Julian is going to pass the third grade no problem. Julian talks in a way that everyone understands all the time. The only bad thing left about Julian is the food in the closet, and he's returned most of it to Person by now. Julian is almost a normal kid. Julian is leaving me behind.

"Put it back," I say.

Person holds her hand out. "Sweetie?" she says. Julian takes the roll from his pocket and hands it to her.

He sticks his tongue out at me and he hates me and I don't care because at least we are the same again. Both trouble. Bad. Onlys.

* * *

I'm being buried in rolls. Thousands of rolls are falling all over my face and body and bed. They're filling my room. They aren't all-the-way real and I can't feel them or smell them or taste them but they're here in the darkness and they'll suffocate me anyway.

Down the hall, Julian is screaming for a roll. That's in my imagination. I'm imagining him screaming for a roll. In my head, he's terrified he'll never eat again because that roll isn't hidden in the folds of his pants or the back of his shoes.

He's crazy. Food is one thing we don't have to worry about here.

But he's a kind of crazy I understand.

I crawl out of the bed and my socks slide across the gold carpet in my room.

Dad and Person kissed me good night hours ago. The water has stopped running and the TV is turned off and everything is quiet except for the rolls and Julian's screaming, which I know are in my imagination but in some ways they're real.

I tiptoe into the kitchen.

When Person adopted us two years ago, we moved into this apartment in New Jersey. She had just moved in too. She bought the apartment for us even though she didn't know who we were yet, which is something she tells us all the time like it's super important but it makes me feel squirmy because I can't figure out what it means.

It felt like a huge apartment for three people and then Dad moved into Person's room when they got married, but there's still lots of space. I have my very own room. It's off of the living room and kitchen, which is one big room with a counter in the middle where Person and Dad chop vegetables and I do my homework. At the end of the living room there's a little nook with our table where we eat breakfast and dinner. And past the nook there's a hallway with two more bedrooms and the bathroom.

I have to be very quiet when I sneak into Julian's room at night because it's right across the hall from Person's.

In the kitchen, I open the breadbasket and pull out a roll. This is allowed. *You are always allowed to eat food in the kitchen and the kitchen will always have food.* Person tells us that all the time because it's supposed to make Julian stop hiding bread and carrots and chocolate bars and yogurts in his closet. It won't ever work, not all the way. I could tell Person that, but it's the sort of thing that would come out the wrong way and get all confusing.

With the roll in my fist, I tiptoe into the hallway and put my hand on Julian's doorknob.

That's when I hear Dad talking.

"I thought we were going to tell them today," he whispers.

Person sighs. "Me too, Jon. Me too. I wanted to. I just . . ."

"Chickened out?" he asks.

Them is us. Me and Julian. Them is always us.

"I got worried when Cheryl called," Person is saying. "I'm not sure I'm ready to . . . I . . . what if it destroys them?"

"You have to have a little more faith in them," Dad says. "They've proven they're pretty resilient."

"Resilient," Person says quietly. "But . . . we've all been

working so hard at it. Things are going better than ever. You see the progress they're making. Julian showed me his whole closet tonight—he only has four pieces of food hidden in there. And he showed them to me! He's starting to trust me. Us. And Flora's progress report this week showed only two missing homework assignments. And did you hear her today? Asking me to *explain*? She's learning how to communicate with us . . ."

It sounds like Person is almost crying, which is impossible because Person doesn't cry. Even when I scream "I hate you" to her face, she doesn't cry. Even when Julian killed her goldfish—on purpose—she didn't cry. Person feels good stuff or else she feels nothing.

But no. I hear sniffling. She's crying.

"I know I have to tell them," she says.

"We're running out of time," Dad says.

"I know, I know. But—" She gasps a huge sob and I feel tears building in me too. I have to go away before the tears come out. I haven't learned to cry quietly. "I feel so selfish," Person says.

I hold my breath to keep all the tears inside until I'm safely in the bathroom. Then I turn on the water and I breathe deep deep deep like Dr. Fredrick taught me. I stand there and breathe breathe breathe until the crying stops.

It's not happening again, I tell myself.

It will never happen again.

You have to believe.

It's the only promise Person has ever asked us to make.

She said, "Believe me. Just believe me that I'm here forever. The moving is over. I'm your mom forever," she said. "Just promise me that you'll try your hardest to believe. If you do that, we can get through anything."

So I try my hardest. I tell myself *We're here forever.*

And it's true, so far.

Five minutes later I sink into bed beside a sleeping Julian and press the roll beneath his nose. He jumps awake and grimaces but then he grabs the roll and shoves it under his pillow.

There's some moonlight spilling in through his window, highlighting our differences. Julian is a little darker than me, but we're both darker than almost everyone else we know, and we're both lighter than Dad. Julian is short and everything about him is tiny: his fingers, his feet, his nose. I'm tall and long and skinny. We're both skinny, too skinny, still. Even after two years with Person and all of her food. But if you look at us closely you can see the things that make us brother and sister. We have the same round, brown eyes. We have the same hair that's somewhere between curly and straight, but I keep mine long and tied up in puffs or twists or braids, and Julian keeps his cropped close to his head. We have the exact same smile. Or, we have the same smile when I'm happy and when Julian uses his real smile. So you don't see our smile that much. But when you do, it's exactly the same.

"Thanks," Julian says, squeezing the roll.

"Team," I say.

He smiles. He knows what I mean. I don't need to say things a million times and use all the little in-between words. Julian understands what I mean when only the important words come out.

We're a team. We're Onlys.

I shouldn't have told on him about the roll.

"She said she has to tell us something," I say. "I heard her say that to Dad on my way to your room."

Julian sits up and turns around so he's looking at my face as I lie on his pillow. "No," he says. "It's not—"

I shrug. "I heard. Through the door."

Julian shakes his head back and forth, back and forth.

"I'm sorry. It's . . . a meeting with Ms. K . . . I'm . . . I'm bad." I'm not saying all the words but I know he understands me. It's my fault, whatever Person has to tell us. I'm never going to be the kid Person dreamed about before she had us.

"No. No more moving. Mom promised."

"Are you believing?" I ask him.

In some ways Forever feels like Tinker Bell in the scene from *Peter Pan*. The one when she's dying and she'll only live if you believe in fairies and clap clap clap. We have to believe in it. We have to tell ourselves constantly to believe in it. And the minute we doubt, all the things that come with Forever will slip away.

Julian sighs. "I . . . you . . . Mom . . ." He shakes his head.

I wonder what he was trying to say. Julian doesn't have my problem with the wrong words slipping out. He somehow managed to grow the right lung filters even when we were in foster care.

He says, "Yes. I believe. That's what Mom says. Just believe." He pastes this crazy smile on his face. I hate that crazy smile. The smile has too many teeth and it wrinkles his cheeks even though he's only nine years old and shouldn't have wrinkles.

I haven't seen that smile in a long time, I realize.

That smile means he's lying or close to it. It means he's afraid of the truth.

So I have to tell the truth. "It's hard."

Julian sighs. "I know," he says.

"That's why you hide food," I say.

"Are *you* believing?" he asks.

I shrug.

"I believe, Florey," he says, this time without the crazy smile. "It's just . . ."

"OK," I say. I don't want him to say it. We both feel the same way but if we say it out loud something terrible could happen.

We believe in Forever. We do. But our belief is thin. It's a tightrope suspended above a deep, dark canyon. We stand on it and wobble. The minute someone shakes the rope, we could fall into the dark abyss of foster care.

So yes. We believe in Person. But we can't help preparing for the fall.

"It's different," he says. "It's different this time. Anyway, I know what she's talking about and it's not us moving."

"What?" I say. "How?"

Julian gets out of bed and walks over to his closet. He stands on his tiptoes and reaches into his pile of folded jeans. I expect him to shove his roll right into that spot, but instead he pulls out a few pieces of paper.

"What's that?" I ask.

Julian turns around. He crosses the room and tosses the papers onto my lap.

I look at them. Postcards. A beach scene. A roller coaster. An illustration of fish and crabs. One that's just black with the worlds "MARYLAND AT NIGHT" printed on the top.

"What's this?" I ask.

"Postcards," Julian says. "I found them in the mailbox. Found the first one a few weeks ago. I found this one yesterday." He points to the black one.

"You're stealing mail now too?"

Julian shakes his head. "*I'm* not stealing," he says. "They're ours."

I flip over the MARYLAND AT NIGHT card. There's messy kid-writing scrawled on the back.

Hi, Flora and Julian!

Isn't this postcard funny? I haven't heard from you at

all so I hope you're getting these. We miss you at Gloria's.
We have a new baby now, only a few months old. Sometimes
Gloria lets me hold her. I'll give all of the dogs a pat for
you. I hope you're liking your new mom.

Megan B.

I point at her name.

"Remember her?" Julian asks. "From the last foster house?"

I nod slowly. I haven't thought about her in a long time, but
I do remember. She was a little older than me, pale white skin
with dark brown hair. We used to play together in Gloria's
house, the one with too many kids.

"She was nice," I say.

"She's still with Gloria," Julian says.

"How did she even mail this to us?" I ask.

Julian points to the address part. It's not addressed to our
house in New Jersey, it's addressed to our foster-adoption
agency in Maryland, with a forwarding sticker attached. "The
agency is sending them?" I ask.

"I think so," Julian says. "Here, read this one."

I pick up one with a beach scene on it.

Dear Flora and Julian,

I hope you're enjoying your new family. I just
wanted to tell you that I still think of you often. I
wish I could get up there for a visit, or at least hear
from you. I hope you've received the other postcards
from me and the kids. We are all praying that you're

happy and we all know you're safe and loved. But we
still miss you sometimes.

    Love,

    Gloria

"That was the mom," I say.

Julian nods.

"She misses us?" I say.

I've never thought about the moms we left behind miss-ing us. I've never thought about them even thinking of us. I always thought I was too bad, too quiet, too confused and scrambled in the brain to be missed.

"The kids do too. I've found three cards from Megan B."

He points to another and I flip it over. It has our names at the top and then a hundred smiley face stickers all over the rest of it. I smile back at the stickers.

"That's what Mom's going to tell us. Finally."

I look up from the stickers. "What?" I say.

"That she stole some of these," Julian says.

"But she didn't. You have them."

Julian shakes his head. "We've been living here for almost two years. Do you really think Megan B. and Gloria waited that long to write to us?"

"I don't know," I say. I can see what he means, but I don't want it to be true. I want it to be impossible.

Person can't steal from us.

Person is good.

We're the bad ones who do things like steal.

"Flora, she took some of the cards. This one from Gloria is the first one I found and it says she wrote to us before."

I shake my head again.

"I don't . . . I can't . . . no talking," I say.

Julian sighs. "OK," he says. "But you better talk when Mom tells us about these. The other ones."

I nod.

"You remember Megan B.?" he says. "I don't think I do. I remember Gloria, though. And a kid named Phillip and a tiny little girl named Rita."

"Megan, yes," I say. I'm too tired for full sentences. She had a dollhouse and she let me play with it. We'd spend hours in the girls' bedroom making those dolls walk up and down the stairs.

"Do you remember moving out of Gloria's house?" Julian asks.

"I think it was raining," I say.

"Was that the gray house? Or the brick apartment?" Julian asks.

"There were dogs. Remember the wet dogs? I sort of remember wet dogs. They smelled."

Julian giggles. "That was a good house, right? Gloria's? With the dogs?"

It's something slightly different between us. We both talk about bad houses, bad moms, bad kids. But Julian calls the others "good."

I call them nothing.

Nothing is good if it slips away so often.

I shrug. "I know I liked the dogs," I say.

Julian nods. "You love dogs."

He lies down next to me and tears a piece of crust off the roll. He hands it to me.

"I thought you were saving this," I say.

"We don't have to, Florey," Julian says. He shrugs. "We believe, right?"

I stare at him.

"I might have to stay back in the fourth grade again."

Julian nods. "Maybe Jon is moving out again. Dad, I mean. Back to Elena and Meredith?"

"Maybe something's wrong with Elena," I say. "Or Meredith."

"Maybe she's still sad about the goldfish."

That's not true. The goldfish was over a year ago. But I can tell we both feel better. Person says we can mess up and mess up and no matter how upset she gets we aren't going back to foster care. So we do this when we feel the belief-tightrope start to shake: we list all the ways we could mess up and that she'd still keep us afterward.

"Tell me your first memory again," Julian says.

"OK," I say. "It was a white house. Everything was white. I was standing in a long line, inside a house. And I was small, tiny. It was too bright, so I reached up along the white wall and I turned off the light. I hit the light switch. I remember being amazed I was tall enough to turn off a light. Then someone started yelling at me. I was scared, but I don't remember why. Or where we were. Or anything. I know you were there, behind me in line. Your hand was on my shoulder."

"Why were we in line inside a house?" Julian asks.

"I don't know," I say. "That's the memory. It happened. Ever since then I've been growing." I take a bite of roll. "Tell me yours."

"I'm in a kitchen," Julian says. "You're there too. We're sitting next to each other at a tiny table, but it's OK the table is tiny, because so are we. Everything is white too, the table, the floor, the walls. And there's a lot of kids at the table. And there's a little bit of food in the middle, but there's a lot of kids. And I'm hungry."

"Yup," I say. "It's the same house. Yours and mine. The white house."

Julian nods. "It's the same place. It's where we first were."

We sigh next to each other at the exact same time. Onlys.

"I don't have a second memory though," Julian says. "There's a bunch of like colors and faces and feelings."

"But nothing goes in order," I say.

"We don't even know which parts of it were real," Julian says.

"We just have a first memory. We only know where we started and where we are now."

"With a little Gloria mixed in," Julian says.

"And a little Megan B.," I say.

I don't want to think about Megan B. though. I don't want

to know why Person would hide her postcards, why Person would hide the good stuff. The good stuff is so easy to forget and it leaves my brain with only the bad stuff.

"Another theory," I say. "Do you have one?"

Julian shoves some bread in his mouth and chews, thinking. Finally he says, "Dogs. Maybe we come from dogs."

THEORY #847

We come from dogs, my brother and me. We were roly-poly puppies with a whole bunch of others. We would jump on each other in piles, nipping each other's ears, chasing each other's tails.

But then all the other puppies grew longer tails and ours got shorter. The other puppies learned to bark and we learned to talk. The other puppies walked on four legs but we started to walk on two. Our paws grew into hands. Our snouts became noses.

We spoke.

And when we tried to play with the other puppies, we would yell. Their teeth were too sharp. Their nails were too hard. We couldn't nip and scratch and growl anymore in our human skin.

All the playing started to hurt.

Four

FAMILIES HAVE NORMAL DAYS

"GOOD MORNING, EMILY," MS. K SAYS the next day. She keeps talking to Person.

Person and I are sitting across from her big desk. Person is wearing her blue scrubs because she has a work day so we are here very, very early. Six a.m. Person's shift starts at seven. Ms. K is wearing the dark green dress that she wears every other Friday. I don't think I was supposed to notice that she wears the same ten outfits over and over again but I did. I'm wearing my plaid skirt and white shirt uniform because after this meeting I'll go down to Early Care and then I'll go right into school.

"I'm sorry," Ms. K says.

I scratch my ankle. I'm thinking about Ms. K's green dress and the recent dog theory and how Dad will be the one to pick us up today because Person will be at the hospital until seven tonight but how it's Friday so we'll probably go out to eat ice cream and I won't have to do my home-work to earn *Jeopardy!* family time.

I'm thinking about stolen postcards, even though I don't want to. I'm thinking about how to be a better, normal-er kid to make her happier.

I'm waiting for them to finish the adult chat and talk to me.

"Did you hear Ms. K, Flora?" Person asks.

I look up. "Huh?" I say.

"I said I'm sorry," Ms. K says. "I owe you an apology."

"No," I say.

No one has ever apologized to me. I scratch my ankle harder. I scratch my elbow. I want to take off the skin and scratch the bone directly.

"I do," Ms. K says. "You asked a question yesterday and I think it was an important one. I think I should have answered you or taken the time to understand you. I'm afraid it felt like I was brushing you off. I feel awful. So I thought your mom and I could try to answer you together now. Do you remem-ber the question you asked?"

"About the mice like me," I say right away. The heat of hate toward Ms. K is cooling off.

"Explain?" Person says.

But I say, "I'm not in trouble?"

"Flora," Ms. K says with a smile that cools my blood and warms my heart back into the sun. "I'm concerned about you. That's why I called you in here."

"Oh," I say. I'm sure she can see how I'm glowing. How I'm relieved.

I love Ms. K almost as much as I love Person. But I don't think that's allowed.

"OK," Person says, looking at me. "Explain about the mice. Which mouse is like you?" She points to the mouse cage.

"No, not these," I say. Then I put the words together. It takes a while. "I mean the ones that don't come from another mouse. The ones that come another way. Come to life. Without the other mouse."

No one is smiling anymore. Ms. K and my person exchange a hard look, then talk to me softly.

"What other way, honey?" Person asks.

I shrug.

"Do you mean how we got Pringles in the first place?" Ms. K says.

"Maybe," I say.

"We bought her from a pet store."

"The pet store," I say. "I mean."

"Explain," Person says again. I can tell that she's getting worried or nervous. Maybe it's almost time for her to go to work. I have to use my words. I have to get through this while being as normal as I can be. Normal Kid. I think about being Normal Kid.

"I mean how Pringles got to the pet store," I say.

"Well, she was probably born there," Ms. K says. "I would imagine."

I shake my head. "Not Pringles then. The other mice. The ones like me."

"What?" Person says this time. Not *explain*. Dr. Fredrick told her to say *explain* not *what,* which means Person made a mistake. Both Person and Ms. K made a mistake because of this.

It feels huge and important and impossible.

"Sweetie," Ms. K says slowly. "How would a mouse be like you? What is the similarity you're describing?"

Words rush through my brain and I try to put them together.

Sand.

Dogs.

Television.

Foster kids.

"Like me and Julian," I say.

"Like you and Julian *how*?" Ms. K says.

I'm sweating now. My heart is racing like gym class. My feet are kicking the bottom of Ms. K's desk.

"Hold on, hold on," Person says. "Quick break. We need a reset. Ms. K, would you like to learn how we reset?"

"Sure," Ms. K says.

Together we take three deep breaths, then we count to ten.

It works. No more sweating. No more pumping hearts.

Person takes my hand. "Flora, we want to know what you mean. But we don't mean to be impatient. Take your time. Put your words together slowly. Then we'll figure this out together."

But she doesn't have to say all of that. The reset worked. I have the words ready to go.

I can even speak in full sentences when I have this much time.

"The mice like me and Julian," I say. "The mice who don't come from mothers, who came to life some other way."

Both women scrunch their eyebrows at me in a silent *what*.

"The mice who were never born."

Ms. K and Person freeze and stare at me. Both of their mouths are half open like Ms. K's was yesterday.

"Flora, do you think—?"

I interrupt Person without meaning to, the words are pouring forward. "I haven't figured how we came here yet," I say. "We both remember the same thing first, but we don't know how we got there. How we got into that white house with the table and the line. I have a bunch of theories. But you know. Julian and I always had shifting mothers. We didn't come out of someone the way the thumbs came out of Pringles. We . . . we're just . . . here. We were never babies. We weren't born."

Ms. K and Person haven't moved.

The bell rings.

"I thought maybe if I knew how the other mice got here, the not-born mice, I could get close to figuring out how Julian and I got here."

They still don't move.

Kids come into the back of the classroom and I realize we've been talking all through Early Care and Person will definitely be late to work and she doesn't even seem angry about it. She doesn't seem anything. She's frozen.

Finally she talks to Ms. K, adult chat again.

"Well, good thing it's the weekend. We'll talk about this over the next few days and I'll let you know how it goes."

Ms. K nods.

"I love you, Flora," Person says. She stands and kisses the top of my head and the kids in the room giggle at that but I don't care. "I'm really glad you're my kid. No matter what. Remember that, OK?"

I like when she says these things and kisses me but I always duck away from it because I'm afraid there's going to be a day when she doesn't say those things or kiss me anymore. It's when the best things are happening that it's hardest to believe in Forever.

"You're a great kid, Flora," Ms. K says. "You've grown so much in just the past few months, and I'm thrilled to get to see it. You'll figure out this part too, OK?"

I love Ms. K and I love Person, but Ms. K never promised me Forever. She's trying her hardest to make sure I leave her next month. It's so confusing.

Then Person is gone and Ms. K says to sit down and we have a normal day.

I'm going to miss these normal days so badly.

Five

FAMILIES HAVE THE SAME NAME

IT'S FRIDAY, WHICH MEANS WE HAVE late recess with the sixth, seventh, and eighth graders because we also have music and PE on Fridays. On Mondays, Wednesdays, and Thursdays, I spend recess doing my math homework because I'm so excited and I can't wait any longer to solve a problem with a definite answer.

Sometimes some of the nice girls in my class, like Lisa and Annie, invite me to play four square or draw with chalk and I really want to talk to them but my tongue gets tied and my words get heavy and I listen to them chat and giggle and hope I'll be able to be a girl like they are a girl one day.

On Tuesdays, first, second, third, fourth, fifth, and sixth grades all have recess together because we have PE but no music. Julian and I sit with our knees pressed together and try to pretend we're OK in the middle of a recess with that many kids running everywhere and screaming, which feels exactly like foster care and I hate Tuesdays.

But Fridays are different. On Fridays I have recess at the same time as Elena and not Julian. There's only big kids here and they're quieter and run less so it's not as scary. Today is Friday.

It's my turn to be nice.

I walk up to where she's leaning against a basketball hoop with a bunch of the other sixth graders. They're all taller than us fourth graders, which makes it look like their skirts are shorter. They laugh with their heads back. Their hair is so shiny it looks like it never needs brushing. They make me glad I'm still in the fourth grade.

"Hi, Elena," I say.

She rolls her eyes. Her friends all giggle.

"Go play with Lisa, Flora," she says.

"OK," I say, and walk away.

The same thing happens every Friday, but I always forget until it's over. Because then on Saturday and Sunday, Elena talks and talks to me and stays by my side all day long and Person says "She wants to be close to you, Flora. You should give it some effort" but when Julian is around it's hard to remember to pay attention to Elena too.

Elena and I are sort of friends, I think. I try on Fridays. She tries on Sundays.

One week we'll figure out how to try on the same day.

* * *

In the afternoon, when it's time for religion class, Ms. K walks around the room and gives everyone a marker.

"Now," she says. "There are nineteen kids in this class and each of you came up with four names. So how many names will we have total?"

She's always doing that, shoving arithmetic into a subject where it doesn't belong. Making social studies about phonics or spelling. Forcing grammar into math class.

"Seventy-six!" David yells.

"Good," Ms. K says. "But raise your hand."

"But if there's two," I say. Then I realize my hand is still down. I'm not working very hard on hand-raising today.

But Ms. K doesn't remind me. She says, "What's that, Flora?"

"If there's two. Like two Minnies."

The class is silent. I'm sure they're staring at me. I'm not making sense again. Like always.

But Ms. K says, "Oh yes, that's a great point, Flora. There will be seventy-six names, but some of you may have come up with the same name, at which point would there be more or less than seventy-six?"

Hands go up.

I say, "Less."

Ms. K looks at me like she wants to tell me to raise my hand but her tongue is too exhausted from saying those words over and over for the past nine months. She nods.

Then she finishes handing out the markers and explaining that in a minute we will all get to go find our spot on the boards around the classroom and write our list of mouse names. There's a buzzing excitement everywhere in the room. Everyone wants to write on the board. It's the most fun thing we get to do.

We all want our own mouse names to be chosen.

Ms. K explains that she's going to be the first judge of new mouse names. She'll go around with an eraser and get rid of names that are not appropriate, which include names of real people and names that are mean and maybe some other names.

Then she says "GO" and we all rush to the boards.

My spot on the board is next to David's because my desk in the front row is next to his too. When we scribble side by side, he leans over to me and whispers, "She never tells you to raise your hand."

Which makes me freeze with my marker halfway through the *u* in Julian.

"Yes," I say. Because Ms. K tells me to raise my hand all the time. More than anyone else. Mostly that's because everyone else is better at it than I am.

"You get away with everything," David says.

"I don't want to go anywhere," I whisper back. I don't want to get away with anything or without anything. I want to stay right here and keep having normal days with Person and Dad and Julian and Ms. K and Dr. Fredrick and Elena and even

David who I don't care about at all. I just want us to stay in one place.

"What?" David says. "You don't even make sense. Jeez."

He shakes his head. He's trying to be mean to me but I don't care. There's no room in my heart for one more worry when Person is stealing postcards from me and mice are born to regular mothers and I'm not going to have Ms. K as a teacher anymore if I do my best like I keep promising I will.

David writes the rest of his list. He's writing in purple. I'm writing in red so my letters are brighter. I make sure they're neater too.

David's list says
1. Slimy
2. Rolly
3. Orange
4. Doofus

My list is much prettier and I think the ideas are better too.
1. Julian
2. Person
3. Ms. K
4. Castillo

A minute later we all sit and watch, leaning out of our desks to see closer as Ms. K walks around to the boards and erases different names. I can't wait for her to get to mine. I'm sure my list is the best and I will get to name all of the mice.

When she gets to David's, she erases *Doofus* right away without saying anything. After a second, she erases *Slimy* too. Then she says, "Rolly and Orange, explain those to me." She pronounces *Rolly* like *lollipop*.

"ROLL-y," David yells. "Because they rolled right out of Pringles."

The rest of the class laughs.

"Hm," Ms. K says. "And what about Orange?"

David shrugs. "My mom gives me orange juice every morning. It's my favorite juice. I figure it could be my favorite mouse too."

Ms. K smiles. "That's what we're looking for," she says. She winks at him. She erases "Rolly" but David beams anyway and I feel itchy because when she winks at me and says those nice things to me I sort of hate it but that doesn't mean I'm OK with her being so nice to someone else.

Even though I also like that she's nice to everyone, even David who is the Mean Boy in the class. She's nice to everyone which proves she's nice for real and it's not that she feels sorry for me.

Julian and I are confused about this. We want people to feel sorry for us, until they do. Then we want them to stop feeling sorry for us. Then they stop. Then we want them to feel sorry for us again.

Ms. K moves on to my list. She erases *Ms. K* and *Julian*.

"But," I say.

Ms. K shakes her head. "No naming mice after real people

we know, remember?"

I nod but my heart is sinking. She's using her Warning Voice. David got a wink and I get the Warning Voice.

She says, "Where did you get the idea to name a mouse 'Person'?"

I don't want to answer. No one knows that Person is what I call Person who is the best person ever. Not even Julian.

Plus, I'm mad at Ms. K now and I don't want to say anything to her.

I shake my head and she erases the name.

"What's this?" Ms. K asks, pointing to the one and only name left on my list.

"Castillo," I say. "The old one."

Ms. K turns. She looks at me softly. That look on her face is her version of Person's *explain*.

I put the words together.

"Our old one. Last name. Before Baker."

I'm sure she's about to erase it, but instead Ms. K starts blinking a lot. She turns and picks up the red marker and puts a star next to *4. Castillo.*

"You all might not know this," Ms. K says to the class. "But when a child is adopted, like we all know Flora was, she changes her last name so that it will match the name of her new parents. So before Ms. Baker adopted Flora, she was Flora Castillo. But now she's Flora Baker. So, what do we think of this as a mouse name, class?"

"That's really special, Flora," a girl behind me calls out.

"Yeah," someone else says.

Then the whole room is clapping and I'm happy and warm and terrified and cold and melting.

No teacher will ever make me feel the way Ms. K does. Worth the work. Smart. Real. Why can't she be my teacher forever?

In the end the four mice are Orange, Duck, Chips, and Castillo.

Castillo is just one of the slimy purple thumbs, but I can totally tell which one he is. I think he's the cutest.

After school, Julian, Dad, and I are in the ice-cream shop, sitting at our favorite booth in the back on the right. Julian nuzzles into Dad's big shoulder. Dad is so much bigger than Julian it almost looks like they're different creatures. Like Dad is a pit bull and Julian is a Shih Tzu.

"Don't you love getting ice cream with us, Dad?" Julian asks.

"You know I love it," Dad says. He slurps a bit of his milk shake. "I only wish my Elena could be here too."

Julian looks up with the biggest smile on his face before digging his spoon back into his strawberry supreme. It's his real smile, not his crazy one. He's a sponge soaking in the love, the closeness, the family. Julian has always been a sponge but in the old days, when there was nothing for him to soak up, he was such a dry sponge parts of him were starting to chip off, parts of him got left behind in every house we were in and out of.

"Want a sip of milk shake?" Dad asks me, even though I have a sundae in front of me.

I nod. I suck a big mouthful up the straw. I love the way the malt coats the back of my throat. "Thanks," I say.

I try not to think of what I heard him saying last night. He said, "We're running out of time." Why would they be running out of time to tell us about the stolen postcards? What could the deadline be?

I can't think about it.

I have to believe. I have to work hard to believe.

We've been doing Ice Cream Fridays with Dad since we called him Jon, before he married Person. We've been doing this for longer than we've done anything.

I have to believe we'll be back here at this ice-cream shop next Friday and next-next Friday and next-next-next Friday. Forever.

Julian and I sit on the couch watching cartoons while Dad clunks around behind us making dinner. Julian shifts to lean on me like usual and his pocket goes *crunch-crunch-crunch*.

"Pocket," I say. Julian freezes with his big brown eyes, wider than usual.

I reach for his pocket and pull out a pack of sugar, a pack of ketchup, and a chicken nugget from the cafeteria lunch today.

He looks at me and shrugs like it's no big deal.

"I'm not in trouble with Ms. K," I say. "I got to name a mouse Castillo even."

I back away from him with his treasures in my fist. Julian lunges for them.

I don't know if he understood me, but Julian never asks me to explain. He either knows what I mean when I speak, or he's so used to not understanding me after all this time of being Onlys that he lets the words wash over him.

He lunges again for the cold chicken nugget in my hands, throwing his body across mine.

"No!" I say. "Stop!"

"You guys OK?" Dad calls.

Julian and I sit back up and get quiet. Dad is the soft one. He's all ice cream and no punishments. But if he catches us doing something bad he'll tell Person and then we'll get sent to our rooms without each other or, worse, have to see the look in her eye when she talks to us about making choices.

"Good," we call.

Dad goes back to clunking.

I lean back over to my brother and whisper into his ear. "You have to stop. No more food." He looks at me so alarmed that I say, "No. You can still eat. Just no more food in the closet."

He still looks as scared. "Why?" he asks. He's crying now. Soaking up too much love is dangerous for a sponge. It'll leak right out of you once the ice cream is gone.

"You were getting better," I say. "You were returning the food."

"She's stealing from us," Julian says. "The postcards."

"Ms. K isn't mad at me," I say. "She wasn't mad."

Julian nods.

"It's not me," I say. "Whatever Mom was crying about. It's not me."

Julian nods again.

"It's you."

"You think it's the food? She's crying about the food?"

"Yes," I say. "Or the faking happy. The lying. She was crying about you."

"But then . . ." He stops talking. He reaches for the ketchup, sugar, and chicken and I hand them over. He clutches them to his chest. "I need them," he says.

I don't understand this. It looks like he's hugging garbage.

"We have to make Mom happy, Julian," I say. "We have to work hard to make her happy."

Julian lowers his eyebrows. "That's really what you think?" he asks.

I nod.

Julian bites his lip. "I'll try," he says. "I'll try for you, Florey."

Before he turns so that Dad can see his face, he pastes that crazy, lying smile on again.

He walks into the kitchen and I hear the whoosh of the food going into the garbage can.

When he sits down again, his fingers play with each other. His breath is heavy and fast. He hates giving the food up.

I hate myself. And Person. And I hate the hate.

"Team," I say.

We're in this together. It's the only thing I've ever been able to do for Julian. It's the only thing he's ever been able to do for me.

He leans against me again and I don't even ask him to change the channel. We're Onlys. Sometimes we can forget that now that we're in a huge apartment where we sleep miles away from each other and we have all these other Ms. Ks and Persons and Dads and Elenas in our lives.

But I love the moments like these. Julian's little body making my right arm fall asleep. Julian's breath even with mine. Julian and me, the only steady things in the constantly shifting universe.

THEORY #300

We come from the television, my brother and me.

We were once the happy kids inside your screen. We were cartoons with funny voices that other people spoke for us. We were dancing teenagers with scripts that told us what to say.

We were thought up by someone else for someone else.

It's why we don't know how to be on our own.

Six

FAMILIES HAVE SERIOUS TALKS

WHEN PERSON GETS HOME SHE PULLS me into my bedroom and we both sit on my bed, facing each other. She has her hands on top of mine. She's looking into my face like she's searching it for diamonds.

This is how Person likes to have Serious Talks. This is *not* how I like to have Serious Talks. It's the opposite. Person likes everything to be still and everyone's eyes to be right on each other. I like everything to be moving all around us and my eyes to be anywhere but her face because I might need to escape the seriousness in a second if things go a bad way.

"Let's talk about what you said in your classroom today, Florey."

I relax because I'm not about to find out she stole from us. Even though I'm starting to believe it.

"We weren't babies," I say.

Person nods. "OK. Do you believe you were ever any younger?"

I laugh. "Yeah," I say. "Before my birthday. And the birthday before that."

"Yup," Person says.

"And in a few months when it's Julian's birthday, he'll be older too. And he was also younger."

"Correct," Person says.

"But we weren't babies."

She's doing this thing where she bounces her eyebrows. I think she does it when she wants us to think whatever she's talking about isn't that important to her, even though it is. It's a weird kind of lie, those bouncing eyebrows. "If you go back enough birthdays, you get to when you were a baby. And if you go back all through your birthdays, you get to the day you were born."

I'm shaking my head.

"You don't think so?" Person asks.

"Nope. It's different for us," I say.

Person lowers her eyebrows. They aren't bouncing anymore. "Why do you say that?" she asks.

"I don't know . . . ," I say. "I guess . . . we never had a birth mom. Most of the other kids when we were in foster care had birth moms. They had visits. They had bio relatives sending them birthday and Christmas presents. They had these books full of, like, pictures and letters and birthday cards from their first family."

"Lifebooks," Person says, nodding. "I'm sorry you don't have a Lifebook, Florey."

I shrug. "We don't have a first family."

"But . . . you did," Person says.

"Did what?" I ask.

Person's face is getting red. I can see some beads of sweat along her hairline.

"You did have a birth mom," Person says. "Of course you did."

I tilt my head. She's never told me that before.

"Who was she?"

Person sighs. Her face gets even redder. I wonder what's wrong.

"Flora . . . You were born. You live with me now, but on your birthday, you were born. That's why we call it a birthday."

Person doesn't say anything about this birth mom. I'm pretty sure that means she doesn't exist after all.

I shake my head.

"Why do you think you were never born?" Person asks again.

I think and think. And think. She asked the same question, which means I need to answer it in another way.

"Were you born?" I ask.

Person nods.

"So you remember being born. I don't," I say.

Person laughs like I'm being cute when I'm not being cute. "No," she says. "No one remembers being born."

"So how do you know you were then?" I ask.

Person gets quiet for a long time. Her eyes go off of me and I feel my jaw relax. I didn't even realize I was holding it so tight.

"Maybe I know we *weren't* born the same reason you know you *were* born," I say.

Then I follow Person's eyes to Dad in the doorway.

"That's a very good point, Flora. I'll have to think about that," she says.

Dad says, "We'll figure this out . . . We still have to tell them." He says it like I'm not there. It's like I'm eavesdropping even though I'm right in the room. Part of me wants to ask him what he means, but most of me doesn't want to know. So my lung filters work for once and I stay quiet.

"I know," Person says.

Dinner that night is honey-mustard chicken casserole: Julian's and my favorite. We sit around the table in our usual spots. Person, me, Dad, Julian.

As Dad is spooning casserole onto each of our plates, Person clears her throat. "OK, my lovelies," she says. "We have to talk. I have some news. Some big exciting news. But before we get to that, we have some things to straighten out."

Julian's eyes are huge across the table. The beginnings of

tears glitter on the outside of his lashes even though he's also smiling. She's going to tell us something big, we can feel it. The ground shakes under our feet, tremors from the Creature of Change who is treading too close to us again.

"So," Person says. "Let's talk about how we all got here."

Dad clunks the casserole down in front of me and I barely notice how delicious it smells.

"Every single person—every single creature—" Person starts.

But Julian doesn't let her continue. He cries out, "We don't care! We forgive you, OK? Just let us stay here."

I start to shake. *No!* I beg him in my head. *Believe, Julian. We have to keep believing!*

Person's mouth drops open. Dad falls into his seat at the same second Person is out of hers with her arms thrown over Julian's shoulders.

"Jules." Person does that thing with her voice where you can tell she's angry but her anger isn't pointing at you, it's more like it's pointing behind you, holding you up. "That is not what's happening. You guys are mine," she says. "Forever. I mean that. You'll live with me until the day you aren't kids anymore, and maybe even after that. I'll be at your graduations and your weddings and you'll be with me at Christmas and Thanksgiving forever, OK? I'm your mom."

Somehow, as she was talking, Dad got up and put his arms around me too, without me even knowing. So now he's holding me and Person is holding Julian and I wonder if that means we're split up too. That we aren't holding each other now in this new family.

Julian isn't crying anymore. Person isn't talking. We freeze for a minute until she looks at Julian and says, "Got it?"

He sniffles and nods.

Then she turns to me.

"And you, Flora?" she asks.

But me? I don't know. How does she believe in Forever? How is Forever until-the-end something you believe in?

I shrug. "What is it then?"

Person and Dad go back to their seats.

"What is what?" Person asks.

"The whispers," I say.

Julian kicks me under the table. "What?" I say.

"It doesn't matter. You heard her, Florey. We're not going anywhere," he says.

"I heard the whispers!" I insist.

"Explain?" Person says.

She's eating. So is Dad. They do this sometimes. Try to act the most normal when I'm being the most weird. Like normal is contagious.

Julian spears a chunk of chicken. "Flora heard you whispering last night," he says. "But it doesn't matter why."

"Before the mice," I say.

"We have to tell them," Dad says.

Person takes a big shaky breath like she's nervous. But that's impossible because Person is never nervous.

I guess she is now though. I guess she really did steal those postcards from us.

"OK, kiddos," she says. "Here's the deal. Julian, Flora, Mom, Dad. We're a family forever."

"And Elena," Dad says.

Person nods. "And Elena. Elena, Julian, Flora, Mom, Dad. Family. Forever."

But they've already lost me because I don't understand why they keep saying Elena is family like the rest of us.

"Nothing will ever change that. But just because something will never change doesn't mean it can't grow, right?"

Julian's lips spread into a slow smile "Grow?" he says.

My heart is racing.

"I'm so glad to see that smile, J," Person says. "In six months we'll be Elena, Flora, Julian, Mom, Dad, and Baby. Forever."

I'm shaking. It's tiny shaking. Maybe it's only my inside organs shaking. Maybe Person and Dad can't see the shaking.

"What do you think, Flora?" Dad asks.

I think I'm shaking.

I don't know how to feel. That's a change. That's the opposite of Forever. It's not the change I was afraid of, but . . .

I shrug.

"You OK?" Person asks.

Am I? I nod.

"Any questions from you guys?" she asks.

"Is it a boy or a girl?" Julian asks. "And where will it sleep? And what will we name it? And can I hold him?"

He's smiling still, but the smile is fake. Of course he can talk, he's lying. I'm only quiet because I'm trying to figure out the truth.

Person laughs. "I don't know, we haven't decided yet, need to know if it's a boy or girl before we name it." She pauses to smile at him. "And yes. You will both hold the baby. It'll be your brother or sister."

My heart is beating so fast. I put my hands on the table to try to hold myself still and on the earth. I don't know why Julian seems so happy. I don't know how I'm feeling.

"It'll be a baby?" I ask.

Person turns. She puts her hand on top of mine and my heart slows. It shouldn't though. She's the one changing everything. She shouldn't calm me down.

"Yes, Flora, a baby," she says.

"Not adopted?" I ask.

And she gives me a half smile like she does sometimes when she's been trying and trying to understand me and finally she does. "No, not adopted this time," she says. "This baby is in my body right now."

I nod. "So it'll be a born baby?" I ask.

Person's hand is still on me. "Flora-girl," she says. "All babies are born, OK? You and Julian were born too."

"Nope," Julian says. It's a cheerful noise. He's covered in honey mustard and happily bouncing on his seat while he eats. My dinner is cold in front of me. I couldn't even eat it now if I tried because Person has my eating-hand.

Person looks at him. "What did you say?"

"Not Flora and me. We weren't born. We're different."

Dad's eyebrows are so low they almost cover his eyes. Person's mouth won't close. They don't look angry, though, just curious.

"Flora, Julian," Person says. "All babies were born. Even you. I promise."

She finally lets go of my hand and I pick up my fork and dig into my casserole. It tastes good even cold.

"Not us," I say.

"We were never babies anyway," Julian says.

"Where did you come from then?" Dad asks.

I smile. I love this game, and now we can play with Person and Dad too. "I think maybe we came from the bottom of the ocean," I say.

"I think maybe we came from dogs," Julian says.

"Or maybe the television," I say. "We came right out of it."

"Or we crawled out of the horizon," Julian says.

We try to tell them about as many of the theories as we can remember.

Person smiles and says, "That's very creative. You two are so smart."

"But you were born," Dad says.

Julian and I shrug across the table. They can think what they want. We know the truth.

It's midnight and I'm in Julian's room, sitting on the floor with him, our knees pressed against each other's, the way we always sit when the ground is shaking.

"Do you think the baby will love us?" Julian asks.

"Love us?" I say.

"Yeah," Julian says. This matters to him. Some baby not-born that will-be-born.

To me the baby is change. I'm not even thinking of it as a person yet.

But Julian. He wants to love the baby.

"Like Person?" I ask.

"Yeah, like a person," Julian says. "It'll be born and then it'll be a person. Like all normal kids."

My face burns. I used my secret inside-my-head name for our mom.

"I mean, do you want the baby to love you like Mom? Or like me?"

"Like Mom," Julian says, scrunching his eyes and moving his head back and forth like I'm being ridiculous. And I am. Of course.

We're Onlys.

I calm down a little.

"Maybe," I say, because I don't care if some stupid baby

loves me but I can tell that Julian does. "Maybe it'll love us like Mom."

Julian sighs. "I'm trying to figure it out, you know?"

"Figure what?" I ask.

Julian shrugs. "Whether it's worth it. Thinking about the baby. Worrying about the baby."

"I'm only worried about Mom," I say.

"Huh?" Julian says. "She'll be fine. Women have babies every day."

"No. Loving. I'm only worried about Mom. Loving still . . ."

Julian is staring at me. His eyes are extra dark. His knees press into me. He's begging me not to say it. He's daring me to say it. It's the most awful thing I can say, but I say it anyway.

"I'm only worried about Pers—about Mom loving us, still."

I thought I never really believed Person with all her "forevers." I thought I wasn't good at believing. But now, now that everything is changing, I realize I must have started to believe her somewhere in me. I must have thought deep down that we were enough for Person, somehow. But how could we be? Not Julian and me with the failing in school and the unable to talk and the hiding food. Not Julian and me who have no memories and no history. Not Julian and me, people who were never born.

"Also," Julian says. "She still didn't tell us about the post-cards she stole."

"Also that," I say.

We're quiet after that, but we sit and we sit together while the night moves around us. We sit with our knees pressed against each other. We connect each other to this house, to this family, to this planet.

And I know, deep in my heart, that there was only Julian at the beginning.

There could be no birth mom.

There could be no other story.

It was Julian and me, me and Julian.

Flora and Julian Castillo, the never-born siblings.

THEORY #3

The stork messed up for my brother and me.

They say the stork is a legend but they say a lot of things and none of them explain how Julian and I came to life. So maybe the stork is real. Maybe the stork uses his big beak to stitch up babies, to connect their fingers to their hands and their toes to their feet. Maybe the stork sits on babies to keep them warm the way Pringles sits on the new mice.

And then the stork drops the babies into homes where moms wait holding out their arms. And if the babies fall into the right place, boom. That's their family. That's when they're born.

But the stork missed with Julian and me. He stitched us too late. Our fingers were too big. Our heads were full grown. And when the stork dropped us, we landed outside a mom and outside a house. We landed somewhere where there was no one to say "hey, look, kids!" and so we grew. I grew a little faster. Julian stayed a bit behind.

We grew in that abandoned spot, that empty yard or parking lot or mountain or desert where the stork dropped us by accident. We grew bigger and stronger and we slept sitting up with our knees pressed together. We fed each other and talked to each other. We grew and grew until the Division of Family Services found us and said, "If you don't have a mother, that means you're ours."

Julian and I are just like everyone. Or we would have been. If the stork didn't mess up.

Seven

FAMILIES WORK HARD

THE NEXT DAY IS SATURDAY, WHICH means the court says Dad gets to take care of Elena, so she comes over even though Mom is at the hospital and Dad is at the fire station, both at work.

Meredith, Elena's mom, drops her off and our babysitter, Elliot, lets her in the front door. Julian and I are on the couch watching the dancing teenagers on television but we only get to watch for ten more minutes before it's screens off until *Jeopardy!*

Elena comes and sits next to us on the couch.

It takes me too long to realize I should say hi.

"Hi," I say.

She smiles at me like she didn't on the playground yesterday. "I just got four new nail polishes from my mom," Elena says. "Do you want me to paint your nails? I'm getting really good at it. I practice on my mom all the time."

I don't say anything for too long.

"You can paint mine," Elliot says, and he waves his fingers at us from his seat next to the couch.

Elena giggles. "You're a boy," she says.

"Boys can have painted nails," Elliot says.

But I think he's only offering because I usually say no. That's what happens every Saturday. Elena comes in with some idea of something we can do together, something that doesn't involve Julian. And if Person and Dad are here they nudge me so I say OK. And if they aren't here, I say no because I feel too weird sitting in a room without Julian when it isn't even school or nighttime.

But today I think about how I felt on the playground yesterday when Elena wouldn't even smile. And how I thought maybe one day we'll try on the same day.

Maybe that can be today.

So I say, "If boys can have painted nails, you can paint my nails and Julian's."

Julian smiles and nods and Elena says, "Woo-hoo!"

It feels good to make someone so happy just by offering my nails.

Mom gets home at seven. Dad comes in with a pizza at seven thirty. We sit in the dining room and Elena talks-talks-talks about nail polish and Julian and I show off our nails. It's a very normal Saturday night. Dad goes back to work. Mom tucks me into my bed and Elena into the pullout next to me.

It's not until I fall asleep that I realize it was too normal of a Saturday.

I didn't think about babies or postcards all day.

And Elena didn't say anything about the baby, and no one said anything to Elena about the baby.

Did they forget to tell her?

On Monday, Ms. K sticks a Post-it to my desk about fifteen minutes before recess. We're supposed to be reading silently. I have my book open in front of me but I'm letting the words swim. Last week, I tried hard to make the words make sense during silent reading time.

This week they keep sailing off the page.

Ms. K lets us read whatever book we want, which means we should be able to enjoy it. That's what she says. And last week I really cared about what was going to happen to Nikki Maxwell on the pages of this book, but today I don't care. Nikki isn't real. I am. Nikki doesn't have a baby showing up ready to make everything change and destroy her life. I do.

I care about Ms. K though so I'm able to read the note.

It says, "See me at recess."

By the time I put the words together, she's telling everyone to line up and go outside. I stay in my seat and Ms. K comes and sits next to me in David's desk.

When Ms. K asks me to see her at recess, it's similar to when Person and I have to see her before school. It's good because she cares. It's bad because it doesn't make her happy.

It's bad because it doesn't make Person happy.

It's all very confusing.

Ms. K says, "How did you feel about your spelling test this morning, Flora?"

I shrug.

She says, "Did your mom or dad review the words with you last night like usual?"

I nod. They did. Last night, after Elena went home, Dad and I sat at the counter in the kitchen with flash cards and flipped through them over and over until I could spell all ten words perfectly.

"What happened?" Ms. K asks.

She hands me my test. It's a list of words in my sloppy handwriting with a row of perfectly neat red *X*s next to it. I got eight words wrong. I got only two right.

Ms. K already limited my test. Everyone else has twenty words, but I only have ten. She recites my words every other word so I have longer to write. She did all of this stuff for me and I still messed up.

"I don't know," I say.

"You've gotten perfect scores on your spelling tests all month," Ms. K says. "What happened this week?"

I shake my head. Nothing happened. I took the test. I knew the words last night. Now I don't.

"Look at this word," Ms. K says. She points to number four. It looks like ✗4. *Anxous.*

"Can you tell me what's wrong with it?" she asks.

"No," I say.

"Can you tell me how to spell anxious?" Ms. K asks.

"A-N-X-I-O-U-S," I say.

"Right," Ms. K says. "Did you say the letters in your head like you did last week?"

I shrug. The truth is I don't know. Did I? I barely remember taking this test. I've been thinking about the baby all day.

"You don't remember?" Ms. K asks.

"I don't know," I say. "Probably not."

Ms. K nods. "OK, Flora. I want you to get some recess time. But is there anything you'd like to tell me? Should I have more understanding here as to why you failed this test? Why you refused to read aloud in social studies today and why you stared into space during independent reading time? Remember that in order to pass fourth grade, you need to pass almost every test and assignment in between now and the end of the year. Should I know anything that might stop you from being able to do this?"

Yes: you should know my person is going to be someone else's mom. You should know I couldn't make her happy enough. You should know that I didn't want to mess up trying to make Person happy by not making you happy too.

Those words are too heavy. I shake my head.

She says, "There's nothing?"

I can't. I can't tell her any of it.

"No," I say.

Ms. K nods. "You've made some huge strides over the last

few months, Flora, but I need you to really focus on these last few weeks of school. You're passing fourth grade by the skin of your teeth right now. You really need to work hard and pass almost every assignment until the end of the school year if you want to go on to fifth grade."

"I know," I say.

But I don't want to go on to fifth grade. I'm trying hard to do it because I want to make Person happy more than I want Ms. K to be my teacher forever. And I want to make Ms. K happy too. But it's so confusing that making Ms. K happy means leaving her. Especially when Person promised no more changes. Forever.

How do I believe in Forever if it doesn't include Ms. K?

Person picks us up from school and as soon as Julian and I crawl into the backseat of her car, she says, "We're going to see Dr. Fredrick."

Dr. Fredrick is a counselor that Person took us to when we first moved in with her, and then again when Dad moved in with us. His job is to help us learn to trust other people. For a long time, we saw Dr. Fredrick after school every Friday. We haven't seen him the past few weeks. He said it was a good time for us to take a break and focus on family at home. He said we were all doing well.

I guess we aren't doing so well anymore.

"But it's Monday," I say.

"Why?" Julian says.

Person turns to look at us. Her face is red and sweaty again. "To be honest," she says, "I need some help."

I shoot Julian an alarmed look, but he has that lying smile on his face and that makes me feel even more lonely. He wears that smile all the way into the parking lot, out of the car, and down the hallway to Dr. Fredrick's office.

Dr. Fredrick's smile is the opposite of Julian's: very real. He says "Flora," and then "Julian," He only needs to say our names to make us feel like he's happy to see us. He has short black hair that's gray in a couple of places and tiny glasses that match the black part of his hair. He's Japanese, like Brian from school.

We chat for a few minutes and I feel a little more relaxed.

Then he says, "So I hear you guys are going to have a new brother or sister? How are you feeling about that?"

I look at Julian. He knows I can't answer a question like that. He knows my words will get stuck. But he doesn't say anything either. He has that crazy smile pasted on his face so hard I want to shove him.

"Does that scare you?" Dr. Fredrick says. "I'm sure you're worried about what it will be like, how your mom and dad will have time for you, how your daily routines might change . . ."

Dr. Fredrick has a soft voice that makes even me answer him. I used to find myself mid-sentence without even realizing I'd opened my mouth. But today my mouth stays closed.

"Julian," Person says. "Tell Dr. Fredrick what you said about when you were a baby."

Julian turns to look at her. "We weren't babies," he says through that awful smile.

Dr. Fredrick's eyebrows jump a half a centimeter and I jump in my chair I'm so surprised. He doesn't let anything but kindness show on his face. I've never seen him move his eyebrows except to say hello.

"You weren't?" Dr. Fredrick says. "Why not?"

Julian shrugs.

"Flora," Person says, nudging me, "you said something about how you don't remember . . ."

She nudges me with her elbow again. I'm confused. I feel like she wants to rush this meeting with Dr. Fredrick along, but she also said she wanted to come here to get some help. How is he going to help her if she rushes us right out of here?

"Don't remember what?" Dr. Fredrick says.

"Tell him," Person says.

Dr. Fredrick looks up at her quickly. "Remember to be patient with Flora, Emily. She needs time to turn her feelings into words. Sometimes when a child experiences a lot of trauma, it can take longer for the words to come."

I finally find my voice. "Being born. I don't remember it. Or being a baby," I say.

"Me either," Julian says.

"Ah," Dr. Fredrick says. He thinks for a second. Person taps her foot. "Do you believe in other things you don't remember?"

"Huh?" Julian says.

"Like when you were moved from house to house. Do you remember all of that?"

I feel Person shifting and shifting in her seat beside me.

"No," Julian says.

"No," I say.

"Do you know how many houses there were?" Dr. Fredrick asks.

Person crosses her legs. She uncrosses them. She rubs her sweaty forehead.

"No," I say.

"What do you know?" Dr. Fredrick asks. "What do you remember?"

"There were a lot of houses before our home now," I say. "Like, more than two."

"But less than ten," Julian says. "Right?"

I nod. "Probably."

"Great," Dr. Fredrick says. "What else do you remember? Which house was the best house?"

"Some were nice . . . some were . . . not," I say.

"Yeah," Julian says. "Gloria's was . . . sort of, neither."

"Yeah," I say. "She was just . . . busy."

Dr. Fredrick nods. "And who else?"

I lean around Person to look at Julian. He's doing the same thing to look at me.

"We don't remember anyone else," Julian says. "Not like names or faces."

"Just . . ." I can't even finish. What do I remember? It's all in feelings. I remember leaving. I remember hugging. I remember crying. I remember being carried on someone's shoulders and I wish I knew who the someone was.

"But you know there was more than Gloria?" Dr. Fredrick says.

"Yeah," Julian and I both say.

"Maybe being born is like that," he says. "Something you can know happened but something you don't remember."

"No," I say. Because that wouldn't make sense. It's OK for foster parents to disappear, but real moms don't. The only thing that would make sense is that there was no first mom.

"Well, why not? No one remembers every minute of their lives, but all of the minutes do happen . . ."

Dr. Fredrick is talking and talking. I'm letting the kindness of his voice lull me into a trance while I ignore the words he's actually saying because they don't work for me.

"Look, guys," Person says, interrupting. "I need you to know you were born. I mean, the circumstances . . . we don't know them. And . . . we're all a family now, right? So maybe it doesn't matter so much but—"

"No!" Julian says, so loudly. I jump out of my seat, ready to cover for him, to protect him. Then I remember Person is there and I don't have to. I sit down slowly while he's still yelling "No! No! No!" The smile is gone. I forgot to be ready for this. I forgot how that fake-lying smile is always followed by the truth shouted way too loudly. "No! No! No!" he yells. "You're not even talking about the important part!"

"Julian, lower your voice," Person says, too calmly.

"No! No!" he screams.

"What's the important part?" Dr. Fredrick asks.

Person says, "Be quiet, Julian."

Julian is screaming now. "The postcards!" he wails. "I want to talk about the postcards!"

"Postcards?" Dr. Fredrick says.

I start to shake. I don't want to know about the postcards. I don't want to hear that Person lied to me and stole from me. As long as she doesn't admit it, I can pretend it's not true.

"Lower your voice," Person says. "We can't talk about anything if you're screaming."

"What postcards?" Dr. Fredrick asks Person.

Julian is still screaming "NO!" and "POSTCARDS" and "SHE STOLE THEM" and "GLORIA MISSES US!"

Person is trying to shush him but he keeps screaming.

I'm pretty sure I'm about to float away. I'm pretty sure my brain can't handle this much screaming and anger between people I love and that my body will stay here but I'll float at the ceiling and rejoin them at home.

"What postcards?" Dr. Fredrick says again. I'm still in his office. But I'm sure I'll float away soon if he doesn't do something.

I hope he does something. Dr. Fredrick does not like when I float away. He says that's one of the reasons I have so much trouble remembering all of the things that happened to us and all of the places we lived.

Person looks at him like he's crazy to try to talk to her in such a normal voice while Julian is screaming his head off.

"It's OK for him to scream," Dr. Fredrick says. "Sometimes we need to scream."

Person's eyes are so huge. Her face is sweaty. I wonder if screaming is hurting the baby. I wonder if the baby has ears yet. I wonder if Person is more worried about the baby's ears than Julian's feelings.

"Tell me about the postcards," Dr. Fredrick says.

Person's eyes are so huge. She looks like David did when Ms. K caught him writing on his desk in permanent marker.

Finally, I answer. "Julian found some postcards from kids in our old home and he thinks there are more and that Mom stole them."

Julian stops screaming. "Yeah," he says.

Person stutters. "You found them?" she says. "How?"

Julian shrugs. "In the mailbox," he says.

"She's still writing to you guys?" Person says. "I don't understand. You've been with me for almost two years now."

"Do you guys like these postcards?" Dr. Fredrick asks. "The ones you've seen?"

"Yeah," Julian says. "Gloria says she misses us."

"Megan B. says they have a new baby," I say.

Person keep shaking her head.

"Are your kids right?" Dr. Fredrick asks, looking at Person. "Are there some postcards you haven't shown them yet?"

She wipes her forehead. "Shouldn't we have this conversation . . . confidentially?"

I grip my chair. I don't want to be sent into the hallway to wonder what they're talking about.

"Actually," Dr. Fredrick says, "I think it's important that they hear the entire conversation so they can be reassured there are no secrets."

"No secrets?" Person asks. She sounds angry. She sounds like she loves secrets.

"It's their story, Emily. You need to go home and give them the postcards."

"You're saying it's my fault?" she asks.

"It's the same thing we always talk about. Remember the roles?"

Julian and Person and I all nod.

"Everyone has a role when it comes to families," Dr. Fredrick reminds us anyway. "Emily, it's your job to be absolutely trustworthy. You need to give Julian and Flora every reason to trust you."

"I know," Person says quietly.

"And Julian, it's your job to try to trust. To act like you trust and let the trust follow sometimes."

"To stop hiding food in my closet," Julian fills in. "To tell the truth."

Dr. Fredrick looks at me.

"And Flora, it's also your job to act like you trust and to let the trust follow sometimes," he repeats, like always.

"It's my job to talk when I have something to say," I recite. "Even if it takes a long time."

We used to talk about these roles all the time. It makes me feel calm to be reminded of them. It means I don't need to work on fixing the whole family: Person and Julian and Dad and me. I only need to talk, and to try to talk even when I don't want to. That's just one thing instead of a million.

"You missed an opportunity to earn trust by hiding those postcards," Dr. Fredrick says to Person. Julian smiles at me, a real smile. Only Dr. Fredrick can make us feel better while at the same time pointing out how Person isn't perfect.

"But . . ." Person's quiet now. "Gloria let them go. And I'm their mom now. It's . . . over. Right?"

Dr. Fredrick shakes his head. "Their story is connected. The parts before they met you are connected to the parts now. Just like the parts of your story before you met Jon are connected to your relationship with him now. We all need our story."

"Our story?" I ask. "We have a story?"

"Sure, you do," Dr. Fredrick says. "Somewhere it's recorded exactly where you lived and who you lived with. Emily, didn't you see a file?"

Person shrugs. "Their records were . . . abysmal. There were a ton of unfinished sentences and questions marks. I don't know . . . everything. I only know. Well, I know about Gloria. And the family before . . . and, well, a little bit. I know only a little bit. I don't know anything about their birth mom, except that they're biological siblings."

"You need to tell them everything you know," Dr. Fredrick says. "There's going to be a baby in the family. They'll watch this baby growing up and know everything about it. They need to know as much as they can about themselves."

"I . . . I'm sorry about the postcards," Person says, but she's still looking at Dr. Fredrick, not at us. "But I really don't know too much."

"They need those postcards," Dr. Fredrick says.

Person is quiet for too long before she turns to us and takes our hands.

"I'll give you guys the postcards when we get home, OK?"

It's weird for my hand to be in hers when I'm feeling mad at her. There's another weird feeling in my heart too, like a worm crawling around in the sadness and angry. I think I sort of feel sorry for Person.

"But . . . It's a sad story," she says, turning back to Dr. Fredrick. "I thought . . . I thought I was doing the right thing."

Dr. Fredrick nods. "Flora," he says. "Are you surprised that your story before you came to your mom's house is a sad one?"

"No," I say. It's the only thing I knew for sure. Sadness.

"Julian, are you?"

"No," he says.

"I know you want to protect them, Emily," Dr. Fredrick says. She's crying now. I never knew it was possible to be mad at someone and also love them this hard. I want to give her a hug and slap her in the face at the same time. "But you only denied them access to their life's history. You didn't protect them from the sadness. That sadness lives in them. They need to know where it came from."

Person moves our hands to her face so she can wipe her eyes. I feel a tear trickle onto my finger.

"I don't . . . I don't know too much."

"Well, start with the postcards. Start with what you do know."

"Please," Julian squeaks.

"OK," Person says.

Dr. Fredrick smiles. "OK, so why don't we all leave this office today with a renewed commitment to the roles of trust. Can we all do that? Can you commit to filling your role as much as possible and watching the trust follow?"

"Yes," Person says.

"Yes," Julian says. "If I get the postcards."

"Yes," I say.

We get up to leave, but Dr. Fredrick keeps talking.

"And Emily? They may need more. If they ask to look for more, do it in an age-appropriate way. Do it in a way that fits into your life. But you're pregnant now; I can't imagine any of this getting any easier for these two until they get some answers."

Person nods. "OK," she says. "We'll see what we can do."

The next thing I know we're all hugging. I'm not sure if I'm still mad at Person or not. I'm not sure at all.

The rest of the week in school is the same. Person says there are a lot of postcards, it's too much for one day, so she starts giving us one every night at dinner. In school, I'm thinking about postcards and babies and stories. I'm thinking about Gloria and Megan B. and the white house I lived in when I was very small and the person whose shoulders I rode at one point.

I'm thinking about Person and how we made her life a whole lot harder right when there's a new baby so we should be trying to be easy.

I'm not thinking about school.

I keep messing up. Calling out. Failing tests. Ms. K has conversations with me a few times, then she gives up.

Inside my head I beg her not to call Person. Not to make Person upset too. Or worse: not to make Person give up like she did.

I want to be a better daughter for Person, a better fourth grader for Ms. K. I just don't know how to do better.

Friday night, when I'm alone in my room again, I dream about Castillo the Mouse.

I'm holding him in my palm, the cute slimy purple lump of him, even though Ms. K said we aren't allowed to hold them yet. But that's OK because I can't get in trouble for things that happen in a dream.

He's there in my palm and then poof he's gone.

I wake up, and I'm already sitting. My heart is racing. He's gone.

But I know he's not. I know he's still in the tank in the

classroom being nursed by Pringles. So why is this so scary?

Then I think about Ms. K in the classroom. I hear her saying, "No names after a real person, Flora."

But Flora Castillo was a real person. Flora Castillo was me for most of my life.

And I was allowed to name a mouse *Castillo*.

Does that mean Flora Castillo isn't a real person anymore?

I get out of bed and sneak though the living room/kitchen to Julian's room.

When we first started living with Person, I would sneak to his room all of the nights. When she didn't give us back after Christmas, I would sneak out about three-quarters of the nights. And then after the summer, when we'd been here a whole year, I got down to half the nights. After our second Christmas with Person, this past one, I got comfortable. I dug myself a spot in my bed like it would always be there. I started telling on Julian when he hid food. I thought I never believed Person about Forever. But now I think maybe I did. Maybe I believed her a little bit.

I thought Forever meant No Changes Ever Again.

Can Forever mean something else?

I'll probably start sneaking out all the nights again.

I open Julian's door and—too loudly since it's the middle of the night—I say, "What happened to Flora Castillo?"

Julian steps out of his closet. He has his hands over his mouth.

"You mean you?" he says. "You're right here."

"I mean Flora Castillo. Girl. Not mouse."

Julian rubs his face. "Are you sleepwalking, Florey?" he asks.

"No," I say. I cross the carpet until we're almost nose to nose.

Julian was in his closet.

There's a brown crumb on his chin. There's another on his cheek. His skin almost camouflages them, but I see them there.

His eyes are big, like he's scared of me.

"You!" I say.

His eyes fall to his feet.

"You said you would stop," I say. We have to be normal kids now. We have to act like we trust Person even when it's hard.

The baby will always trust Person.

"Sorry," he says. He shrugs.

"We have to be perfect now," I say. "We have to be easy."

"I don't have to be perfect, Florey," Julian says.

"There's a baby coming," I say. "We have to be perfect for Per—for Mom."

"That's not normal. You shouldn't have to be perfect for your mother."

My face is hot. I'm so angry. He doesn't get it. "We're already making her so uncomfortable with the postcards," I say. We can't ask for more than that. We have to take up less space in her life, not more.

"You heard Dr. Fredrick. She owes us those postcards!"

he says. He's almost shouting. He's the one turning this from discussion into fight.

I walk over and grab at the brownie in his hand. It breaks so that I'm holding most of it, but he still has a chunk. "You don't need this," I say.

"Give it," he says. "Give it, Florey."

"Why do you need it if—"

"Because what if the baby eats everything?" he asks all of a sudden, the words coming out too hard and fast. "What if another person means there's not enough food? What if Mom comes up with a rule that says we can only have as much food as we can fit into one hand like that one mom that time. What if my hands start to shrink again and what if I'm always always hungry and never never have anything to eat?"

"There wasn't a mom with a food and hands thing," I say.

Julian nods. I'm just a year older than him but he's still much shorter than me. His eyes are huge. Scared.

"You heard Mom," he says. "She doesn't know anything about this baby. She doesn't know where it'll sleep. How does she know what it will eat? How does she know that she'll love it the same as us? . . . She loves us, I think, usually, but . . . Love doesn't matter to family. You know that."

"Why aren't you saying this to Mom?" I ask. "You're supposed to try to trust her."

"Me?" he says. "You're the one who can't say anything half the time."

"Yeah," I say. "But at least when I talk it's the truth."

He shuts his mouth.

"Why do you fake that smile all the time?" I say.

Julian looks at his toes.

"You have to stop stealing and lying."

"I can't," Julian says.

"You have to!" I say.

"I *can't*!"

We are on the verge of being too loud. It's midnight. We could get caught.

"If you don't stop . . ." I can't finish.

"What?" Julian says. "If I don't start acting like I trust her all the time, Mom won't love me anymore? Or she'll love me less? Or something?"

"Just try?" I say. "Try to stop?"

"Maybe I don't care!" Julian yells. "I don't have to make her love me. Who cares if she loves me?"

"Us," I say.

"Who cares if she loves us?" Julian says. Then he takes a huge bite of brownie and chews it right in my face. "She says we're here forever, so that means it doesn't matter what we do, right? So what if I smile when I don't know what else to do? So what if I hide food and eat it at midnight? What do we need love for anyway?"

He reaches out and takes the rest of the brownie from me, shoving most of it in his mouth.

"Julian . . . ," I say. "We have to . . . we're supposed to . . . team."

"Sorry, Flora." Julian polishes off the brownie and balls up the wrapper. "I just don't care."

We are Onlys. I'm supposed to be scared when he's scared. But right now I'm too angry to be scared.

I march out of his room and down the hallways back to my own bed. Suddenly I don't care about mice *or* Floras named Castillo.

I don't think Julian and I fought before we got here. I don't think I was ever angry at him before.

He's going to mess up everything.

Maybe I didn't know how to be mad at him before, but now I do. Maybe that's one thing Person gave me.

I think I like it.

Eight
FAMILIES ARE PEOPLE WHO LIVE TOGETHER

THE NEXT DAY, SATURDAY, ELENA COMES over again. This time she's coming for two nights since Monday is a holiday from school. Elena has come over almost every Saturday and Sunday since Dad moved into Person's room. Elena also calls Dad *Dad*. But she calls Person *Emily*.

She says I'm lucky my dad and my mom live in the same place.

I say she's lucky she's known her dad and her mom her whole life except I never say that out loud because there are too many important words in that sentence. It's the most important sentence ever and so the words would never get out in the right order so that Elena would understand them.

Elena is Dad's other daughter but she's not really my sister or foster sister because she doesn't live here.

Elena is my friend. She says *sister*. I say *friend* but I only say it in my head the same way I only call my person *Person* in my head. I say friend because I've had a lot of sisters and they were all sort of broken like me. And Elena is nice and normal with pretty hair and sixth-grade friends with short skirts and I've never had a friend before.

She calls Julian her brother but she's more mine than Julian's. When she comes over she sleeps on a pullout in my room. And she shares her things with me. And she always wants to play with me without Julian and I always say no, we have to play with Julian and it goes around and around like that.

But today I'm mad at Julian and I don't want to see him at all.

Person has a shift at the hospital so it's just me and Julian and Dad and Elena at lunch. Afterward Dad says, "Do you guys want to go to the park?"

"I want to play alone with Elena," I say.

"You do?" Elena asks. Her eyes are bigger than usual. I've tried to play with her every Friday at recess for almost the whole school year, but I've never said it in those words.

"I want to go to the park!" Julian says. He looks right at me. I'm still mad at him and I realize now that he might be mad at me too even though that seems like it shouldn't be allowed. He's the one who's messing up. I'm the one trying.

"You guys can go to the park," Elena says. "I'll stay and play with Flora."

Elena is one year older than me but she's already in the sixth grade. And the park is right behind our house. Still, I'm shocked when Dad says, "OK."

"What do you want to do?" Elena asks when we're alone in my room.

She's always asking stuff like that. Like I'm the leader. Like I'm the real girl. When Dad and Person got married, she whispered to me, "I was so upset when my parents got divorced but you made it OK. Now I get a sister."

I know she'll go with it when I say, "It's a secret."

Elena nods, seriously. Her skin is almost as dark as mine and she wears her hair in a bunch of twists like I do, sometimes. But her eyes are gray-blue. She says she's mixed—black and white. Because both of her parents are also mixed—black and white. Person is white and Ms. K is white and Dr. Fredrick is Japanese and most the kids at school are white except Hannah and Quentin are black and Emilio is Latino and Brian is Japanese. Person says Julian and I are also mixed in some way just like Dad and Elena, except probably with some Spanish thrown in. But she doesn't know how or why or mixed of what exactly. Julian and I are Onlys and we don't know what else we are so I always end this conversation as quickly as it starts.

"It's important but I can't tell you why and you can't ask," I tell Elena.

She nods again.

"OK, come on," I say. I pull her to Julian's closet. I'm really going to do it. I'm going to get all of the food out and make sure he can't ever put any more in. I'm going to do what he can't. I'm going to force him to trust our person.

We stand and look at it. The closet is big and his clothes and shoes take up only a quarter of it. The rest is empty. There are shelves on the left where T-shirts and jeans and shorts are folded. There are a few hangers on the right. There are five pairs of shoes lined up neatly on the floor.

"Is that a candy wrapper?" Elena asks, pointing to a fold between two of his jeans.

I nod.

"He's hiding candy in here?" she asks. She dives for it and pulls out a Milky Way. "Score!" she yells, ripping open the wrapper. "These are my favorite. Want half?"

I stare at her dumbfounded. It hadn't even occurred to me to eat the food Julian was saving in here. That seems somehow worse, a greater violation, meaner, than throwing it away.

But no. It's his fault. He needs to trust, or at least act like it. He needs to work harder for Person because we keep asking her to work so hard for us.

That's what Dr. Fredrick said: stop hiding food, stop lying, and the trust will follow. Act like you trust your mother, and when nothing terrible happens, you actually will trust her. Or something like that.

I open my palm and Elena puts half the chocolaty-caramely-goodness in it. We munch together, then I say, "We get all of the food out of here. We put it in your bag and you take it to your house and throw it away there Monday."

I expect Elena to ask why. Anyone else would ask why. But

she says, "You mean my *other* house."

"Sure," I say. I'm always forgetting that Elena thinks she's a part of this too. This Person-Dad-Julian-Flora thing. She's only here every seventh night but she says *my*.

"My room."

"My family."

"My dad."

"My stepmom."

"My remote control."

My person and my dad both say she's right and I like Elena (sometimes) so I don't bother to argue with them. But I've been in lots and lots of families and the only definition I've come up with is this: families are people who live together. So, Elena doesn't count.

"OK," Elena says.

We tear through each of Julian's shoes. We run our fingers through the folds of all of his T-shirts. We empty the pockets of his pants and shorts. We uncover a pile of food. Stuff that's normal, like two more candy bars (that Elena eats) and four granola bars, and a few packets of trail mix that Person likes to keep in her purse. And stuff that's definitely stale now, like rock-hard slices of bread and halves of Pop-Tarts. And stuff that's gross, like moldy slices of cheese and green chicken fingers from the school lunch.

"Why does he keep all this?" Elena asks.

I shrug. She'd never get it. She'd never get anything.

She thinks Julian and I are lucky.

But the pile is too big. It's big enough to bury my feet in. A few weeks ago, Person said Julian was getting better, that he was showing her his closet and only hiding a few pieces of food in it.

He's getting worse since we found out about the baby.

He's worse and I'm worse.

I don't want to be worse. I don't want us to be worse.

"He has to stop," Elena says. I nod. I don't think she knows what's coming in six months. I'm pretty sure Dad and Person haven't told her. Yet. She just thinks Julian's closet is gross.

"I won't say anything," Elena says.

I smile.

Elena throws her arm around me and we drag the pile of food to my room and hide it in the back of her overnight bag. Doing that with Elena made it almost fun. It made me almost forget that these pounds and pounds of food are going to destroy our lives.

The next day Person is home from work and the sun is shining so when Elena asks for a picnic at the park, Person and Dad get all excited and start pulling things out of the fridge, making sandwiches and shouting about lemonade.

Actually, Elena said, "Can we have a picnic in the park like we used to last year?" Even though I think we've only had one picnic ever.

After a while, we pile out of the apartment and walk down a little hill toward the pond at the back of the park. Julian

is carrying a cooler since we didn't have a picnic basket. I
have a blue bedsheet since we didn't have a red-and-white
checked blanket. Elena has a pitcher of lemonade. Person and
Dad walk behind us, holding hands. The sun massages my
face. I'm in sandals for the first time all spring so I can feel the
grass tickle the sides of my feet. For a second I wonder if this
is what Person means by family. People who do things outside
together just because they're close by each other and the sun
is finally shining after a long winter.

But that definition is too confusing. Because I'm glad to
be with Julian but I'm still mad at him for faking happy with
Person and for stealing food. And because I love Person but I
don't love the baby inside her, at least not yet. And because I
don't understand Elena at all. So she can't be my family.

I'll stick to my definition. Families are people who live
together.

Once we're settled on the sheet with plastic cups of lemonade and slices of sandwiches and a huge bowl of strawberries
between us, Person says, "So, kiddos, should we tell Elena the
good news?"

That's all it takes and Julian is jumping up and down. It
makes me so mad at him. It's all fake, all that jumping. And
the cheering.

"We're gonna have a baby! We're gonna have a baby!"

He's almost too loud and jumpy to understand what he's
saying. I narrow my eyes at him.

"What?" Elena asks.

"Julian and I are going to have a brother or sister. It'll be born," I say.

"And you," Dad says loudly. "Of course, baby. It'll be your brother or sister too."

"I know," I say. "It'll be my brother or sister. A baby."

Elena is shaking her head back and forth. "No," she says. "He means *mine*. It'll be *my* brother or sister. Wait!" She turns to Person. "You're pregnant?"

Person nods. "You'll be such a great big sister, Elena," she says. "You can hold the baby and sing to it."

"You're pregnant?" Elena says again, more loudly. Then she laughs. "I thought you were getting fat," she says. She smirks toward me.

I sort of thought Person was getting fat too, but I don't think it's funny. Who cares if she's fat or skinny, as long as she's mine.

"Elena!" Dad says. "Apologize."

Person laughs. "It's OK, Jon. She's right. I am getting fatter. I'm eating for two."

Elena meant it to be mean. I'm pretty sure Person knows that. But she pretends not to care. Or she doesn't care. I can never tell when someone is pretending.

"When?" Elena asks. It sounds like the sun and the strawberries aren't making her happy anymore.

Julian sits back down and starts eating quietly. I see him sneak a few strawberries into the pocket of his cargo shorts. He'll try to hide them later. And he'll probably find out all of his food is missing.

"Five and a half months from now," Person sings.

I watch Elena's face as it shifts through a lot of expressions. She says, "They knew already?" nodding at Julian and me.

Person and Dad look at each other and sort of freeze like that.

"When did you tell them?" Elena asks.

"Only a few days ago, sweetie," Dad says. But I'm good at math so I count in my brain. Ten. It was ten whole days ago.

I don't say anything.

"Why?" Elena says. "Why didn't you tell me first? Or at least at the same time?"

No one answers. They look so confused about this, but the answer is simple: they didn't tell you because you weren't there.

"I'm sorry," Dad says. "We should have waited." He pauses. "I'm pretty excited to see you hold a baby."

Elena's face does that shifting thing again. Sad. Angry. Sad. Happy. Confused. Sad. Happy. It finishes on happy but after all the shifting I don't think the happy is real.

"I hope it's a boy," she says. "Then I'll have a real brother."

"Elena!" Dad says again. Even though Julian and I don't care about this. "Julian is your real brother."

"He's a stepbrother," Elena says.

Julian and I freeze. We don't call Elena our sister but we've never thought about her like a stepsister either.

"You all share a dad," Person says. "So—"

"Nope," Elena says. "We don't really share a dad. They don't even know their dad."

Julian and I look at each other. He raises his eyebrows.

When you and your brother are Onlys it gets lonely being mad at him. I decide it's over. I have the food. His closet is empty except for clothes. I don't have to be mad at him anymore.

"Stepbrother, stepsister," Elena says again.

It seems like Elena is trying to be mean but she's failing because we don't care about stepsister, foster sister, friend. We only know she's not one of us.

I shrug. "OK," I say.

"No, not OK," Person says. "I mean, there's nothing wrong with stepsisters, but that's not what you guys are. That's not how it works. Julian and Flora are adopted by both me and your father. There are no steps here."

"You!" Elena says. "You're my stepmom."

"Oh, well, that's true," Person says.

"You're my stepmom," Elena says. "And you're their mom."

Person says, "Yes."

"Then how aren't they my stepbrother and stepsister?"

Person and Dad stare at each other.

I don't even know why we're talking about all of this. I thought we were supposed to be talking about the baby.

"Sometimes I hate how confusing this all is," Elena says. Her voice sounds more normal. Dad throws an arm around her.

"I know," he says. "But, are you excited for your new brother or sister?" he asks.

Elena shrugs under his shoulder. "The baby will be more mine though, right? More than theirs?"

She's looking at her dad, but Julian says, "No!"

"Yes!" Elena says. "He's my dad's *baby.*"

I watch Julian get angry. I feel calm. At least he's real when he's angry.

"He's going to live with us!" Julian says. "He'll be more ours. Mine and Flora's."

That's true. Elena will only see him once every seven days because he won't even go to St. Peter's school with us. Babies don't go to school.

"No!" Elena screeches. "He's, like, my dad's actual baby."

"He's our dad too!" Julian says.

Person is trying to shush us but it doesn't work.

"I mean for real. He's really my dad. And the baby will be the same way. Like made of my dad."

"Well, he's coming out of our mom!" Julian yells. "He's inside her right now."

"God, you guys don't get it," Elena says. "She's not your mom like that. She didn't have you."

"Have us?" I ask. I'm calm.

Julian has all of our anger. I let him have it.

"You weren't born from her," Elena says. "The baby isn't really related to you at all."

"We weren't born from anyone," Julian says. "So what?"

"Huh?" Elena says. "What do you mean you weren't born from anyone?"

"We weren't like *born* like that," Julian says, still angry though.

"You were like grown in a test tube or something?" Elena says, looking at Person.

"No!" Person says.

At the same time, Julian and I say, "Maybe."

Person is trying so hard to keep her voice calm and quiet like it always is, and also to be sure Elena can hear her. She says, "Flora and Julian are a little confused right now. Of course they were born—"

"No we're not," Julian says.

"Dad!" Elena screams.

"Elena, shh," Dad says.

She turns to look at him. "Dad, they think they weren't born?"

"We're still figuring some stuff out," Person says.

"I can't, Dad. Really? You have kids who think they weren't born?"

"Elena," Person says. "After adoption people can be confused—"

But Elena isn't looking at Person anymore. She's looking at her dad and right now he really does seem like he's more hers than anyone's because they're talking with their eyes the way Julian and I can. And their eyes are both the same mix of gray and blue and Julian's and mine are just brown, unlike anyone else at this picnic.

"How am I supposed to be happy about this, Dad?" she

says. "I'm still getting used to Julian and Flora. Now there's another one? You want me to be happy? You barely even see me anymore! You won't care about me at all now!"

She takes off into the park and Dad runs after her.

Julian sits and freezes that crazy smile on his face. He picks up a strawberry. I pick up my sandwich. We munch.

Person says, "You guys OK?" And we nod.

It's sort of nice to be the calm ones for once.

There's a hand shaking my shoulders. It's the middle of the night. "Florey! Florey!" Julian is whispering.

It takes me a second to figure out what's going on and where I am. I half sit with my wrist rubbing my eyeballs. "Julian?" I say.

"Shh!" Julian says.

Suddenly I'm scared. It's never Julian in my room. It's always me in Julian's room. It has not been Julian in my room since—

I jump out of bed and leap toward him. I throw my arms around him. "They started again? Is it the baby?"

Julian pulls back. "Huh? What started? What about the baby?"

"Nightmares," I say. They used to be so bad. They were the screaming, shaking kind of nightmares. They are in my memory as long as I can remember. I would hear Julian when he had a nightmare no matter where I was, in any room, on any floor, in any house we lived in and I would try and try to wake him up but it was always too late. The nightmares always won.

Julian had nightmares here too. He had them for so long. I don't remember why they stopped, how they stopped.

I guess they didn't stop.

"Another nightmare," I say. "Because of the baby?"

Julian shrugs my arms off of his shoulder. "No," he says. He glances at Elena. "She is my nightmare. And she's real."

He points and I see Elena sleeping on the pullout next to me, her breath going in and out evenly.

I almost jump. Tomorrow is a day off from school which for some reason means Elena spends both Saturday and Sunday night at our house. I had forgotten she was there.

"Huh?" I say. I have no idea what he's talking about. I wonder for a second if that's what it's always like to talk to me.

"She stole my food," Julian says.

And like that, I remember. I feel my cheeks burn, but Julian doesn't notice.

"She stole it all," he whispers. "She doesn't care if we eat or not. She doesn't care about us at all. She stole it all, Flora. Every piece from every little pocket. How did she know? How did she do that? What if . . ."

My heart is hammering. I should tell him. Explain to him I was mad. But I'm not mad anymore. I should grab the plastic garbage bag full of old stale food out of Elena's backpack and give it back to him.

But I'm frozen. I can't.

Person says she'll love us forever, but she's about to have a real baby. She already has a real baby—inside her the way we never were. A real baby who will trust her so easily because it won't have another choice. Or another mother or mothers who make it hard to trust your real mother once you find her.

I can't let Julian keep stealing food. I can't let him keep messing this up. We have to deserve Person.

"Do you know where it is, Flora?" Julian asks, a pleading tone to his voice.

I shake my head. Elena shifts in her sleep and we both freeze and stare at her until it seems for sure that she fell back asleep again.

"Then you're going to help me get her back, right?"

"Get the food back?" I ask.

Julian shakes his head. "She probably threw it away. I have to start all over. But . . . you'll help me get her back," he says, nodding to the lump on the bed next to mine. "She's not our sister anyway."

I nod. "I'm your sister," I say.

"Team," Julian says.

"Team," I say.

I hope he never finds out it was me.

Nine

FAMILIES HAVE RECORDS

AFTER ELENA GOES HOME IN THE morning, Person sits us down at the kitchen table. There are no plates or food. Instead, there's papers.

"OK, kiddos," Person says. "Here it is."

"Huh?" Julian says.

But I nod my head. I can't ask too many questions.

Person gestures at all of the papers spread out across the table. "This is everything I know about you guys from before I met you. Where you lived. Who you lived with. Why you moved."

Julian lunges at a paper and grabs it too quickly. "Really?" he says. "You know all of that? And it says we were born?"

I pick up a paper too, but it's rows and rows of black letters on white paper. It's a code. I don't even see my name on it. I see a lot of "seven-year-old girl."

What if we were born? What if these papers say we were born?

I'm not sure I want to be born, really. That would lead to so many more questions. Like . . . where is that mother?

"Oh, guys, I'm sorry. I'm doing this all wrong. I don't . . . this stuff. It's hard to talk about . . ."

"Huh?" Julian says again.

"I talked to Dr. Fredrick again yesterday," Person says. "And he said to show it all to you. But he made it sound so easy."

We don't say anything.

"I didn't know you'd ever want to know this stuff," Person says. "So . . ."

"It's OK, Mom!" Julian says. His smile is real. He lunges for another paper. "Look at all of this. You know all of this. You must know everything."

Person glances back to the papers. "Oh . . . ," she says. She does not sound happy. "I guess to you this might look like a lot, all this paperwork. But it's actually not a lot. When I said this is all I know, I mean it's limited. I know very little. The foster care system failed you guys in a lot of ways, and one of them is that it didn't keep your records correctly."

"Explain?" I ask.

"But what *does* it say?" Julian says.

"You really want to know?"

We nod. Of course we want to know. This is our lives. This is the answer to all of the questions. This is the light in all of the dark spots. This is the white house. This is the shoulders I sat on.

"OK." She sighs. "Well, I've been through the mess of these papers several times, and it all comes down to this: before me, you lived with a single mother with a lot of foster children."

"Gloria," Julian says.

"Yes," Person says. "She was supposed to keep you very temporarily, but you ended up staying there for eleven months."

"That's almost a whole year," Julian whispers. I don't know if he thinks that's too long or too short for his memory. I'm not sure which one I feel either.

"Before that," Person says, "you guys lived with a woman who intended to adopt you."

At that, our eyes go wide.

"I take it you never knew that?" Person says.

We shake our heads. She intended to adopt us . . . and then didn't? We were that awful?

I start to shake.

"OK," Person says. "Well, that woman—I don't know how to say this."

"You have to," I say. I don't mean to say it. My lung filters fail me again.

Person doesn't look angry at me, just sad. She says, "That woman would have gotten all of the files about what happened before you went to her. And now they're nowhere to be found. I mean, the agency should have kept them too. But apparently neither that woman nor the agency can find them.

I've been fighting to reclaim them for years but . . . I can't get anywhere."

"Why?" I say.

Person lowers her eyebrows at me. "Why what?" she asks.

I mean, why would she fight to get records of our lives if she didn't want us to have them, but before I can put those words together, Julian speaks.

"So these don't say we were born?" he asks.

"J, baby." Person sighs. "You were both born."

"Tell us about it then," Julian says. "Where? When? With who?"

Person shakes her head. "I . . . Look . . . I . . . We know your birthdays, that means you were born. OK? Do you guys believe me?"

"I'm sorry, Mom. I just . . ."

"We can't," I say.

I wish I could believe her. It would make her so happy if I did.

"Is there anything you guys remember?" Person asks.

I nod. "White."

"Yeah," Julian says. "We started at a white house. It was white inside. Flora remembers turning on a light switch while standing in a line."

"Inside the house?" Person says to me.

I nod.

Julian's still talking. "And I remember a tiny table. I was sitting at the table. Flora was standing and reached up to turn on a light switch. So we weren't babies."

Person nods. "Most people's first memory is from when they were between two and three years old. So I bet that's when you guys lived in that house. The white house, as you say. But you were babies before that," she says. Her eyes are big and serious and begging.

We don't say anything. It feels good that Person believes us about the white house. I wish I could believe her back and make her feel this good.

"Maybe the person in the white house knows," I say.

"What?" Person asks.

"Yeah," Julian says. "If we find the white house, maybe they'll tell you that we weren't born. That we just showed up there."

"Sweetie," Person says. She takes Julian's face in her hands. "You didn't show up as a toddler inside a random white house."

"Maybe it wasn't random," I say. My filters are so open. I can't stop the words.

"Yeah," Julian says. "Maybe Gloria or someone knows where it is."

"I want to find it," I say. And I want to see Gloria again. And play with Megan B. and her dollhouse. But I don't say those things out loud.

"Do you guys want to write back to Gloria? And this little Megan B.?"

But we're shaking our heads. It isn't enough.

"I want to find the white house," Julian says.

"Me too."

Person looks so worried.

She rubs her forehead. I try not to see how we're making it sweat. I try not to worry about the baby inside her and how it'll never make her look for white houses or ex-foster moms or beginnings. That baby will always have a beginning.

"I wouldn't even know where to start looking for that place," Person says. "But if you ever want to write back to Gloria or any of the kids at her house, tell me. I'll make it happen."

Jen

FAMILIES STAY ON THE SAME TEAM

I'M AT THE WHITE BOARD IN my classroom first thing Tuesday morning, the second-to-last Tuesday of the school year, marker in hand, waiting for Ms. K to finish writing out a division problem so that I can loop to the answer. I can't wait to loop to the answer. I'm very good at looping to the answer.

Ms. K calls this Review Tuesday. She has one row go up to the board to work on a problem while everyone else works in their seats. Then we rotate so everyone gets a chance on the board. Since I'm in the first row, I get to go to the board first, and the board is the most fun, but I like Review Tuesdays, all of it, even the part when I'm in my seat.

The morning was hard. Hard to pay attention to stupid things like unpacking my bag and greeting Ms. K when the sun is shining through the windows and Julian wants us to find the white house and so do I and when Person says we can write back to Gloria now but also I hurt Julian and he doesn't know it.

Ms. K writes

$$23 \overline{)1245}$$

My marker starts moving right away. My marker moves fastest. My marker is always moving fastest in math and never moving fastest not in math.

I grab the answer from the string of numbers on my board and circle it.

"Fifty-four, remainder two!" I shout.

"Oh, oh, oh," Ms. K says quickly. "I'm sorry, I forgot to tell you. No remainders. You know how to do the whole thing now. Drop your zeros. Find the decimal. Round to the nearest hundredth."

"OK!" I say.

Ms. K comes up and whispers something in my ear but I'm too busy dropping zeros like a genius to hear her.

I'm still the first to the answer.

"Fifty-four point one three!"

"That's correct, Flora," Ms. K says. "But please don't shout out the answer. Other students might still be working on it."

I look at the rest of the board. Everyone else is still working. Most of them have only gotten to the *1* and some haven't even gotten past the *4* yet. I don't understand how so many of these kids who are so good at hard stuff like reading out loud and timed writing responses are also so bad at math.

The first row sits and I pick up my pencil as the second row goes to the board.

Ms. K writes

$$473$$
$$\times 1655$$

Multiplication! And with two fives! Even easier.

My pencil moves across my paper fast as lightning. I circle the answer. Everyone at the board is still working. Some of them are only on their second round of addition. I need to say my answer. I can't wait that long.

"Seven hundred eighty-two thousand, eight hundred fifteen," I say. I don't shout it this time. I say it nicely.

Ms. K comes over and squats in front of my desk. She can do this because she's wearing her every-other-Tuesday khakis and blue blouse today. "Flora," she whispers in her Warning Voice. "I'm proud of you for getting the answers correct, but I expect you to follow the rules and wait until I ask for the answer to shout it out. We need to respect the students who are moving more slowly. OK?"

I nod. But she doesn't get why it's so hard for me.

The thing about math is that numbers are better than words. I can give the answer and it will always make sense, even if it's wrong (which it usually isn't) because the answer is a number. No full sentences. No important words sneaking out before they'll make sense.

"This is your final warning," Ms. K whispers so no one

else can hear. "If you call out again, that will show me you are unable to participate in class today and you'll have to go finish your math assignment with Mr. Jackson."

The third row is at the board and Ms. K writes

$$47\overline{)215}$$

My pencil is moving and I realize for the first time today that I'm not thinking about Julian or Elena or Person's baby or where we'll go at the end of the school year. My pencil is moving. I am my pencil moving.

I have 4.574 circled.

I tap my eraser against my paper.

All around me pencils scratch. Markers move against the board. At least two of the kids have wrong answers already.

Scratch-scratch-scratch.

I have the answer. I want to say it. I don't want to wait.

Scratch-scratch-scratch.

When I wait for anything, bad things wake up in my head. Like the time Julian was caught hiding food at one of the foster homes where the lights were hardly ever on. Or when we were really little and there was a girl who would pull my hair and I never said anything because back then I didn't have any words at all.

I don't want to think about these things. I want to think about my circled 4.574. I want numbers. More numbers.

The *scratch-scratch-scratch* goes on around me. I feel the

numbers build in my throat. I feel them bouncing at the back of my teeth.

If I call out the answer, Ms. K will send me to Mr. Jackson, the principal, and that wouldn't be good because then I'd be away from Ms. K. But usually that also means I get a private moment with her at the end of the day. So maybe it would be OK. Maybe it would be better than waiting.

Finally Ms. K goes back to the board. She says, "Raise your hand if—"

"Four point five seven four!" I shout.

"Flora," Ms. K says. "Please go to Mr. Jackson's office."

The look on her face does not say, *Let's have a private meeting later.* It doesn't say, *I know you're trying your best for me, Flora. I want to help you try your best forever.* It doesn't say, *I love you, Flora.*

She doesn't even look disappointed, which is a kind of love. She looks exhausted.

By the time I get to Mr. Jackson's I'm almost in tears, but Ms. K has emailed him with a Review Tuesday worksheet for me to do while I sit here so I'm OK. The math keeps the bad stuff out.

A few minutes before recess, Mr. Jackson comes and sits next to me in the little room outside of his office. He's a big man with huge shoulders and a bald, white head. He has gray glasses that barely look different from the skin on his face. He's also wearing a gray suit. He's a very gray person.

"What happened today, Flora?" he asks.

I don't answer. My words are stuck again and his question is not a math problem.

"Ms. K had said you've been improving. She said that if you finish the rest of the year doing as well as you've been doing the past few months, you'll probably advance to fifth grade."

I still don't say anything.

"We didn't think that would be possible during the middle of the year. I'm incredibly impressed with how much you've improved."

I shrug.

It's not like I can say what I'm thinking: I don't like switching teachers. It feels too much like switching mothers.

But I'm trying hard to pass fourth grade anyway.

I love Person too much not to try.

"You understand?" Mr. Jackson asks.

I nod.

"Good," he says. "So then I take it that this little trip to my office was a fluke?"

I tip my head. I don't know what it means.

"I take it you won't end up here again."

That's fine with me. I want every extra minute with Ms. K.

I nod again.

"OK, go enjoy your recess."

I dash out the door. I wonder if Mr. Jackson noticed that my words were stuck.

* * *

When I get outside, I'm only a few minutes late. Recess has just started. My heart is already speeding up, happy, because it's Tuesday, which is a Julian-at-recess day and an Elena-not-at-recess day. I run out to the blacktop and look for him at our typical spot under the basketball hoop, but he's not there.

I scan the crowd for his brown hair but I don't see him with the other fourth graders or the little kids. When I finally find him, he's standing in a circle of Elena's friends.

Elena's friends?

The sixth grade is at recess today? But it's Tuesday. Their schedule must have changed.

I start to shake immediately. I didn't want to see Elena until I was supposed to have to see her on Friday. I didn't want to see Julian and Elena in the same place until it was Saturday afternoon when Person and Dad would be there to keep us safe.

But I see them now. And even though I don't want to, my legs start running toward them.

Julian is yelling.

The sixth graders around him are all laughing.

"FLORA!" Julian cries toward me. "FLORA!" He looks so tiny standing in the middle of all those laughing sixth-grade girls.

I sprint across the parking lot like it's on fire. I'm next to him with my arm around him. I'm trying to hold him on the earth. His brain is spinning, I can tell. I'm trying to be the point for his compass.

"What happened?" I ask.

Julian is shaking under my arm.

Elena laughs. "It was you, Flora. It was your idea."

"No," I say without even hearing her. She's standing a few feet away from us, but it's still like she's trying to wiggle her way in between us even though I don't know how or why. I want to kick her.

There's bad in my blood: she hasn't done anything but love me but I hate her anyway.

"WHERE IS IT?" Julian screams.

It's not until Elena starts laughing that I rewind and hear what she just said. *It was my idea.*

He's so angry his face is sweaty, his fists are clenched, he's almost vibrating under my arm. But she's still laughing. The rest of her friends seem to fall away so it's just the three of us in this corner of the blacktop. Julian shaking and shouting. Elena laughing. Me frozen.

Her laughing isn't like at a cartoon when it's actually funny. It's the laughing of the girls in school. It's the mean kind of laughing.

"This is about the food?" I ask.

She's still laughing. It's the laughing *at.* She's laughing at my brother.

Julian puts his hands on my shoulders and shoves me away from him. I trip into Elena and both of us fall on our butts.

"Where is it, Flora? What did you do? Weeks, it's taken weeks," Julian shouts.

Elena is laughing. I want to hit her.

Julian is crying but not like he used to. Not soft and quiet and scared. It's loud and violent. His tears are poison.

"How could you, Florey? You? YOU?"

Each time Elena laughs, my fists get tighter.

"First Mom steals from me, and now YOU?"

"Mom?" Elena says through giggles. "Emily stole something from you?"

We try to ignore her.

"You knew we needed it. We NEED it. Everything is . . ."

Julian doesn't struggle with words the way I do. But he can't say what he wants to because Elena is here, laughing.

"It's . . ."

I can fill in the blanks anyway. He doesn't need to say it.

Everything is . . . dangerous.

"It's . . . ," Julian says again. He's hiccuping sobs now. I hate myself. I hate him. I hate Person. I hate Elena.

"It's gross," Elena says through those laughing-at chuckles. "Right, Flora? Disgusting. That chicken finger was *moldy*."

I swivel my back and head so I can see her face. Her eyes are sparkling. Her mouth is open. She's happy. Julian is as angry as I've seen him—angry enough to kill another goldfish—and it makes Elena happy.

"It was so gross!" she gasps between laughs.

Her teeth are right there, jammed into the middle of her laughter.

"Florey," Julian sobs. "You're the only person who . . . I can't believe you would . . ."

Elena laughs. She speaks. "You're right though, Julian. We shouldn't have stolen that food. You're going to need it when the new baby comes and Dad and Emily forget all about you guys."

"I can't believe you did this to me, Florey. You. YOU!" Julian is shaking.

Elena keeps talk-laughing. "It's not like your mom's going to love you anymore when there's a new baby. Believe me. I was replaced with you guys. Now we'll all be replaced."

There are teeth in the middle of her laugh. All I can see is her teeth.

Those teeth don't need to be there, I think.

"Maybe you guys should go back to foster care and let us be a normal family."

Then *zoom*, I'm punching her. I don't remember deciding to do it. It doesn't feel like a choice. The minute her tooth breaks the skin on my knuckles I realize that yes, I've punched someone before. Somewhere. Some time.

Now Elena is crying and Julian is on my back like he's trying to hold my arms still even though I'm not going to punch her again or anything. It feels good. The place on my right hand where my blood is flowing out over my fingers feels like it's always needed to exhale. "When have I done that before?" I ask Julian.

"Florey," he says. He's still crying. But it's the other kind of crying now. The old crying. Elena is crying much louder.

Suddenly she yells, "MS. K!" and Julian and I look at each

other shocked. It was one fight. One punch. I didn't even suc-
ceed in knocking out her tooth. I'm the only one bleeding.

"MS. K!" she yells again.

We've never heard a kid call for a grown-up after only one
little punch.

Ms. K, who is the teacher on duty at recess, comes running
over to us and it's all *Flora, why are you bleeding?* and *Julian,
are you alright?* and *Elena, what are you doing over here with
them?* and *Flora, why are you bleeding?*

I say, "Her. I punched her."

And then I float away. I don't know where I go but that used
to happen all the time and it might be why I can't remember
anything in the right order and with the right details.

I float away. I'm gone. I'm nowhere.

THEORY #7

We come from blood, my brother and me.

All humans have blood, but most of them are made of their parents. Not my brother and me.

There was a time when we were tubes in a hospital, bubbling side by side, until a clumsy nurse knocked us over and we were puddles of blood on the floor. The nurse turned to find a towel to wipe up the mess, but when she turned back around, we'd already slithered away. We slid down the tiled floors of the hospital hallways, two red patches, close but not touching. We got out the door and out the parking lot and onto a school playground where kids were having recess.

"Gross!" said one.

"They're disgusting!" said another.

We grew veins to hold the blood. They still said "gross." We grew bones for the veins to wrap around. We grew muscles for the veins to hide behind. They still said "gross."

We grew skin and nails and eyes and noses and fingers and faces and feet.

We grew everything until we were trapped somewhere deep inside these new bodies.

Even now, they still say "gross."

That's the theory. We come from blood. That's why it feels so good when we bleed.

Eleven

FAMILIES DIVIDE LOVE INTO FRACTIONS

ELENA, JULIAN, AND I SIT IN a row outside of Mr. Jackson's office. His assistant told us that he's in a meeting so we need to sit and wait.

I tell her I don't know why Julian and Elena have to be here. I'm the one who punched. But she says we should all wait.

We're quiet while she sits at her desk typing and glancing at the clock every few seconds. But then she steps into the hallway and Elena leans over to whisper to us.

"It's not going to be the same, guys. I hope you know that."

We stare straight ahead, ignoring her, so she keeps going.

"Take it from me. I've known Dad and Emily longer than you have."

I still don't look at her, but in my head I admit that that's true. Person knew Dad before he was even divorced from

Meredith, when Elena was still small. Then later they fell in love and got married. After we were around. And Elena has known Dad all her life because she's a usual born-baby.

"Babies are expensive, I hope you know," Elena says. She looks at Julian. "You aren't going to get as many birthday presents as you did last year. I hope you're ready for that. And you guys can't ask for so much stuff. The money has to get to another person now. A cuter, smaller, more expensive person."

I file that away. Elena is talking like she's at our house on the weekend: real talk, friendly talk.

"And it's not just money. I was there already. So I know."

Now I can't help it. I say, "Huh?"

"Before you guys came along, Dad loved me more than he does now. I got one hundred percent. Then he had to split it up with you guys so now we each get only a third of his love."

"Thirty-three and a third percent," I say.

"Huh?" Elena says. "Flora, I try with you, but you're so weird sometimes."

We don't say anything for a while.

"So what do you think is going to happen?" she says finally. "There's going to be a new baby and we'll be down to only twenty-five percent each. Probably less because the baby will be new and cute and too little to even make any mistakes so he'll take up more than his fair share of Dad's love. We aren't going to be important anymore."

Elena is talking so quietly I can barely hear her even though her face is right near mine.

Julian breaks his statue pose to glance at me. I know what he's thinking.

Twenty-five percent of Dad's love isn't that much less than 33.33333 . . . That's OK.

But Person? We need all her love.

We sit in silence, letting Elena scare us for a few minutes. Then Mr. Jackson calls us into his office.

We stand in a row lined up in front of his desk.

I tell him the same thing I told Ms. K. "I punched her."

"I'm surprised you're back so soon, Ms. Baker," Mr. Jackson says. "Elena and Julian, why are you here?"

"Oh my God, you were here already today?" Elena says.

Her voice is so much meaner than it was a minute ago. I wonder which one of her is pretending.

She's still talking. "What's wrong with you?"

I don't know anymore. It used to be foster care was what was wrong with me. But foster care ended almost two years ago and I'm still wrong and broken. I feel wrong-er and broken-er than I did last week, even.

"That's enough, Elena," Mr. Jackson says, and she shuts her mouth. "I can see you're having no problem speaking so I assume your sister didn't do any permanent damage."

I'm not her sister.

Elena shakes her head.

"Good," Mr. Jackson says. "So, Flora, can Elena and Julian go back to class?"

Why is he asking me that? I shrug and then they're gone.

I sit in his office for hours and hours and hours with no math, with nothing to keep all of the bad stuff from haunting my brain.

I'm in the living room on the couch with a blanket and a pillow and Person at my feet. "I just can't figure out . . . I don't . . . punching isn't . . . Well, jeez, Flora, you already know it's wrong so what am I supposed to say to you now?"

Then she gets up and she's in her room and I think she's crying again and I made everything worse instead of better and it's another day closer to the baby showing up.

Elena is right. Why would Person still want some punching, food-stealing, broken kids when she's going to have a real baby?

I lie and stare at the ceiling. I'm numb, mostly. My hand hurts, but the pain is good. My heart doesn't hurt the way it did when Julian was crying, and the not-pain is also good.

I'm supposed to be sad or something about a time-out on the couch but it's not that bad.

"Are you asleep, Florey?" Julian asks, walking out of the bathroom. He has finally stopped crying.

I prop up my head. Words are too tired. Even *No, I'm awake* won't come out of my mouth.

"I think that was our first fight. Was that our first fight?"

I nod.

He stands to go, then turns back to look at me. "Is the fight over?" he asks.

I don't have the words to say it. I shrug.

"Yeah. I can't tell yet either," he says.

Then he's gone and my head falls back on the pillow.

I'm not sure how long I lie there, numb, before Person walks back into the room. She looks more awake and more mom-ish than she did before my time-out.

She sits on the couch and hands me the phone. "You need to call Elena and apologize for punching her. We do not punch or hit or hurt in this family."

I rub my knuckle under the blanket. The pain sings back to me. It's not bleeding anymore but it still feels bad and good, both at once. The harder I press on my knuckle, the more I think about a stupid cut. The more I think about a stupid cut on my knuckle, the less I think about change and Person forgetting to love us and Julian messing everything up and all the things that cut a thousand times deeper than Elena's tooth.

Person holds the phone out to me. I shake my head.

"You're not going to call her?"

I shake my head again.

"Flora, did you punch Elena?"

I nod.

"Why?" Person asks.

But I still don't know. And even if I did know, I've lost my words. They're buried so far inside me now. My tongue is tired and heavy.

It's been a long time since I lost all of my words. Person likes when I speak. Dr. Fredrick says I need to speak even when it's hard; that's trust. I always try. But right now I can't try at all.

"Why?" Person asks again.

Really, I should have punched Person. She's the one changing everything on us. She's the one breaking all her promises. Elena doesn't even matter. She's only here once a week.

I can't answer, so I shrug.

"Do you want to apologize to your sister?" Person asks.

I nod, but then I get up and leave. I can't.

That night I sneak into Julian's room with a Pop-Tart. I watch him roll over in his bed. His eyes are on me as I walk over to his closet and open the door.

Say something. Say something. I'm begging him. But only in my brain because my voice won't work.

I slip the Pop-Tart between two T-shirts on the bottom shelf. I turn. He's looking right at me.

Talk. Talk. Talk!

I'm not even sure which one of us my brain is urging.

We stare and stare until I'm sure the sun is coming up.

Then Julian rolls over so he's facing the wall and my

already-broken heart breaks all over again.

Person wants me to apologize to Elena. But Julian is the one I really need back.

I can't apologize. I can't answer Julian. I can't reply to Person when she asks if I want more milk with dinner. For two days, I can't speak.

Twelve

FAMILIES DO NOT INCLUDE FOURTH-GRADE TEACHERS

MY VOICE COMES BACK IN THE middle of math class on the second-to-last Thursday of the school year. I think Ms. K is happy when I yell out the first answer, because she smiles. But when I can't keep quiet after two more answers, she sighs and gives me several corrections in the Warning Voice.

At the end of the day, I'm still packing my backpack after the rest of the kids have left the room.

"Flora," Ms. K says. "Sit down for a minute."

"I—" I say. I don't know what to say. My words are mostly back, but the word "Sorry" is huge and clumsy and I can't get it through my throat. Even for Ms. K.

"Come here," Ms. K says.

I can tell that she wants to have a conversation the way that Person does: with her eyes right on me and her voice super serious. I don't think I can handle that.

"Can I hold Castillo while we talk?" I ask.

The mice are getting bigger now. We can hold them away from Pringles for a few minutes.

Ms. K looks at me seriously before she says. "Sure, OK."

I go over to the mice tank. I use the lotion next to it to disinfect my hands so that Castillo will be safe while he's with me. Castillo always walks right over to me when I put my hand in there. Then I carry the little warm bundle of him over to Ms. K.

I sit in the chair next to her. She smiles at me. I watch the white mouse wiggle through my right hand, then I put my left hand in front so he has somewhere to walk next.

I don't want to be mad at Ms. K. I'm so tired from being so angry. I want to crawl into her lap and take a nap. But you don't do that with teachers; you do that with mothers. And my person is going to be more somebody else's mother than she is my mother. It's going to hurt like when Ms. K winks at David. Worse.

"You've been having a rough week, huh?" Ms. K asks.

I shrug. But she looks at me until I nod.

She knows me. She knows I always tell the truth even though it sometimes makes no sense to her. She knows if she waits and rearranges my words she can learn everything. But I don't want her to know everything. I don't trust her as much anymore.

She's been trying all year to not be my teacher anymore. She treated me as well as Person did, but without any of the promises.

Too confusing.

I put Castillo in my lap and watch him run over the folds of my skirt.

"I see," Ms. K says. "Sometimes when we're having a rough time, it can be even harder to do the right thing in school."

That isn't a question.

"Math?" I say. Shouldn't we be talking about what happened in math class?

Ms. K doesn't know what I mean or else she ignores me.

"Did your mom talk with you about your birth?" Ms. K asks.

"No," I say.

Ms. K seems shocked. "She didn't? Why? What happened?"

Ms. K sees that there are tears in my eyes.

"You can tell me, Flora. I know something is wrong. You have to tell someone. What happened this week?"

I want to now. I want to try.

"Trouble," I say.

"You got in trouble?" Ms. K asks. "For what you told me about not being born?"

"No," I say.

"For what, then?" Ms. K asks.

"I . . . Julian . . . Elena . . . fighting . . ." There are too many words. All the words from the weekend fill me up from the inside. They get jammed in my filters.

"Fighting?" Ms. K asks. "Like a fist fight? Again?"

"No!" I say. "Just one. Just me."

I pick Castillo up. Maybe I can tell him the story. Maybe I can pretend Ms. K isn't here and I'll be able to find the words.

"Just one what? I thought you said Julian and Elena were involved."

"No." I want to answer her. But I stutter. *No* is the only word I can get out. "Food . . . ," I say finally. "Food . . . my brother . . ."

I'm holding Castillo too tight, I think. He wiggles in my palm.

"You got into a food fight?" Ms. K looks utterly confused. I don't want to make her confused. I don't want to be jammed.

"OK, let's reset like your mom showed us, right?"

I nod and I let Ms. K take the mouse out of my hands and we take our deep breaths. Ms. K says, "Flora, I know you're a bit confused about your family and where you come from, and I have to imagine you would be. But I want you to know that I see a lot of mothers and fathers in this job, and yours love you. They love you and Julian as much as any other mothers and fathers I've met."

I will not cry. I will not cry.

"Now tell me what's going on. Tell me what made it hard for you to be your best-Flora-self today?"

"It's Thursday," I say.

Ms. K nods.

I speak slowly. "Almost the end of the school year," I say.

"You're upset about the end of the school year?" she asks.

Relief floods me. *Yes. I'm upset about the end of the school year. The baby is coming. I have to go to fifth grade. Normal life is almost over.* Someone finally understands me.

"Are you worried that you will have to repeat the fourth grade?" Ms. K asks.

I shake my head.

Ms. K is thinking. "Are you worried about having a new teacher when you get to the fifth grade?"

"Yes," I say.

"Are you trying to make it so that you have to stay in the fourth grade?"

"I got the right answers!" I say.

But I have been calling out more. I wonder if part of me sort of wants to make Ms. K mad because part of me is so mad at Ms. K.

Mad that she loved me and the love is going to be over.

"School is fine," is all I can put together.

"So it's home then?" Ms. K asks.

I nod. I can feel the words freeze in my gut. They poke into my stomach lining. They're cold and uncomfortable like I swallowed a whole bag of ice cubes.

"What's going on at home, Flora?" Ms. K asks.

"I . . . a fight . . . food . . . end of the . . . I . . . you . . . a . . . see . . ."

The words I do have dissolve into solo letters and I can't get anything out even if I wanted to. Maybe if she didn't want to send me away to fifth grade I could tell her. Maybe if Ms. K loved me enough to be my mother, to promise Forever, I could tell her. But now all I have are letters.

There are more letters and more words. They're building up inside me but they refuse to leave my body. They jam on top of each other like a million-car pileup on the freeway until my face is hot and my throat is sore and I know that when I finally do cry it won't be tears falling out of my eyes but letters.

If I was like Julian, I would lie. I would paste on a fake smile and tell her I'm fine. But I don't want to lie. I want to be the kind of person who tells the truth, and who has the words to do it.

Ms. K keeps trying to say "Flora . . ." and reword the question, but I don't need the question reworded, I don't need her to say anything. I need to get my words out.

"I . . . a fight . . . the food . . . the closet . . . my brother . . . Elena . . . I . . . a . . . couch . . . a . . . candy . . . my brother . . ."

She's shaking her head. I'm giving her everything but she's getting nothing. I feel like I'm going to break in half trying to make myself make sense.

"Flora?" a man's voice says. I turn. Dad and Julian are standing in the doorway.

"Hi," Ms. K says. "Come on in. Flora is just trying to tell me about what's going on."

"Oh," Dad says. "I'm sorry. I didn't mean to interrupt. Jules and I were waiting in the car-pool line until it seemed like just about every kid was gone and I still didn't see our Flora come out so I thought I'd come up and check on her."

"She's here," Ms. K says. "She had a rough day."

"Yeah," Dad says. "Well, we're all having a rough week, but we'll be alright."

But I barely hear any of this because I'm staring at Julian, who is leaning against Dad, staring back at me.

Finally I rush at him and he rushes at me. I throw my arms around him. He throws his around me.

"I'm sorry!" I say.

"I'm sorry!" he says.

My tears are real tears, not word-tears, but they are also relief and I feel all the words inside me poof away. I thought I needed to tell Ms. K everything. Turns out all I needed was my brother.

"Team," we say at the same time.

On Friday, Dad doesn't take us straight home. Instead, he pulls into the parking lot outside of Dr. Fredrick's office. When we get to the waiting room, Person is there. She stands and stretches her arms for a hug like we're at home and this is all super normal. Julian and I don't say anything about how un-normal it is.

After a few minutes, Dr. Fredrick comes out of his office. "Hello, Flora and Julian!" he says. "I'd like to speak to your mom and dad for a minute before I call you in. Is that OK?"

We nod.

When they go behind the closed door, Julian whispers, "What do you think they're talking about?"

"Us," I say.

"But last time Dr. Fredrick said no secrets."

I shrug. So much for that.

"Do you think what Elena said is true?" Julian asks. "That there's less of everything because of us? That there'll be even less with a new baby?"

"Maybe," I say.

"Are you worried?" Julian asks.

I look at him. His face is open, no crazy smiles, so this is my chance. "Yeah," I say. "There's this new baby that's going to come from the inside of . . . Mom. And we didn't. I think she'll realize all of the ways we're so . . . like . . ."

"Confused?" Julian says.

I nod.

"And . . . hard to deal with?" he says.

I nod.

"The new baby will be so easy," I say. "Mom will know everything about it. From before it was even born."

Julian stares into the empty waiting room for a full minute before he says, "We have to try to be easy too."

"Yeah," I say. "Exactly."

A few minutes later, Dr. Fredrick opens his door and says, "Come on in, guys!" He has a big smile on his face, a real one. Julian's lips spread into his fake smile and we follow Dr. Fredrick inside.

All of us sit in Dr. Fredrick's office: Person, me, Dad, Julian. Every time I'm here it's like there are more and more people.

Julian and I don't say anything while Person catches Dr.

Fredrick up on everything that's been happening. She tells him about showing us all of the papers that are supposed to be our whole life but really said almost nothing. She tells him how we've now read all of the postcards from Gloria and Megan B. and how she offered for us to write them back, but we never did. She starts to tell him about how I punched Elena, but Dr. Fredrick interrupts.

"Is there a reason you guys don't want to write back to your old foster mom and foster sister?"

But it's not that we don't want to write back to them. It's that we want to *see* them.

"Nah," Julian says. "We're good." He pastes on that fake smile again but I'm not mad about it this time.

I have to lie too. I have to pretend I don't care about Megan B. or Gloria or the white house or the shoulders I once rode on anymore. If I want 100 percent of Person's love, I have to give her 100 percent of mine. So we have to stop asking for things.

"You seemed so curious about it last time I saw you," Dr. Fredrick says. "You seemed downright angry that you had not had access to your past. And now you don't want to connect?"

Julian shrugs. "We saw the postcards. We feel better."

"Flora?" Dr. Fredrick asks.

He's staring right at me. He's very smart. He'll totally see that I'm lying.

I manage to squeak out a "yup" but it's high and crooked.

"There's something else going on here," Dr. Fredrick says. He looks at Person. "What do you think could be happening?"

"Is it really impossible that the postcards were enough?" Person says.

Dad sighs.

I want to sigh too. Moments like this—when Person can't read my mind, when she can't find my heart—are the most lonely.

"What?" Person asks Dad.

"I, um . . ." He trails off.

"Tell me," Person says.

I shift in my seat. Person and Dad almost never fight but when they do it starts like this. Like Dad saying nothing and Person begging for words. Like Dad not agreeing with something, and Person wanting to know why but also being mad at him before he even talks.

"What do you think, Jon?" Dr. Fredrick asks.

Dad looks at Dr. Fredrick when he answers instead of Person, even though it's clear she's the one he's really talking to.

"I don't know. There's a lot going on. My daughters are fighting with each other. We have a new baby coming. And they just found out that some of the people from their life before us still miss them and think about them . . . I don't know that postcards *can* be enough."

Julian leans across Dad to raise his eyebrows at me. He's saying *DAD gets it? Dad gets it when Mom doesn't?* I raise mine back, but then we both shake our heads. No matter how much we want to see Gloria again, no matter how much we want to remember, no matter how much we want to know where we came from, we can't ask for anything. We have to be easy. We have to be normal.

"And then there's the whole 'born' thing. I mean, we don't have any baby pictures. These are my kids. I want to see their baby faces. I want to retrace their steps. I want to know."

"You weren't there, Jon," Person says. "You don't know how it was."

"But *they* were there," Dad says. "They know . . . I really don't think we're going to shock them with their own lives."

"He's right," Dr. Fredrick says.

"So, what?" Person says. "I should force them to write a postcard to this woman when they say they don't want to?"

I'm sitting on my hands so that they don't start twitching with everything I want to write, everything I would if I could.

"Why don't you ask them what they do want?" Dr. Fredrick says.

"I want to see it!" I say before I can make my gates stop the words from coming.

"Floral!" Julian says.

"Oops, I mean . . . I want . . . I want to see the postcards again."

"Yeah, me too," Julian says.

"What did you really mean?" Dr. Fredrick asks. "You want to see your old house?"

I bite my lips to keep my voice from saying yes.

"We don't need that. We're happy here. Right, Mom?" Julian says.

Person looks at him, then at me.

"You guys want to go back there?"

Julian doesn't say anything. Neither do I.

"What's going on?" Person asks. "Why aren't you telling me what's on your minds?"

I swallow more words. Dr. Fredrick says, "Remember that these are kids who have experienced trauma, Flora especially. It can be hard for her to express herself because of her traumatic history. We need to be patient with Flora."

"I know," Person says. She takes a deep breath. "I'm sorry, guys. You can tell me. I promise it's safe. You can tell me what you're thinking."

It feels safe again but we still don't say anything.

"You know," Dr. Fredrick says. "Sometimes you might want something, or even need something, that your mom has a hard time giving you. It's OK to ask for it anyway. I'm not talking about a cookie or a toy . . . I'm talking about a real deep desire."

Person nods. "You guys can ask for anything. You know that."

Except we don't.

"There's not a baby picture," I say. "But if there is, I want to see it. And . . . I want to see younger pictures of me. If there are any."

"Me too," Julian says. "I want to know . . . whatever. I want to know what we can. I want . . . I want to stay with you. I want to live with you, but . . . I want to know . . . about before."

Person's eyebrows knit together. "Then why did you say you didn't need any of that?"

I shrug.

Julian's lips curl back into the crazy smile and he says, "Because we don't. We don't *need* it. We're happy. Right, Florey?"

He went from truth to lying so fast I'm dizzy.

"No," I say.

"What?" Person asks. "You're unhappy? What's making you unhappy?"

"Not unhappy," I say. "Just no asking."

I missed a few words in there, I think. My words are getting heavy again. This is a scary thing to talk about.

"No more asking," I say. "Just stay quiet."

"What?" Dad says. "You're allowed to ask about your past. You can ask us every day if you like."

"Asking for," I say. "No asking for."

"What?" Dad says.

Person says, "Explain." I feel like she's reaching out again. I feel like her heart is getting a little closer to mine, which would mean it's getting a little further from the baby's, and I like that.

"There's a new baby," I say.

"Floral" Julian says.

"I need . . . we need . . . normal. Easy. We're normal and

easy. You can . . . you can just take care of the new baby. We'll be . . ."

"We'll be fine! We're happy! We're all totally fine and happy! Right, Mom?" Julian and I are saying the same thing, but somehow mine is a truth and his is a lie.

Person's face comes apart. Of course it's still together, but I can see something inside her rip into two.

"Guys," she says. "You don't have to be happy for me. You're allowed to ask me for things. You need to ask me for things. You're my kids. I want . . . I want to give you everything. I mean, nothing will change that. Not one baby. Not one hundred babies."

Her eyes are wet. I don't like that we made her cry. I scoot closer to her and put my head on her shoulder and then she turns and hugs me and it's the tightest, warmest hug ever.

"I wish I knew how to do this better," she says.

Dr. Fredrick says, "That's a pretty nice hug. I think you're doing a lot of things right."

"I wish I could crawl into your heart with a Dustbuster and tidy it up," Person says. "I wish I could get in there in a way that you knew I always, always will be."

She's still hugging me.

"You know," Dr. Fredrick says. "I think that's exactly what Flora and Julian are asking for. To go back through the steps of their life and put things in order. To tidy up their hearts."

Person starts crying for real now.

"I know it's hard," Dr. Fredrick says. "But it's important.

And remember that just because something is scary and difficult in the moment doesn't mean it's bad. We usually feel better after the worst moments. Sometimes we need to go through the dark tunnel in order to see the light."

Thirteen

FAMILIES HAVE STORIES

AFTER DINNER THE NEXT NIGHT, JULIAN and I hand dishes to Person and she rinses them and puts them in the dishwasher.

"Ask her," Julian says. "Ask for the story."

I hand her my plate, then turn quickly so I can't see her face. "Tell us again?" I say.

"Tell you what?" Person asks. She leans over and puts a plate in the dishwasher. We still haven't talked about how I punched Elena or how I spent days and days not talking at all or how Dr. Fredrick wants us to go back in time and Person is afraid to do it, but also Person still has her contacts in her eyes and she smiled with her whole face at dinner and Dad had to work tonight but when he left they said Person will be here tomorrow, which means she has the day off so maybe she's in a little bit of a better mood.

"Tell us again," I say, wandering back over to the table. There's almost nothing left on it but I don't want to have to look in her face when I ask or when she answers. "The story."

"How you got us," Julian says. He always finds the words I'm missing.

"Oh!" Person says. "OK. It's been awhile since you've asked for this one but you know how I love to tell it!"

Julian smiles at me. I smile back.

Person still loves the story, one checkmark in the box for We Are Lovable.

"When your aunt Alice had baby Cate, your cousin, I got to thinking how I would probably be a good mommy too," Person says.

She always starts at this part of the story, even though it doesn't seem to have much to do with us. And she always calls these people "your" meaning ours even though we only see them a few times a year and don't know too much about them.

There are all sorts of connections in the world. People are connected to people and then other people. And some of these people are connected to me even though I haven't met them. Or don't remember them. I don't think I'll ever understand it all.

The only connection I understand without trying is Julian.

"But Cate's not a baby anymore," Julian says.

He always says that. We have a script for this story. We've told it so many times it's worn thin and comfortable, like a T-shirt tumbled and tumbled in the dryer until it's soft and settles right on your shoulders like a second skin.

"No, Cate's almost your age now. I had to wait years and

years and years for my dreams to come true with the two of you." Person is talking loud, over the running water and the clinking of dishes. Julian and I are both circling the table picking at nothing, pretending to be busy so we can draw the story out.

My favorite part comes at the end. My favorite part is why Julian wanted to hear the story today, I'm sure of it.

"What did you do while you waited?" I ask.

"Well, I had a lot of preparing to do to become a mommy by myself," Person says. "First I went to meetings with lots of professionals who love kids like you so much they dedicate their lives to you."

I always imagine these professionals as men in black suits with no faces. They have never fully existed. I've never seen their faces so how can they love me? But they've always been a part of our story.

"They said, 'Emily, you'd probably make a good mom, but we need to be absolutely sure because children are super precious and important. So we're going to make you fill out a ton of paperwork that proves you've always been a good person. And we're going to make you take classes to be sure you're ready for our particular kids. And we're going to make sure you have a good support system so that any kids you adopt are coming into a full community.' All that sort of thing."

"How did you do all of that?" Julian says.

"How long did it take?" I say. I want to skip to the end. I want to hear the last thing she says, the thing that always makes me feel good.

"It took months and months," Person says. "First, a bunch of people came to my home. They went through all of my drawers. They looked in my refrigerator and said 'Oh good, you have some healthy food for kids!'" Person chuckles.

"The food you fed us on the first day?" Julian asks. He twists to look at her.

Suddenly the three of us are sitting on the sofa, Julian and me on either side of Person, leaning into her. How did that happen?

It's warm and happy. It's good.

Person only has two sides. How will we all lean on her when she has three kids?

"No!" Person says. "That's why I laughed when he said that. Why would it matter if I had healthy food for you? I wouldn't meet you for years still. Those social workers are a funny bunch."

"Then what happened?" I ask. I want to stay in this moment forever. I never want to leave my person or her couch. But I also can't wait to hear the end of her story.

"What else did he say?" Julian asks.

"He said, 'Ms. Baker, your paperwork says you're interested in a sibling group of school age children, but I'm sorry, your apartment is too small. I can license you for one preschool child or baby, but not two or more older kids.'"

"And did you say OK?" Julian asks.

He likes the whole story. I'm warm and happy. I tell myself

to stop rushing it along.

"Nope." Person plants a kiss on both of our heads. "Somewhere in the universe I sensed you two or something because I said, 'Then I guess I'll have to move!' and he said 'Really? You're going to move out of your home?'"

She squeezes us a little closer.

"He couldn't believe I would move for you guys. Isn't that silly? We love our home but we love our families more. Or at least we should."

I don't know who the *we* is because Person was all alone when all this happened.

"And then you moved here," I say. "To our home."

"And then I moved here. Then another social worker came through and gave the whole rundown again. She said my home was good to go and sent me out to classes."

"What kind of classes?" Julian asks. "What did they teach you?"

"They're supposed to teach you how to be a good mom or dad. They taught some good stuff—science-y stuff. Like psychology, which is the study of human minds. And neurology, which is the study of—"

"The human brain!" I shout.

"Good job, Flora!" Person says, squeezing me tighter. I never get in trouble for calling out when I'm at home. "And human development, which is the study of . . ." Person pauses for me on purpose.

"The way we grow," I say.

"That's right!" she says. She's proud. I'm glowing.

"What else did you have to do?" Julian asks.

"I had to turn in all sorts of papers. I had to use my birth certificate to prove that I'm a US citizen. I had to use my mortgage papers to prove that I owned this apartment. I had to get fingerprinted at the city office to prove that I'm not a criminal."

We always chuckle at that. How could Person be a criminal? It's ridiculous.

"And then they said, 'OK, Ms. Baker, you're all set. We'll let you know when we have a match for you.'

"And then I waited. And waited."

"How long did you wait?" Julian asks.

"Almost another year! Can you believe it? I waited and waited and waited. You guys were out there and—"

"We were waiting too," I say.

I've never said that before. It's a new thread in the T-shirt. Person freezes. She turns and looks at me and her eyes get so dark I'm sure she's going to cry again, but her arm stays heavy and solid on my shoulders and she stares and stares and stares.

"You were. You were waiting," she says. "You were at Gloria's, and you were at the other house before that while I was doing all of this preparation. And you were waiting."

Something big is happening. It's so huge I'm going to drown in it. Something big and huge is suffocating us.

Julian rescues me like always. "Then what?" he asks.

I breathe deeply. I need her to get to the end of the story. I need to hear the magic word.

"And then," she says, "one day they finally called and said 'We have a little boy and a little girl, brother and sister. They love each other a lot. We want someone to adopt them together.' And it was like fireworks exploded in my heart. It was like a key turned in a lock. It was . . . ," Person says. "It just was. Finally, after all that waiting, it was."

I'm almost crying now. Because for Person the waiting was over in that minute. But Julian and I were still waiting when we got here. Waiting to have to go away again. Waiting to not be here anymore. Waiting for something bad. And just when we thought we weren't waiting anymore, now we are again.

Waiting for a baby, a new person. Another change.

"So I ran around like crazy," Person is saying. "I wanted to get you everything in the store. I had to set up your rooms so that you would love them. It was October so I wanted to be sure we had Halloween costumes ready to go! It was going to be Flora's birthday the next month so I wanted to get started planning a party. I wanted to be sure I had good food in the fridge!"—Julian and Person laugh, I focus on not crying—"I asked all sorts of questions about your favorite colors and your favorite toys and your favorite foods and I called everyone I knew and said 'Guess what, I'm going to have two kids!' and made them all help me so you'd love everything about it when you finally got here. I still had to wait weeks and weeks to meet you even though I was your mom already." Person stops. She looks at me again. "The waiting was so hard."

That's another new part of the story.

"And you were waiting too. We were all waiting. I wish we could have those days of waiting back, Flora. I wish you never had to wait for me."

Person ignores that there are a few tears leaking now. I'm avoiding her eyes. She knows I don't want to talk about the tears.

Person says, "And then I met you!" She's smiling so big at this part. "The social worker finally brought you here. And you guys came stumbling in my apartment with nothing but the clothes on your back and a garbage bag full of clothes and toys in your hands. You didn't look at me or smile. You were so scared! And so was I. I saw your little faces and I just thought, I love them already." She takes a deep breath. "Then I thought, you better be good at this, Emily."

She squeezes us close. I'm almost done crying. The part I love is coming. The part is almost here.

"The first thing we did was sit at the table and eat some pizza. I asked about your favorite foods and colors and toys in case the social workers had gotten anything wrong—and I learned a lot of new stuff. Julian, you answered all the questions. Even the ones about Flora. Flora, you wouldn't even look at me. You kept your eyes on your shoes the whole time. Julian, you kept asking for more and more pizza!"

He laughs.

"But then?" I say.

Here it comes. The best part.

"Well, Flora, you remember that first pizza dinner, right?"

But I shake my head. I don't remember any of this.

Person looks alarmed. "You don't?"

I shake my head again. "I remember the story," I say. "The way you tell it."

But I don't remember being there. I was probably terrified. I had probably floated away to the ceiling.

"But you don't—" Person shakes her head like she's clearing it and I'm relieved. I want her to get back to the real story. I don't want all these new parts. I need to hear the last word.

"Well, anyway, you didn't talk to me for days, Flora. Weeks, really. You didn't look right at me again after this for a long time. But that night, about halfway through your first slice, Flora, you finally took your eyes off your shoes. You looked at Julian, and then you looked at me."

It's almost here.

"All of our eyes connected for the first time and I thought—"

This is it.

"I thought, yup, I'm a mom now."

I wait. I look at Julian. He looks at me.

Person squeezes us close again. She plants a kiss on each of our foreheads one more time.

Then she whispers that final magical word.

"Forever."

I turn those words over in my brain. I wait for them to have the calming effect they usually do, like rubbing a smooth stone in your hand with the back of your thumb.

I'm a mom now. Forever.

I'm a mom now. Forever.

After another big squeeze, Person stands and says, "It's almost seven. Who wants ice cream?"

We both sort of nod, dazed.

Person sits on the edge of my bed. I'm in my pink pajamas with the cupcakes printed on them. They're soft against the skin on my legs and stomach and arms. I'm settled into the nest of my bed. Person is stroking my hair.

"You seem to be feeling better," Person says.

I nod against the pillow.

"I'm so glad," Person says. "I always want my kiddos to feel good all the time, even if that's not possible."

The rhythm of her hand on my head is putting me to sleep. She starts at the part, then her fingers trace my hair down to my ear and then to the back of my neck. Then she starts over again. *Part-ear-neck. Part-ear-neck,* I think, getting sleepy.

"You know you're going to have to apologize to Elena though, right?"

Boom. I'm awake. My eyes go wide. She's still stroking but it feels like she's scratching me now.

I shake my head.

"You do. You two are sisters. Sometimes sisters fight but we need to try to work it out."

"No," I say, sitting up.

"No?" Person says. "No, you will not apologize?"

I meant *No, we aren't sisters*. But I nod.

"Why?" Person asks.

"I punched her," I say.

"I know," Person says. "That's why you need to apologize."

I shake my head.

Person sighs. She looks tired now. I bother her all the time. I can't be the perfect apologizing sister. I can't be the great fourth grader who will definitely pass and go into fifth grade. No wonder she needs another kid.

"Baby," Person says heavily. I love when she calls me that. It's almost like I got to be her baby. But now I know I wasn't a good enough baby because I was already big and now she doesn't want me like that anymore and now the word is half like, half hate and it's like ants are crawling between my bones and muscles. "Do you know that punching is wrong?"

"Yes," I say.

"Do you know why?"

"Hurts," I say.

"Yup, exactly. You hurt Elena. Do you know that?"

I think about the blood. It was her tooth on my knuckle. I'm the one who was bleeding. I think about her tooth jammed into that laugh and about her laugh stabbing Julian and how we had stolen all of Julian's food.

Did I hurt Elena when I punched her? Do I care if I did?

"I needed to," I say.

"You needed to punch her?" Person asks. "Why?"

I don't say anything for a second and her eyes turn from tired to wanting.

"Tell me why, baby. I know it might not be in words right now, in your head, but put it in words. I want to understand."

What happened when there was no Person who wanted to understand?

"Why did you need to punch her?" Person says again.

Because the skin on my knuckle needed to breathe. Because I was so guilty for hurting Julian. Because she says I'm lucky to have you which sounds to me like I don't deserve you.

Because sometimes I believe that.

I say, "She was laughing at Julian."

Person raises her eyebrows. Her eyes are calm now. "Oh," she says.

She puts her arms around me. It's like the filters that I don't have fly open. I can't stop the words from coming.

"For the food," I say. "She was laughing at him for the food and . . . and gross. She . . . gross. She called him gross. And laughed. It was like . . . she said laugh. She says . . . gross. Mean. Too mean. I . . . I was the worst. But the laughing. It was like Julian was . . . food . . . broken. She doesn't . . . she can't . . . she's not . . ."

Person's arms are tight around me and she's rock-rock-rocking me back and forth on the bed. "Shh, shh," she says. "OK, now? Shh."

"She's not . . . us," I finish.

Person pulls back to look at me. "Well, she is, Flora. She's your dad's daughter. She is us."

But my dad is my dad because he adopted Julian and me when he married Person. My dad is Elena's dad and the new baby's dad for some other reason.

"Listen, Flora. We've all got a long way to go. Elena included. You're right. She shouldn't laugh at Julian. But . . . look. *You* are the one in trouble now. She did something wrong, and you are in trouble. Do you know why?"

"Because I punched her?" I ask.

Person nods. "We've got to get you to express yourself, OK? With words. You can't go around punching because your words aren't coming. Forget about Elena. That's going to hurt *you*."

With my thumb, I rub the spot on my knuckle where a scab is forming. Sometimes I want it to hurt me.

"No more punching, OK? Promise me."

I nod.

I lie back down.

"Will you stroke my head again?" I ask.

Person almost looks like she'll cry. "Of course, baby," she says.

I think about what she said. About expressing myself as her hand goes *part-ear-neck, part-ear-neck, part-ear-neck.*

I have to do whatever I can to make Person happy. I have to tell her.

"Mom," I say. "Sometimes I'm not excited about the new baby."

"Oh?" she says.

Her hand stutters on my head though. She's mad at me. She loves the new baby and she maybe loves it more than she loves me. Probably.

Words rush out quickly. "I mean, not like Julian and the goldfish. I—I'll be careful anyway."

Person whispers in my ear, the most comfortably tickle-y words. "Flora, my Flora, you are not going to hurt the baby. Don't worry about that."

"I know," I say.

Person sighs. Her hand keeps going. I'm almost asleep by the time she talks again. "It's OK if you're scared about how this will be. After now. It's OK if that scares you. But you don't need to figure out how it's going to be, OK? You don't need to work it out. You don't need to take care of anything or anyone. You leave that to the grown-ups, your dad and me."

Don't worry about anything? But if I didn't worry constantly about being good enough for Person, there's no way I'd ever be good enough for her.

"I just . . . ," I say. "I sometimes wish . . ."

Person doesn't urge me on so I know I should stop the words from coming out but I can't because I'm missing the lung gates.

"I sometimes wish the baby would stay inside you," I say. "Forever."

THEORY #31

We come from the chaos, my brother and me.

We were born out of the screams of other kids. We're made of their tears. We grew from their temper tantrums.

We will never escape the chaos because it's what brought us to life in the first place.

Fourteen
FAMILIES HAVE MEETINGS

DAD PICKS US UP FROM SCHOOL the next Friday and then there's only one week left of fourth grade and Ms. K. Maybe. If I do good.

When we get home Person is on the phone in the kitchen so I guess she and Dad both don't have to work today. She doesn't hear us come in because she's being very loud.

"I'm not making excuses for her, Meredith. What she did was inexcusable, but she's my kid and this is how I'm dealing with it."

She's talking to Elena's mom.

"They are *both* his daughters," Person is saying.

Dad puts his hands on our backs trying to rush us through to the other room but we dig our heels into the wooden floor and lean against his hands so he can't push us anywhere too quickly.

"Oh, don't try to out-mom me. We have different kids, different girls. What my kids have been through . . . Those extra eight years give you no authority over my kids and my parenting . . . You have a voice. Believe me you do. We hear your voice loud and clear around here . . ."

Person looks up and sees us staring at her, leaning almost perpendicular into Dad's hands as he pushes us.

She waves her hand in front of her face almost like she's asking him to get us out of the room.

Dad ushers us into the hallway toward Julian's room. The last thing we hear Person say is, "Look, she has to come tomorrow. Co-parenting is court ordered. Why don't you both come over tonight and we can try to make everyone more comfortable?"

We go into Julian's room and Dad rushes back toward the kitchen.

Julian says, "Yes!" as soon as the door closes behind us. He does a little move with his hand in a fist and his elbow going down while his knee goes up like he's a regular happy boy from our school.

"Huh?" I say.

I watch Julian go to his closet. He starts tapping on his full pockets and surveying the hiding spaces as he talks and talks over his shoulders.

"Did you hear her? Did you hear her, Florey? What she was saying?"

I'm still all *huh?* staring at the back of his head as he darts all over his closet pulling food out of his pockets and talking-talking-talking to me.

"She was saying stuff like *my kids* and *don't try to out-mom me* and how you're just as much Dad's daughter as Elena is and how she's a mom she's totally a mom and you know what she needs to be a mom?"

He turns and looks at me. He's rushing toward me, doing a little jig on the carpet.

"You know what she needs to be a mom, Florey?"

I shake my head. Not because I don't know the answer. Because he's wrong.

"You know what she needs to be a mom? She needs us! Us."

I shake my head again. "Not anymore," I say. "She's having a baby."

His face falls so fast.

The door opens.

"Elena is coming over," Person calls in.

Julian and I stare at each other, confused.

"Friday," I say.

"I know it's different," Person says. "Meredith is coming too. We need to have a family meeting. If you want to change out of your uniforms do it now. And, I don't know, maybe . . . think . . . or get . . . or be . . ."

Person interrupts herself, shaking her head.

"Never mind. Just be you. Just be my beautiful babies."

* * *

Julian and I sit on the couch with Person between us. Elena and Meredith sit in chairs next to the couch. Dad paces. He props himself on another chair, then gets back up. He sits on the arm of the couch, then gets back up. He walks over to behind Elena, then to the other side of the couch so he's facing her.

It feels like the quiet goes on too long. The quiet and Dad moving. Like the grown-ups don't know what to do.

Person says don't worry, be a kid. It's impossible.

"Well, let's get to the bottom of this," Person says.

"There's nothing to get to the bottom of," Meredith says back. She always speaks too quickly. It's like her words are all connected by a hard metal wire, the kind that could cut your skin. She has always made me want to hide. But I've never had to be in a room with her for this long before. "Your kid punched my kid in the mouth."

"Flora?" Person says.

I nod. It's true. I did that.

"Well, that was easy," Meredith says. "Your kid punched my kid. We all know it. That's it. I told Jon this situation gets only one strike. I don't want them together anymore. You guys have to find Elena another place to sleep when she comes over here. I want them separated. I never liked the idea of them spending so much time together to begin with but I let it slide because, Emily, you said all of those things about family and I, well, I couldn't speak up without sounding like an awful person, huh? But now here we are. I was right from the beginning." She turns to face Dad where he's now standing behind their chairs again. "Jon, what are you going to do?"

He slumps. "I'm trying here, Meredith," he says.

I want to say, *Fine.*

I want to say, *Elena wasn't family anyway.*

I want to say, *Why does she even have to come back here at all?*

When Dad doesn't say anything else, Person shoots him a disappointed look and says, "I'd like to try to fix this in a way that preserves all of our relationships. I think everyone deserves to have her voice heard."

Meredith almost snorts.

Person ignores her. "I know Flora and Elena fought, but I do think deep down they understand that they're sisters and they love each other."

Person is hardly ever wrong, but she is now. I maybe love Elena. Or maybe I could if I don't. But sisters? No.

She can't be my sister.

Julian and I are Onlys.

Meredith sighs.

Person says, "Flora, will you explain what happened?"

I remember what Person said before bed the other night about how I needed to express myself or else it would hurt me. I have to try to talk when Person asks me to. "The food. The laughing. Julian. Elena was laughing and I—"

Elena's voice is so much louder. "She punched me for no

reason. It came out of nowhere. I was at recess talking to my friends, I didn't even see them walking up to us. Then boom. She punched me."

"That's not—" I say.

"She's lying!" Elena says.

"She punched you while your back was turned?" Meredith says, somehow getting louder and louder.

"No," I say.

"Yes," Elena says.

"She was laughing," I say, all the words coming out without me even trying. I can feel Person smiling at me. "Elena was trying to get me to—"

"She's lying!" Elena says.

But Elena is lying. I don't know why she's lying. Punching is worse than laughing. I'm in the biggest trouble.

Person leans over and whispers to me. "Try again. Explain."

I take a deep breath. "Julian was mad about the food," I say.

"What?" Elena spits. She's leaning out of her chair now. "I don't even know what she's talking about."

And that's also a lie because I know that part made perfect sense if you were there, and Elena was.

"She never makes any sense," Elena says.

"I'm not sure what the point of this is, Emily, but it's not working. Why should my daughter come all the way over here? So she can listen to a girl who assaulted her and who refuses to apologize? I'm not sure the abuser should get a voice."

Person's jaw snaps shut so hard I can hear her teeth clank

together. She stares at Meredith. Her eyes are hard, but it's like she doesn't know what to say.

It's tense and frozen and I want to melt and drip through the floorboards. I can't believe I haven't floated away to the ceiling yet. I rub the scab on the back of my hand but it's mostly healed so it doesn't even distract me.

Meredith motions for Elena to get up but then finally a little voice says, "How about me? Can I talk?"

Julian.

Meredith sighs.

Meredith doesn't know that Julian uses my own words better than I do. That Julian talking is me talking. Julian didn't do any punching so she has to listen to him.

"So . . . um . . . ," Julian says. His voice is small but everyone is quiet and listening. I don't know how he does that. I'm glad he's not smiling. I'm glad this will be the truth. "I don't like to talk about this but for Florey . . ." He pauses and looks at me for a second. His eyes are sad. "OK. I . . . I hide food, sometimes . . . in my closet. Sometimes. I just . . . I . . . put food in my closet. Flora and Elena went to my closet and stole all the food—"

"I didn't do that!" Elena yells.

Dad finally speaks. "Let him finish. Then you can talk, baby."

"Maybe they were trying to help me," Julian says, looking right at Elena like he's the strongest person in the world. "But I got really mad when I found out it was all gone . . . I never thought Flora would do it . . . I went into my closet on that Sunday night when Elena was still here and all of my food was gone. It was totally gone. So I thought Elena had—"

"You immediately assumed that—"

"Meredith," Dad says. "Let him finish."

"I'm sorry, Elena. I thought it was you," Julian says, looking right at her. But he's smiling that crazy smile. The "sorry" is a lie.

"So then when I saw Elena on Tuesday at recess I was so angry. And I ran up to her and started yelling at her and telling her she shouldn't steal and then Flora was there and she was so upset she was crying."

I was crying? I don't even remember that part.

"Elena didn't care that I was shouting or that Flora was crying. Because she was . . . making fun of me. She was laughing."

"I wasn't laughing," she says.

"Yes, you were," Julian says. "And then Flora got mad at her for laughing at me like that so she punched her."

"I wasn't laughing," Elena says, even louder. "God! You're both liars. I didn't even see you guys before Flora punched me in the face."

Julian snorts, which is something else I've never heard.

"Flora, was Elena laughing? Did she have her back turned or did she see you guys?" Person asks me.

"Laughing," I say. I'm so calm I put it into a full sentence. "She was laughing at Julian. It was the mean kind of laughing. She was trying to get me to laugh with her. At Julian."

"Now," Person says, still looking at me. "Is that a reason to—"

But before she can finish, Elena cries out, "I can't believe you're going to take her side. You know she's lying. She can't even—"

"Elena," Person says. "Flora is going to get an appropriate punishment for punching you. It is my top priority to make sure that every member of this family feels safe in this house. There's no punching or hurting in this house. But there's no making fun of your brother, either."

"I cannot believe this!" Elena says.

Person turns to keep talking to me. I feel like she's a wall. I feel like chaos is swirling around her, thick and familiar, and she's a wall built just to keep it from touching me.

Meredith looks so upset I almost feel sorry for her. It's not her fault Elena is lying. And Person is right. I shouldn't have punched her no matter what she did.

But then Meredith says, "Honestly, Emily? This is how you will handle this situation? You barely listened to my kid. And what about you?" she says, turning to Dad. "Is this what goes on here now? Do you never even think about your real kid anymore?"

"Hey, now," Dad says. Then stops.

"Excuse me," Person says. "We don't use that language. They're all real kids."

"But Elena is *his* kid. He's Elena's father," Meredith says.

"He's Julian's father. He's Flora's father. He's Elena's father," Person says.

Meredith stands. Not to leave. Just to make herself bigger or something. "Our kids are not the same."

"What does that mean?" Person says, almost in a growl. She stands as well.

"I've done some reading," Meredith says. "I couldn't stop Jon from marrying you but I did some reading when I found out about it. I had to protect my girl as best I could. You know some things about foster kids? They do more than hide food in their closets. They do worse than that. They lie. They fail out of school. They're violent. They end up homeless or—"

"Meredith!" Dad says. "Stop!"

"At first I was so worried. The girl seemed so weird and the boy killed that goldfish. I was terrified to have my daughter around them all the time." Meredith won't stop talking. "But then they seemed to be getting better. You all almost seemed like a family. And Elena said she enjoys coming here. As soon as I let my guard down, this happens."

"Stop. Now," Dad says again.

But she doesn't. "Emily, it was your choice to accept dysfunction into your family. Jon, it was your choice to marry into a dysfunctional family. But Elena and I didn't get that choice."

Dysfunction. She called us dysfunction. We are dysfunction, the whole word at once.

"Enough!" Person says.

She reaches for us and almost scoots us behind her back

like she really wants to be a wall. But it feels like the wall is falling down.

"We didn't even listen to Elena, you realize that, right?" Meredith is saying. "We skipped right over everything she said."

Behind her mother's back, and with our father staring into the kitchen, Elena sticks her tongue out at us.

"Tongue!" I yell, just as Person is saying, "Elena was lying. She was not sucker punched. She saw them, talked to them, then Flora got angry."

"Tongue!" I yell again.

"What?" Person says, turning to look at me.

"Tongue," I say, still too excited and angry and frustrated and confused to make it make sense.

"Elena stuck her tongue out at us," Julian says flatly.

"Lying! They're lying!" Elena bursts out again. "Mom, they're always doing this. They're always ganging up on me and lying about me and I'm always getting into all sorts of trouble because of the messed up things they do."

None of that is true. We mostly ignore Elena when she's here. We can't gang up on her if we barely even talk to her.

"Elena," Person says. Her voice is almost calm but it's more thin than I've ever heard. "I am trying my heart out here. I'm trying to make everyone feel loved and special and important to this family. I love you. But you need to tell the truth."

"Why do you assume my kid's lying? Why do you think your foster kids are perfect?" Meredith says. "How dare you say you love my daughter in the middle of accusing her of being worse than them?"

Julian and I are specks on the couch. We're dirt. We're nothing. I hope he's floated away by now. I'm still waiting for it to happen for me.

"Enough," Person says again, even though it hasn't worked a single time yet. "And they are my *kids*, period."

"Elena, are you telling the truth?" Meredith asks.

"Yes," Elena says. "Flora is lying."

"Flora is not lying!" Person says.

"How do you know that?" Meredith says.

Suddenly, it's funny. Adults yelling about tongues sticking out and food hidden in a closet. It's gross and funny. It's too familiar but I don't remember why.

But then Person says, "Flora can't communicate well enough to lie."

I've been slapped in the face before. I'm sure of that at this moment. Because those words coming from my person, they feel exactly the same way.

Person turns and stares at me, her face broken. And then she collapses back between Julian and me again, her hands covering her face.

It's quiet for a minute. I'm biting my lip. I don't think I'm crying but maybe Julian will tell me later that I was. Maybe I can't even tell what crying is anymore.

"This isn't getting us anywhere," Dad says. "We should get some sleep and try to figure all this out another time."

"I'm not dropping Elena off tomorrow, Jon. Sue me for all I care, I won't do it. And I know you're supposed to have the first two weeks of summer, but no. No way. This is unacceptable. My daughter does not have to pay the price for your choices."

Dad sighs. "That's not how we see it, Meredith. It's good for Elena to have siblings . . . We're all still . . . working."

Elena's looking at her shoes now, almost like she's shy.

"Jon . . . it's . . ." Meredith is not as loud anymore. "Elena is a child. This is too heavy. She shouldn't have to be involved in all of this. I . . . I'm trying. I'm trying to be a good mother and I . . . I can't drop her off tomorrow. I can't leave her for two whole weeks when she feels this way."

Dad sighs. "Elena, honey," he says. "Do you mind staying with your mother this weekend? And then when school ends, Emily is going to take Flora and Julian on a little trip down to the beach in Maryland."

Julian leans across Person to raise his eyebrows at me.

His eyes say *we're going back to Maryland?*

Mine say back, *the trip we accidentally asked for?*

Dad is still talking. "We've had this planned already. We were all going to go and hang out on the beach but . . . what if you and I stay back? We can have some dad-daughter time like the old days and hopefully Flora and Julian can feel a little better. Then we'll work on getting everyone together again."

I don't know what Elena says because sirens blare in my brain.

She's taking us that soon? We're going to see Gloria and Megan B. in just a week? Right after my last week of Ms. K, Person is going to take us searching for the white house?

Miraculously, Meredith doesn't yell. She says something else I can't hear over the noise in my head. She stands and puts on her sweater. She holds Elena's hand. Person and Julian and I stay frozen. Dad follows Meredith to the apartment door. He gives Elena a long hug, then Meredith shoos her away. Before she leaves herself, she turns and says, "You broke our family. I hope you know that, Jon. Forget the divorce, we all survived that. But when you adopted those children, you broke our lives."

"Meredith, leave," Dad says. "They can hear you."

But we didn't need to hear that to know it's true.

Sitting in the middle of us is the woman who is supposed to be our final human mother.

It looks like we broke her too.

Fifteen
FAMILIES ADJUST (FOREVER)

MONDAY MORNING I WAKE UP WITH a headache that goes *boom boom* between my ears and a stomachache that comes from when your stomach won't stay still even when you're just lying in your bed.

I stare at my hard-boiled egg. I think about telling Person there's no way I can eat it. I think about telling her I don't feel well and asking if I can stay home.

In the end I let Julian steal my egg and hide it in his closet.

It's another quiet morning. Saturday and Sunday we managed to go grocery shopping and play board games and all the usual stuff, but we did it quietly. Person confirmed that we start our hunt for the white house and all of the other foster houses this weekend, and Julian smiled at me and my heart raced in my chest, both excited and scared.

I wander into the classroom to start the last week with Ms. K and I don't even feel like looking at her. In my backpack, there's a pile of blank worksheets, an assignment notebook listing assignments without a single initial next to them. I didn't even think about homework last night. Person didn't even mention homework last night.

I drop into my desk and float to the ceiling. My head hurts too much or my stomach is turning over too often so it's sort of good to float away now. I wish I was able to float away on Friday when Meredith was yelling and everything awful was happening. I wish I was paying attention now when it's the last week of fourth grade and the last chance to show Ms. K and Person that I'm normal and lovable and smart.

When I come back it's because I'm doing a long division test and that's something I can actually think about without feeling like I want to disappear. It's fun. My pencil goes all over the paper. My hand is quick-quick-quick. My brain works. Answer. Answer. Answer.

I realize I missed Ms. K collecting all of our homework this morning. I missed it when she said I had to stay in from recess to work on it. I missed her disappointed look.

And as soon as I realize that, the bell rings for recess. My test is complete and flipped over on my desk so the back side is up, the way Ms. K likes, but around me pencils are still moving and kids groan.

"I didn't get to finish!" Sue says.

"Me either, Ms. K," David whines.

"OK," she says. "If you'd like to work during your recess, I'm not going to stop you. If you'd like to hand in your papers as they are now, go ahead outside. The rest of you work until you're satisfied, then come and hand in your paper and go outside."

About half the class leaves right away. I stay. I watch Ms. K work at her desk. I wonder what she said to me this morning. I know I'm not allowed to go to recess if I don't have my homework done, but I don't know what else she said.

I didn't do it on purpose but I don't want to go to recess anyway. I don't want to go anywhere except back in time to before we found out about the baby.

I watch Ms. K. She writes something on the top of a piece of paper, flips it onto a new pile, and looks at a different piece of paper on her desk. She seems to have forgotten about me.

One by one, kids get up and hand in their papers.

Sue.

Greg.

Annie.

She says, "Thank you, enjoy your recess," to each of them, like they are each the most special kid in the world. It's hard to watch since I'm apparently invisible and she forgot all about me.

Finally, it's me and David left and then even he goes to hand in his paper.

"Thank you, David. I'm proud of you for working hard on this," Ms. K says. "You have about eight minutes of recess left. Go run around! It's a beautiful day."

That makes me look out the window. The sun is shining.

The sky is blue. Why don't I ever notice when it's a beautiful day until someone points it out to me?

David is still heading out the door when Ms. K finally sees me. "Flora?" she says.

I nod.

"You're still working on your test?" she asks.

"No," I say.

"Come hand it in and get out to recess then," Ms. K says. "It's a beautiful day."

I shake my head.

"No recess for you today?" Ms. K asks. "Why not?"

Has she totally forgotten about me? I feel empty.

"Homework," I say.

"Oh," Ms. K says. "Do you remember what I told you this morning?"

I shake my head.

Ms. K comes over and sits in the little desk next to me, David's desk, even though it's for kids and she's a grown-up. Then she stands back up, crosses the classroom to the mouse tank, and comes back with Castillo in her hands.

As she lets the mouse crawl over to me, she says, "Your mom emailed this morning. She said you guys had a rough weekend and you didn't get to your homework. Is that true?"

I nod. "Sorry," I say.

Ms. K sighs. "You've been working hard to become a great student so I'm really sorry that something interrupted you this weekend. But I do understand family emergencies. Do you want to go to recess?"

I shake my head. Now that I'm back in my body and now that the math problems are all answered, my headache and stomachache are back. Elena is at recess.

"Do you want to talk about it?" Ms. K asks.

No. I don't want to talk about it. But Person told me to talk more. Maybe if I talk more to Ms. K she won't be as eager to get rid of me. Castillo nestles into my palm, making me brave.

"Too many changes," I say.

"Ah," Ms. K says, nodding. "You mean fifth grade? Or the baby?"

My mouth drops open. "You know?" I say. "About the baby?"

"Your mom told me last week," she says. "I understand it might be scary, Flora, but you'll be an excellent big sister. You already are."

"Thanks," I say. But she's talking about Julian. It's different to be Julian's sister. I can never be anyone's the way I'm Julian's.

I take a deep breath. I'm going to do what Person says. I'm going to express myself.

"Will you be our fifth-grade teacher?" I ask. "Please?"

Ms. K smiles. "No," she says. "I need to stay here and teach the fourth grade. You deserve a fifth-grade teacher who is used to the fifth grade, who knows what she's doing."

I shake my head.

"But thank you, Flora," Ms. K says. "That's a huge compliment that you'd like me to be your teacher again."

"Yeah," I say. Except now I'm mad at her. I don't want her to be my teacher again, exactly, I just want her to stay. I want to see her every day. I don't want another person to come into my life and go away.

It's so hard to believe in Forever when it only counts for some people and not all of them.

That night I get up to sneak into Julian's room like usual. At least that's what I tell myself I'm doing.

But when I pass outside of Person and Dad's room, I stop. I press my ear against the door. I still don't hear anything so I lean into the door until it cracks open a little bit.

Then the whispers filter out.

I don't think I did this at any of my homes before. I don't think I bothered to worry about when we were leaving or where we were going. I sat and shook in the certainty that we were leaving one day.

Dad is talking. "I know you're worried. I'm also worried . . . but I want to know. Don't you?"

I hear him kiss Person, a short kiss. Maybe on the cheek or forehead.

"I should want to know everything . . . I can't think about some of the stuff, though."

"It's tough," Dad says.

"I'm awful," Person says.

Person is not awful.

"This is one thing and it's a tough one and you're going to do it anyway," Dad says. "You can't force yourself to want to do it."

"They need something. I don't know what it is, how to give it to them. They both think they were never born. They've started the erratic behaviors again. We have to do something about all of this . . . Maybe . . . Maybe Dr. Fredrick is right, but . . ."

Dad sighs. "How did this stuff start up again? I thought we were through the rough patch, the adjustment."

"The adjustment will last the rest of their lives," Person says.

I gasp so loudly I freeze to make sure they don't hear.

I can't believe Person knows that. That she admits it.

Person says she's here forever, but I know Person doesn't still live with Grams who used to be her mom. And Ms. K doesn't live with her mom either. And Dad doesn't live with his mom, especially since his mom is dead. So Forever doesn't mean what it is supposed to mean and adjustment will happen over and over again and it's always going to hurt and I'm almost crying because it's such a relief that Person realizes this even if I have no idea who else she means or what else she's talking about.

"The only thing I'm worried about is the message it sends," Dad says. "To separate them. To take Julian and Flora away right when things get a little rough."

"I'm not taking them away to separate them from Elena. But I think we're giving all of our kids what they need. Julian and Flora need their history, or something. Elena needs some time with you. They'll forgive each other, if we let them do it on their own time. I'm sure of it."

"I guess it's hard to forgive anyone when you don't have a sense of who you are," Dad says.

"I know this isn't the way I'm supposed to think but . . . The one I'm worried about is me," Person says. "I . . . I have to see all of it."

And then I know why I'm nervous. Because, yes, I want to see Gloria and Megan B. again. I want to know everything that happened to me. I want to know where and how and why I got started on this life. But I don't think I want Person to see all of this. The thought of Person in Gloria's house makes me itchy.

Person doesn't belong anywhere near the chaos and dirt of foster care. And when she sees it, will she start to think that I'm dirty and chaotic too?

"Do you think the baby brought up all this stuff? Do you really think they think they weren't born?" Dad says.

"Well, how about you, do you think you were born?" Person asks.

"Huh?" Dad says. "Yes."

"Do you remember being born?" Person asks.

Dad chuckles. "No," he says.

"Do you remember being a baby?"

"No," Dad says.

"So . . . then how do you know you were?"

He thinks a long time. Then he says, "There were pictures, of course. And my mom told me stories. The stories are there before my memory starts."

"Exactly. Flora asked me that question and I've been thinking of it ever since."

"God, I hope we find them a baby picture," Dad says.

I'm beaming. Person remembered what I said word for word and she's still thinking about it weeks later.

I feel like the smartest ex-foster kid in the world as I sneak into Julian's room and curl up on the bottom of his bed.

I don't feel as smart when Ms. K hugs me good-bye on the last day of school. I'm heading out her door and she puts her arms around me and hands me a card.

But it's not that special because she's doing the same thing for everyone as everyone heads out the classroom door for the last time.

But it's also sort of special because at least I'm last. At least I get the most time with Ms. K out of all of these classmates. I want to make her smile one more time but she's already smiling.

"Oh, Flora," she says. She hands over the card. "I'm really proud of you, you know? I've so enjoyed being your teacher. And I am hoping and praying you've passed all of your tests this week and you'll be onto bigger and better things in the next year!"

"Fifth grade?" I say.

"I don't know yet. I still have some papers to grade. We'll know for sure next week. But you worked so hard. I'm hoping for you!"

She's smiling but I don't want to see it anymore.

I barely hug her back and then I'm in the hallway and Ms. K is gone for the summer and maybe forever.

When I get into the hallway, I open her card.

Dear Flora,

I am so proud of everything you accomplished this year. I will miss you a lot when you move on to the fifth grade. But you know who won't miss you? Castillo the Mouse. He'll be the fifth-grade class pet! You're so good to him, I knew he deserved to be with you another year!

Love,

Ms. K

THEORY #1046

We come from the horizon, my brother and me.

The slippery line between the earth and sky. The slice of desert or ocean that's the farthest you can see. The spot in your vision that is always, always moving.

One day the seagulls were flying over the waves; the snakes were slithering over the desert sand; the pine branches were bending across the trunks of their trees; the mountains were darkening, all turning toward the sun while it was setting. They noticed two dark dots on that faraway line.

"Those dots are in the sky," the seagulls said.

"No, they're resting on the sand," the snakes said.

"No, they're dancing on the mountains," the trees said.

"No, they're hanging from the clouds," the mountains said.

But the seagulls and the snakes and the trees and the mountains and all of the creatures were wrong.

We were in the horizon itself. We were crawling out of the place where the earth zips itself shut. We were in the sky and the clouds and the waves and the desert and the forest and the mountain range. We were everywhere and nowhere.

We were exactly where we've been every day since.

Sixteen

FAMILIES TAKE VACATIONS

THE CAR IS STUFFED WITH EVERYTHING we could possibly want (except Dad). Person is in the front seat, driving. In the seat beside her is her iPhone and her iPad that she keeps offering to let us play on because it's going to be a long drive from New Jersey to Maryland.

Lilian Samuels is singing and bopping around on the stereo, her cheery voice filling the car because I once said she was my favorite when Elena asked and I knew that she was Elena's favorite. Lilian Samuels used to be OK but now I love her because I know that Person is playing her just for me and this is yet another thing she listened to me say and then remembered.

And the backseat is scattered with food. There's juices and sandwiches and oranges and grapes in a cooler. There's bags of pretzels and chips crinkling in the middle seat between us. There's gummy worms and Tootsie Rolls and M&M's

sliding around at our feet.

Julian is staring at the food with big eyes as I watch the road zipping by my window. Every time I turn my head to look at him, he's holding a different snack. Not eating. Just holding.

I know Person put all of these snacks back here to make him comfortable. We already ate a big breakfast and she said we'd stop for lunch around noon.

"You wish all of this food was hidden in your closet instead of here where everyone can see it, don't you?" I say, joking.

But Julian is serious. He shrugs with guilty eyes.

Which means he *would* prefer to have all of these snacks hidden in his closet rather than here for him to take any time he wants and which also means I'm never going to quite understand his thing with food. It's weird that our things aren't the same. We were always together. We have the same blank history. Either he should be terrible at talking or I should be obsessed with hiding food in my closet.

We stop for lunch somewhere in Pennsylvania. We're at a real restaurant where a person comes over to your table and asks what you want to drink like we're visiting our aunt or something except that the waiter has a little notebook and I know Person is going to have to pay for it in the end.

"So," Person says as we wait for our drinks and look over our menus.

I decide on a cheeseburger. It's the cheapest thing on the menu. I don't want to be too expensive for Person.

"Have you guys ever stayed in a hotel before?" she asks.

I shrug.

Julian says, "I don't know."

And then the waiter comes back. "Anything to eat, folks?"

Julian orders chicken fingers and mac and cheese on top of the soda he already asked for. I shoot him a look but he doesn't seem to notice.

It's not fair to Person. It shouldn't cost her so much money—food and gas and a hotel—for us to find our histories. Not when normal kids like the one inside her, and Elena, come with their histories already attached.

"You don't know if you've ever been to a hotel?" Person says when the food is ordered.

We stare at her. We keep telling her that we don't remember anything but it's like me and those concepts from Earth Science—she can't quite grasp it.

"Listen, guys," she says. "I want us to have some fun on this trip, OK? I mean, there will be some tough stuff. We all know that. But tonight we'll check into our hotel in Maryland and then wander down to the beach. It's only a few blocks away. And there's a pool too. I want us to have fun. Whenever we can. It won't be fun the whole time, but when we can have fun we should try. Right?"

Julian and I look at each other and sip through our straws. We don't know what Person is talking about. She sounds stressed. My heart speeds up. Is stress contagious?

The waiter comes back over and puts the cheeseburger in front of me.

"Can I get you another Sprite, buddy?" she asks.

I stare at my brother. I make my eyes say, *No, no no. No more Sprite. You've already asked for too much.*

Julian has chicken in his mouth but he nods.

Now I want to kick him for real.

I wonder if there's anything I do that threatens our place in Person's heart, anything he can see but I can't like the way Julian fakes happy and the way he eats and eats and eats without thinking about who is paying for all the food.

"Last Sprite, OK, J?" Person says. "I want to get there before the pool closes tonight so we can't have too many bathroom breaks."

"OK," Julian says through a full mouth.

I can't help it. I add, "Plus, it's expensive. All this food and drinks. And the trip. All of it. We don't have to make it cost more for Mom with stuff like extra sodas."

"Flora." Person says my name like I'm in trouble. I look at her, my heart now racing. "I want you to try to stop that, OK? I know it's hard to stop a habit that grows and grows, but I want you to try."

"Stop what?" I ask.

Person smiles. "Stop being so responsible." She chuckles. "Now that's not something most parents have to tell their fourth grader . . . or fifth grader."

She looks happy now. Happy about this bad habit of mine. I'm so confused. I want to be her normal fourth grader but I also want to make her smile like that.

"Huh?" I say.

"Be the kid," Person says. "Let me be the grown-up. I'll worry about money and food and where we sleep. You worry about as little as possible."

"Oh," I say.

"It's hard for you to promise to do that all the time. So just give me these two weeks, OK? I promise I won't spend more money than I can." She turns to Julian. "I promise you'll have plenty of food. There will be some hard and tough and uncomfortable moments, but I promise I'll follow them with something fun or healthy. Let me take care of you. Let me be your mom. Like Dr. Fredrick says: I'll earn your trust. You work on giving it. For two weeks."

We stare at her for a few minutes. I feel my heart rate falling.

Is that all I have to do to make Person happy? Just stop worrying? It sounds so nice. It also sounds impossible.

When the waiter comes back with Julian's second Sprite, I say, "Can I please have a glass of milk?"

Person looks at me with a smile so big I think her face will burst. "Good job," she says.

I look at Julian. He's shaking his head at me like I shouldn't have ordered the milk when he's the one who ordered two Sprites plus two whole meals.

Don't worry about that, Flora. Person says not to worry.

"I think it would be a lot easier to not worry at all if I knew exactly what we were doing," I say.

"I was just getting to that," Person says. "We're doing

exactly what you asked. We're visiting all of your old homes, your foster homes, starting with Gloria's."

I thought we'd start at the beginning looking for our histories. I thought we'd start at the sea or at outer space or at the bottom of the ocean or at the horizon. But no.

We're starting in foster care.

"Gloria," Julian says. "With too many kids."

"And dogs," I say.

"Yes," Person says. "We don't know enough to start anywhere else, really. We'll start there and work on piecing together your story. That's what Dr. Fredrick says to do."

My heart speeds up. My brain can't help worrying. I tell it to stop. *Stop worrying. Stop worrying.*

"But the file leaves off after just two homes," Julian says.

Person nods. "I know," she says. She takes a deep breath. "But Dr. Fredrick says to keep looking. We'll ask Gloria what she knows. We'll ask everyone what they know."

She's nervous. She doesn't want to know what they know.

"Maybe we can gather enough information to trace back to all of your previous homes," she says, forcing a smile.

"The white house?" I ask.

I want to see it. It's so weird to want something Person doesn't want to give me. Something bigger than an extra bowl of ice cream or more screen time. There are other things I need in this big way: hugs and the same bed every night and enough food and to stay near Julian. But those are all things Person wants to give me. It's so weird to have this big need that she doesn't want to fill.

Dr. Fredrick says it's OK, but when Person smiles that sadly it doesn't feel OK.

"We're going to try to go all the way back to the beginning, piece by piece."

"The beginning?" I say.

Person nods. "When you were born . . . which you were. I just have to find a picture. Or someone who knew you as babies. You'll see."

It seems so important to Person. I wonder why this matters more than anything else. More than me passing fourth grade. More than Julian being normal about food. More than us being good to the new baby. But it's the one thing I can't even try to do for her. I can try to express myself. I can try to pass fourth grade. I can try not to worry.

I can't try to be born. Why does being born matter?

That night I'm snuggled into the big bed in the hotel. Julian is propped up on his elbow beside me. We've just said good night to Dad on FaceTime and now Person is reading to us from a funny book she brought called *Joey Pigza Swallowed the Key*. I can still smell the chlorine in my hair and my muscles feel delightfully tired from the long swim we took when we first got to the hotel this afternoon.

Person talked on and on about what great swimmers we were. The same way she did last summer. This time she said, "I wonder who taught you to swim."

The words are still going through my brain. Did anyone teach us? Or maybe we came from the water and we've always just known?

Every few sentences Julian and I bubble with giggles at the silly antics Joey gets himself into. And when we do, Person stops reading to smile at us like we are surprises, like we're presents under the Christmas tree that she was sure she'd never get.

When she gets to the end of the chapter, she closes the book and Julian says, "Mom, please—"

"We've got a big day tomorrow," Person says. "We'll read more on the beach in the afternoon."

Julian lies down on the pillow next to me. "What about the morning?" he asks. He's staring at the ceiling. He's nervous. I'm nervous. She's nervous.

I thought I'd be afraid of the beach but when we took a walk on it today, it was OK. I thought I'd be afraid to be back here so close to where so much bad stuff happened to us, where we grew before we became Person's. The Maryland shore.

I don't want Person to answer his question. I don't want to think about the hard stuff we're here to do. Because I feel happy. I feel like I'm on a family vacation like television people go on. I feel like we are a family.

I feel almost normal.

I feel almost real.

"We'll go to Gloria's home. We'll only stay as long as we

need to gather information," Person says. "Then we'll hit the beach."

Underneath the covers I start to shake.

"This is what Dr. Fredrick suggested. It's time for you guys to learn your story. Even if it's hard or uncomfortable, he thinks you guys will get some answers. You'll get some memories with each place we go." She sounds unconvinced.

I shake. I shake. I hope Person can't see.

It's hard enough to want something Person doesn't. But to want something and also be afraid of it, it's so confusing.

We're going to the homes. We're reliving all the change and all the chaos. How can Person ask me to be an un-worrying kid and also take me back to all of these places?

She puts her hand on my head and I'm glad I'm not shaking there.

"And the rest of the days—most of the time—we'll be on vacation. We'll go to the beach and the boardwalk. We'll play games and mini-golf. We'll go to restaurants and swim in the pool. OK, Flora? Then we will all go home together. I will not leave your side. OK, Flora?"

No no no. NO. Not OK.

Except I can't say that because all of my words are stuck.

I know we asked Person for this trip, but now that it's starting tomorrow, I'm scared.

What if once I remember, I don't want to remember anymore, but this time I can't forget?

"We'll have a code word," Person says. "If either of you

get into a situation that you feel you can't handle, you say the word *elephant* and we'll leave immediately. I promise. I won't worry about being rude or anything, I'll just take you right out of there, OK?"

What if my words are stuck?

"And we'll do something fun every day, too."

Person keeps saying that. Fun. How do we have fun in the middle of darkness and chaos? How do we have fun while also watching her learn exactly how terrible it is where we come from?

Believe, Flora. Believe.

When I finally make words they say, "Read another?"

Person knits her eyebrows together. "Another chapter?" she asks.

"Yes, yes!" I say.

"Yes," Julian says.

And then we lie down and she opens the book back up. The funny words wash over me but I barely hear them. Instead I hear Person's voice.

She's reading for me. She's doing this for me.

I'll be OK as long as I'm with her.

Seventeen
FAMILIES HAVE HISTORIES

WHEN WE ARRIVE SATURDAY MORNING, THE house looms over the car. It's not big. I can see that with my eyes. But it feels huge. It takes up my whole vision. It takes up my whole heart.

It's exactly like I remember: blue-gray paneled with a small square front yard that's half grass, half white concrete driveway. The yard is filled with stuff. Old, rusty-looking bicycles. Plastic cars that little kids would sit in and move their feet to make them go. Baby dolls and plastic bowling pins and basketballs and a fake lawn mower. Everything is broken or dented or missing a leg or a door. I even see a lone white sock hanging over the banister that leads up to the porch. There's the pole for a basketball hoop in the driveway, but no backboard or hoop at the top.

Every few seconds the screen door screeches open and a kid spills out. They seem to be everywhere, the kids. All sizes and colors and shapes of them.

On the side of the yard, behind a chain-link fence, I can see three dogs running around back and forth, playing. There's a lot of playing. Kids. Dogs.

I never knew playing could be scary.

"This was your last house. I think you were here for almost a year."

"Yeah," Julian says.

"Yeah," I say. Because I'm remembering some things. I remember the way the dogs used to lick my hands in the mornings and how happy I was when one of them chose to curl up on the bottom of my bed at night. I remember Megan B. and her dollhouse. I remember the swirling chaos around Julian and me as kids careened in every direction.

"It's OK, Mom," Julian says. "We don't need to do this."

He's changing his mind now that we're here, now that we're steps away from Gloria's front door, the front door to our lives Before. I sort of want to change my mind too.

I know that Person will say OK. She'll take us back to the hotel and we'll spend the days swimming in the ocean on a Dad-less family vacation instead of doing what we should. What we need to. Julian and I will pretend it's OK while the holes inside us get bigger and bigger and bigger. Then there will be a baby and Julian will hide more and more food and I will talk less and less and Julian's smile will get bigger and faker and crazier.

I can't let that happen.

Person turns to face us in the backseat. She smiles like she's taking charge. I love that smile. "Let's make a game of it then," she says. "I'm pretty sure I'm right about you being born, but if we gather the evidence in these houses to prove one of your other theories, I'll accept that. We'll look for clues in all the houses. We'll keep track of which theory has the most evidence. We'll assign points. OK? We'll make it fun."

Julian and I don't say anything. We stare.

"Remind me of the theories," Person says.

"Sand," I say. "Television. Blood."

"The horizon," Julian says. "The sea."

"Alright," Person says, turning from the front seat with a smile that's too big to be real, but that's OK because I know she's doing it for us. "Let the games begin."

We get out of the car and all of the kids in the yard ignore us as we approach the front door.

Before Person can ring the bell, a black-haired lady with a baby on her right hip opens the screen door and says, "Julian! Flora!" She looks at Person. "I'm so glad you came back to visit us. Thank you, Emily."

It's Gloria.

My eyebrows shoot up. So do Julian's. I guess I figured the mommies would remember us, especially if we remember them. But I didn't think they'd know Person.

"Come in," she says.

We file into a dark living room. There's no one in here but the TV is on anyway, playing cartoons loudly. We sit on the couch in a row: Julian, me, Person.

"I was so glad when your mom called to say you guys would be visiting. What brings you all back this way?" Gloria says, before she leans forward and mutes the TV.

At that moment two kids bound into the room. I don't recognize them so they must be new. I didn't recognize the kids in the yard either. There were always new kids here. These two are black and one is a girl around six and there's a boy that looks about a year younger. "Gloria!" the girl whines. "Sam took my juice."

She snatches at the juice box in Sam's hand.

"So get another one," Gloria says over her shoulder, without bothering to look at the kids.

The girl snatches at the box again. "But that's the last grape one!"

"We'll have more soon. I pick up the WIC check today. Just get a different one."

"I want grape!" the girl shouts. This time she manages to get her hand on the juice box and squeezes so juice explodes into Sam's face. "Jasmine!" Sam screams. He throws the juice box at her and then puts both of his hands on her shoulders and shoves her into the wall.

Julian starts to shake next to me. I shake back. We're talking in shakes. *Yes, we remember this. No, we didn't want to.*

"That's it!" Gloria shouts. "Outside, both of you! I have company, can't you see?"

She gets up and shoves the kids out the front door and

when she sits back down, Person says, "Well, it's nice to see you, Gloria. I can see you still have your hands full. We don't need to stay long but—"

We're all shocked when Gloria talks again. It almost sounds like she's going to cry. "I know, I know," she says. "*Dios mio*, I know."

"What?" Person asks.

I scoot closer to her. I belong to Person now, not this frazzled black-haired lady.

"I know I have my hands too full," she says.

Person nods. Julian and I shake.

Person says, "So if we could—"

"I'm weak, you know? The county, they call. They say there's kids who need help. I can't say no. I have to say yes. If I don't say yes . . . what kind of person am I? I'm a Christian. I can't turn a child away from my home. But they give me too many. I'm never doing a good job."

Person's eyes are huge. It's like she doesn't know what to say.

"I love these little ones but . . . it's not supposed to be this way. They shouldn't all be here, you know?"

"No," Julian says, and I love him for it. What is this woman talking about?

"I mean, foster care is supposed to be temporary. They're always saying 'Just for a few days, just for a month' so I say yes when more kids need a home. I think, I can handle ten kids if it's only for two days. I think, what's one more for this week?

And then they stay and stay."

"Maybe you should say no sometimes," I say. "You look tired."

My face burns. Stupid lung filters.

Gloria looks right at me. Her eyes are big and brown like Julian's.

"You talked!" she says.

"Yes," I say.

"Flora! You talked. So quickly." She turns and looks at Person. "The whole time she was here she barely talked except to Megan and Julian. Maybe three words in what was it? Six months? Or five?"

"Eleven, I think," Person says.

"Eleven! Eleven months, I had these babies!"

Person squeezes my shoulders. I'm thinking. Gloria remembers me. And I didn't talk.

I try to remember not talking. I try to remember being here. But all I remember is scariness and a few bright memories of dogs and Megan and her dollhouse. I don't remember a routine. I don't remember breakfast and going to school and bedtime and all the normal stuff. I remember stuff from here but I don't remember *being* here.

"Flora's pretty smart. We should all listen to her more," Person says.

"Do you know anything else about us?" Julian asks. "Like do you know how we started?"

Gloria shakes her head. "By the time you guys got to me,

you'd been in care a long time. I'm not sure how you came into care in the first place."

"Do you know anything about their previous houses?" Person asks.

Gloria's eyes get wet again. "No . . . no, I'm sorry. I should be finding these things out. It's just that I have so much . . . and . . . I can't . . ."

"Where's Megan B.?" I ask because we need to change the subject.

She's the one who started this after all, with all her postcards.

Gloria smiles. It looks a little forced. "Megan just moved out! She's going to be adopted. At twelve years old. She's such a good girl, I'm so glad she found a home."

"You don't look glad," Julian says.

"I know," Gloria says. She takes a deep breath. "Megan deserves a home with parents forever. Like you and Julian before her. But I miss her like I miss you." She's looking right at me again. "I love you all. I love all of my babies, I do," Gloria says.

There's something warm in my heart. Like maybe it believes her. Like maybe she did love me when I lived here but my heart was buried too far beneath my ribs for me to even recognize it.

Or maybe she was too busy to tell me.

I think about Sam and Jasmine. There's no way they know she loves them.

Is there such a thing as too busy to love?

"I know you've got a lot going on," Person says. "But do you happen to have any pictures of these two that you can share with us?"

"Oh, oh oh," Gloria says. "I do, somewhere. Of course. Come on. Follow me."

We go with her through the door into the next room, which I know will be the kitchen before I even walk into it because I used to live here.

I used to live here. It's so weird.

"Come on, come on," Gloria says, walking toward her fridge. It's covered in pictures. They are taped on mostly because it looks like she's run out of magnets, and anyway, the pictures are three layers thick. Mostly there are photographs but there are also some drawings and postcards and even report cards. She starts rifling through the top corner and when the baby on her hip cries she jiggles her a little and then keeps rifling.

"Come on," she says. "You guys can help."

Julian and I start looking at the bottom of the fridge since we can't reach the top and Person takes the other top corner. We pull back pictures of some kids to find pictures of others. A picture of a baby boy falls on my head when Person drops it.

Gloria must love all of these kids to keep them on her fridge forever.

But doesn't Gloria realize her fridge is too crowded to see all of the kids she loves?

We look for a minute and it's quiet except the screams and

the barks outside and the occasional crying from the on-her-hip baby.

Then, I pull a picture from the stack at the very edge of the fridge against the floor. It was on the bottom of the fridge, but it was in the front of the stack. At the same time Person says, "I found it!"

"Me too!" I say.

We put the two pictures on the kitchen table and the five of us—me, Julian, Gloria, Person, and the hip-baby—stare at them.

In the one Person found, Julian and I are in the middle of a crush of kids all standing on Gloria's porch. Julian looks at that one and points to one of the kids. "That's Chris. He was my age."

I point to the girl next to me. "That's Megan B.," I tell Person.

Suddenly I miss her. It feels like my heart is ripping apart. I think about her writing me all of those postcards and how it's been months and months or maybe a year since I thought about her but I miss her anyway. I didn't know I could miss someone this way, someone who wasn't Julian.

It makes me a little uncomfortable, like there's pebbles in my shoes.

In the other picture, we're on the sand. Just the two of us. It isn't the beach because there's no ocean behind us. We're just little specks, squatting in the sand and looking at it in our fingers.

Below us is sand. Above us is sky.

"The horizon," I whisper, pointing.

Person laughs. "Point for you guys," she says, like she doesn't really care.

"I . . . ," Gloria starts. "Well, no. You can . . . well . . . I . . ."

I look at her. "It's OK," I say, "Sometimes my words get stuck too. Just take a deep breath and we'll wait for you."

At that, Person and Gloria burst out laughing and I feel my face get hot. I didn't mean to be funny.

But it works because after a minute, Gloria says, "I'd like to offer you the pictures because I know they're important for Julian and Flora to have. But they're my only two of these babies and . . . I know they are your kids now but they were—"

"Oh!" Person says. "How about I take a picture of these pictures with my phone?"

Gloria nods happily and a dog barks at the back door off the kitchen. She crosses the tile floor and opens the door and the dogs pour in.

And they walk.

Right.

To.

Me.

Within seconds I'm on the floor with my face in their necks. They're licking my hands and wiggling around in my lap.

And this. This is remembering.

"Good boy, Francis," I say to the small one. "Good boy,

Sully," I say to the fast one. "Good girl, Cassie," I say to the shy one.

Person has tears in her eyes when she pulls me off the floor.

"Thank you, Gloria," she says, giving her a big hug. "This could not have gone any better."

"Wait!" I say, maybe too loudly. Everyone in the room jumps. "I need one more thing. Do you have Megan B.'s address where she lives with her new parents? I owe her some postcards."

Gloria smiles. "I sure do," she says.

We say our good-byes armed with new pictures and addresses and this weird feeling of warmth that comes when you find out someone you almost forgot remembers you and loves you still.

And then, when we're in the car, the most amazing thing of all happens.

Person says, "Well, Florey. Looks like we're going to have to get you a dog."

Later that night, Person takes us to a place for dinner. She calls it a restaurant but it's hard to think of it like that because the building has no walls. It's just a roof and a floor and a bunch of tables where families crowd around and talk-talk-talk.

"Crabs are the perfect food for a day like today," Person says.

She's sitting on the bench across from us. The table between us is covered with newspaper and the little critters are piled on top of it, pink with white bellies and red powder all over them.

Person already taught us how to crack the claws and pick out the meat, how to lift open the tab on the belly to find all the best meat in the body of the crab.

"Why are they perfect?" Julian asks.

"Because Julian can't steal one and keep it in his closet?" I say, my eyes on the back of my second crab.

But when Person laughs, I look up. I realize that I don't mind her laughing.

Did I just make a joke?

"Why couldn't I hide it in my closet?" Julian says. "It's easier to carry around than that slice of pizza you found in there."

We all laugh again.

We aren't supposed to laugh at Julian and the food. I *punched* Elena for laughing at Julian and the food. But something about this laughing feels different. Whole.

"Well, you can't keep crabs or pizza in your closet anymore or else my dog will find them and he'll eat them and she'll get sick."

I'm saying it to test Person. A dog, my dog, would be unbelievable. Nothing that good will ever happen to me.

But Person says, "That's true, Julian. You'll have to think about that with a dog around."

Julian says, "You just said 'he' and 'she' at once."

I smile as I pull open the back of the shell. "That's because we don't know which one it'll be yet," I say.

Then I realize that yes, I did say both "he" and "she." That's the most confusing thing I said since we sat down, but they both understood me. I'm having a conversation. It's going on and on. And no one has said "huh?" or asked me to "explain."

"No," Person says through the last few giggles. I'm looking at her but she has her eyes on the tiny legs as she snaps them in half and sucks out the saltiest meat. "Crabs are perfect talking food. Your hands are busy. Your eyes are busy. And eating them takes hours. It's easy to talk while you're eating crabs."

I keep my eyes on my own dinner as I de-shell it and begin to wipe out the "crab mustard" with a paper towel.

"Plus, they're delicious," Person says.

I focus on the salty and spicy flavor in my mouth. I'm nervous that talking about talking will make my words go back and get stuck again.

But Person doesn't want us to talk, I don't think, because she keeps talking herself.

"Did you know that my parents drove us to a town near here every summer when we were kids?" she asks.

"Why?" I say.

She laughs. "For vacation, of course. It was in Delaware, actually, but only a few miles from here. Aunt Alice and I would swim in the ocean or read on the beach all day. My parents too, I guess. And then at night we'd walk the boardwalk and eat crabs."

"Vacation," Julian says. "Like family vacation?"

"Yup," Person says. "Those are some of my favorite memories from when I was a kid. So I always dreamed I'd be able to take my own kids back here someday. It's a little weird when you live in New Jersey to drive south, past the Jersey shore, and go to these beaches in Delaware and Maryland, but I always wanted to anyway. I didn't mind the extra hours in the car. Those weeks at the beach were my favorites."

"You always wanted to take kids here?" I say. Suddenly this whole trip feels bigger and more important. Even bigger than discovering where we come from.

Maybe we're making Person happy just by being here.

"Yup," Person says. "You'd never believe how far my jaw dropped when the adoption agency told me I was matched with a couple of kids who live on the Maryland shore! My eyes about bugged out of my head."

"You didn't have to take us here, then," Julian says. "You found us here."

Person reaches out like she's going to pat Julian's head, but then she remembers her fingers are covered in crab gook and red spice and we all laugh again.

So much laughing. I've never felt so much laughing in one day. It's like my shoulders are lighter. It's like there's helium in my brain.

"It wasn't as bad as I thought it would be," Julian says. "I mean, I barely remember Gloria."

"Yeah," I say. "There were always so many kids."

"And dogs," Julian says.

"Three dogs," I say.

"Maybe ten kids?" Julian says. "It always felt like more."

"Yeah," I say. "It felt like so many. Way too many kids for just one mom."

"Yeah," Julian says. "Gloria remembers us though, better than we remember her. And . . . she liked us?"

"She liked us," I say. I'm not sure there are any words in any unstuck place that can explain how big it is that we found someone from those dark unremembered places, someone good, someone who is happy to see us and hoping and hoping that we're happy.

"She loved you," Person says.

When we look up she's looking so serious and the whole thing feels too big again and I get itchy. I wonder if she's right and the crabs really are making us talk.

"Can I see the pictures again?" I ask.

And even though there are still four crabs lined up on her side of the table, Person takes a few minutes to wipe her messy hands and passes me her phone.

I stare at the pictures, flipping back and forth between them.

Even if I'm not a born person, I realize, *I was a person here. I was a person before I was Person's.*

That night, in bed, Julian and I pass the phone back and forth quick-quick-quick as we tell Dad everything that happened that day. We're talking too loudly. We're coming-out-of-our-skin excited. We're like the other kids who were always bouncing everywhere in Gloria's house.

We're like kids.

"That's great, guys," Dad keeps saying.

I have the phone in my hands when I say, "We got pictures! Did Mom send them to you?"

"She did," Dad says. "I'm so glad to see them . . . I wish I was with you all though. I miss you."

Something weird and dark twitches in my heart. I don't want it there after such a good and whole day.

I say, "You and Elena? Today?"

Dad smiles. "We had a nice day. We went to the farmers' market and bought some fresh fruits and veggies. Then we came back here and made a raspberry pie from scratch."

"Cool," I say.

"I sort of wish you guys were here too, for the pie," Dad says. "And that we were there. I miss you guys."

"But if we were there and you were here we still couldn't see you," I say.

Dad laughs and I laugh with him and Julian laughs beside me. I just made another joke. Two jokes in my entire life, both on the same day.

"Good night, Flora," Dad says.

"Good night, Dad," I say. I hand the phone back to Julian and lie down under the blankets. Because Dad's right.

We're finally on a family vacation. We finally feel whole.

But really, we aren't.

THEORY #742

We come from crabs, my brother and me.

We're made of good stuff, but you have to work to get to it.

Our good stuff is cased under hard shells that will cut your fingers and burn your hands when you try to break through them.

Our good stuff is hidden under layers of guts and gross yellow goo that will make you say "yuck" the whole time you're cleaning it away with a paper towel. And just when you think you've gotten all of the bad stuff out of the way, there's more guts, more shells, more goo.

But we're made of good stuff. If you work really, really hard.

Eighteen
FAMILIES HAVE UPS AND DOWNS

"SO THAT'S POINT TWO FOR US," I say to Person, after I finish telling her about the newest theory.

Person is sitting on a low beach chair. Her white cover-up spreads across her bigger belly, and she rests a magazine on it and stretches her legs in front of her into the sand. She isn't actually reading the magazine though. She's talking to me.

I'm sitting near her feet, burying my legs in the sand, letting my hands and arms and chest get a dusting of sand too. Person says she couldn't stand to have all that sand on her but to me it feels warm and the right sort of scratchy. Julian is playing by the shore a few feet away.

We went to the beach in the morning today because we don't have any appointments until the afternoon.

"Uh-uh," Person says. "No way. You can't just make up a new theory and use it as a point for you guys. That's not how it works."

I squint at her. "But why?" I say. "It didn't make sense?"

It felt like all the words were there when I was explaining it to Person. It even felt like they almost all came out in the right order. I only stumbled a few times.

Person smiles. "Actually, it made perfect sense. Except why is it number 742? Wasn't the one before it number 1046?"

"Because," I say, watching a stream of sand fall out of my hand and onto my thigh, "numbers don't always go in order."

"They don't?" Person asks.

I know why she sounds surprised. She knows I'm good at math.

"Sometimes things don't make sense. Like Julian and me. Anyway, you can't stop us from making new theories because we do it all the time and it's one of the only things I know we've always been doing," I say.

Then I think, *Whoa. Those were important words. And they all came out.*

I'm happy but I start to shake anyway. Happy and Scared are so close together inside me. They press up against each other like two people sharing a bed that's too small. I can't wake up Happy without Scared being a little bit disturbed.

I reach over and dribble a handful of sand onto Person's foot so that I don't have to look at her face and see her reaction to all those real words.

But she says, "OK."

"OK?" I say. "So we get another point for the crab theory?"

"Yup, sure," Person says.

I jump to my feet, spraying sand everywhere, but Person doesn't yelp or complain. "Yes!" I say.

"But you know what else that means?" Person asks. She sounds almost serious, but she's smiling.

"No," I say. "What?"

"Well, if you're a crab . . . I just might have to eat you!"

In a flash, Person reaches out over her belly and latches on to my arm. She pulls me toward her mouth and opens it and closes it going "num num num num num." With her other hand, she reaches up and tickles me in the side.

I yelp and twist and squeal and try to get my arm back.

She keep num-ing.

I keep trying to get away but I'm laughing too hard to do it.

I don't know why I'm even resisting.

I have never enjoyed being touched so much as I do in this moment.

That afternoon is our second visit. After we clean up from the beach, we eat lunch and pile into the car. A little while later, we pull in a driveway next to the biggest house I've ever seen. It's the biggest house ever built. Before we get out of the car, I count the windows.

Twenty-two.

Just in the front of the house.

"We lived here?" Julian says.

"How did we even know our way around?" I ask.

I'm getting better at this joking thing.

But Person doesn't laugh. She shifts in the front seat in a way that makes my heart race. "I don't know," she says. "This is the address our old agency gave me and . . . well. Here we are."

Julian looks at me. We both swallow. The shiver in Person's voice reminds us of that bad thing: we're here because we asked for it. Person doesn't actually want to see where we used to live. Person doesn't actually want to know about foster care.

But this house does not look like foster care.

"This is the woman who should have your files. She might have baby pictures. Or she should at least have some information about your biological family."

Biological family. First mother. Those are the things that come with being born. I don't want to think about them.

A white woman opens the door with two packages in her hands, one wrapped in blue, the other wrapped in pink. Her face is familiar: skinny nose, gray eyes, pale skin. I'd recognize her anywhere, but I wouldn't know why until now. She used to be my mom.

"Isn't it lovely to see you two again?" she says.

She's shorter and skinnier than Person. Skinnier than Person ever was, even before the baby. She looks younger too.

"Are those for us?" Julian says, sounding excited.

"Of course," she says. She hands over the packages and opens the door.

"Thank you," I say. I squeeze my pink package. I don't think I want a present from this woman but I'm not sure why. And it makes Person happy when I say thank you.

The woman freezes and turns. "You're welcome, Flora." She seems surprised to see me, even though she must have known we were coming because she bought us gifts. "Follow me to the dining room," she says.

We walk through a big room full of brown wood with a large staircase at the front, then we walk through a living room with a white sofa and a cream carpet, then we walk into a beige room with a long dining room table. Everything is shiny and fancy. I'm nervous to touch any of it.

It seems like everything in this house is made for a different kind of kid. A not-foster-kid kind of kid.

Julian turns to Person and says, "This isn't the white house. We were somewhere else."

"Yeah," I confirm.

Person nods and waves her hands, urging us to sit at the dining room table with the woman. There are glasses of lemonade at four of the twelve chairs at the big table. Julian and I sit together on one side. Person sits across from us. The woman sits at the head of the table.

"Thank you for having us, Marta," Person says. "We thought it was very important to gather as much information about the past as we can."

Marta looks confused. "Well . . . I'll help . . . if I can . . ."

"There's a lot my children don't remember," Person says.

"I don't remember living here at all!" Julian says.

"Me neither," I say. "The house is big enough to get lost in."

Marta looks at me like she's surprised to see me sitting here next to Julian, again. Then she laughs, but it's a fake one. Not mean but strained. "You two didn't live here with me. I bought this house only about a year ago. We lived a bit closer to the shore. And yes, that house was a little smaller."

"Was it the white house?" I ask, but I'm too quiet. I don't think it was anyway. That white house was full of kids: they're in both our memories. This woman doesn't look like she likes kids at all.

"Do you have pictures of it?" Person asks. "The house you all lived in together?"

"I, um . . . ," Marta says.

"And you must have some pictures of them, right?"

"I, well . . . ," Marta says. "You see, they are two children. They had acquired a lot of stuff. I'm afraid I'm not sure. I donated most of it."

"You donated their pictures?" Person asks. She sounds more confused than angry.

"Of course I still have some pictures of their time with me. But, well, the Lifebooks were mixed in with the rest of their books so—"

"Lifebooks?" I interrupt.

"We had Lifebooks? Who made us Lifebooks?" Julian asks.

"I'm not sure but—"

"Did they say where we come from?" Julian asks.

"I don't exactly know," the woman says. "They were mostly pictures. I never got any information about your biological family, though I did ask for it." She says this like she deserves applause just for asking the same question that Person is taking us all around to try to answer.

I raise my eyebrows at Julian. Here's another one. One more person from our past who thinks we were born but doesn't know anything about how or why or where or who else was there.

"Wait," Person says. "Wait. Someone made books of these children, of my children. Someone made them books. And you lost them?"

"Most of their things were donated and—"

"Why would you do that?" Person asks. "I'm not . . . I know there's so many hard things to learn but . . . you donated them? Why? How could they have any value to anyone except these children here at this table?"

"That's enough," Marta says calmly. It seems extra mean to be calm when Person is on the verge of tears.

"Enough? What do you mean?"

"I will not be lectured in my own home," Marta says. "It's hard on me to have to relive any of this."

"Hard on you?" Person asks. "What about—"

"I'll be happy to email you pictures. I do have some of those. It's just, I was so sad when Julian was—"

"Hold on, hold on," Person interrupts Marta. "We want to hear that. We want the story of how they came to live with you and why they left. But first, please, tell me what you know. Where were they before they were with you? Who were they with? What information do you have?"

"I don't have too much but—"

Person interrupts her again, and not so politely this time. "Apparently their files were lost with you and their Lifebooks were donated . . . can you tell us anything? We can't let this be the end of the road."

Person sounds determined. It's like she wants to know what we want to know. It's like she'll say our words for us even if she doesn't want them said.

Julian chugs half his lemonade. I follow his lead.

"Hold on," Marta says. She doesn't look happy. Her face is pinched. I wonder if she ever smiled. I wonder if I used to try to make her smile like I do with Person. "The worker who placed them with me left the agency soon after, but I believe I may still have her personal phone number from all those years ago. Let me go see if I can find it."

Marta leaves the room and Julian and I look at Person. Now is usually a moment when Person would tell us something to make us feel good. It's a moment when she would translate what's happening. But instead she takes a deep breath and stares at her folded hands, not looking at us. Her lips move but the words don't come out. I've never seen Person pray. I don't even know if she believes in God. But it looks like she's praying.

Marta returns with a pitcher of lemonade and refills Julian's glass. "I found it," she says. She refills my glass, puts the pitcher down, and hands a slip of paper to Person.

Person grabs at it. It's like Marta is trying to act like whatever this paper is is no big deal, but to Person it's as important as medicine.

"Thank you," she says. I watch her put it carefully in her wallet.

"Of course," Marta says. It's mean how she's acting like something is no big deal when it clearly matters to someone else. It's like Marta is one of Elena's recess friends. "I'll certainly email you some pictures of the old house and of Julian and Flora during their time with me as well," Marta says. "Will that be all?"

All? I think *No, that can't be all.*

I don't want to sit here and hear about the awful thing I did that meant Marta didn't adopt us. I don't want Person to endure any more of this sixth-grade mean-girl-ness. But we need to know what happened. We need our story.

And it started bad but then it got so good with Gloria.

Maybe it can get better here too.

"I want to know it," I say.

Marta turns to me and says, "Know what, dear?"

"She means why we left. Why we came. When we were here. All of it," Julian says. I didn't need him to be my voice this time, but he's used to it.

"Well, you arrived when you were six, Julian. Flora was seven." Marta is looking at Julian, only, while she talks. Like she doesn't realize I'm the one who asked the question. "And you were here for a little more than a year," she says.

"More than a year?" I say.

Marta gives me that surprised look again.

"I tried, Flora. I really did," Marta says. "So yes, you were with me for a while. I can't believe you don't remember anything I did for—well, anyway, we did the proper slow transition that the experts recommend. So first you came for a weekend. Then a week."

"Where were they in the meantime?" Person asks.

"With their foster mothers," Marta says.

"Mothers?" says Person.

Julian smiles at me. I smile back. We sort of remember. Two moms. Two good moms.

"And you don't have their information?" Person asks. "Their address? Their emails?"

"I'm afraid I don't anymore," Marta says. "You have to understand, this was all painful for me. Saying good-bye to Julian."

I wait for her to say my name. She doesn't.

Person opens her mouth to object. She's getting angry. I'm not used to seeing her angry. But then she closes it because if she says anything we won't hear whatever else Marta is going to say and now I sort of want to hear it even if I don't want Person to hear it.

"I took you guys to the museums," Marta is saying. "We visited Kings Dominion and Hersheypark. We went shopping and got you outfitted for school. I got you toys galore. But . . . you never seemed . . . happy."

"Happy?" Julian asks.

Happy is impossible. We've never been happy.

"There were tantrums almost daily. Julian would put on this smile and then the next minute he'd be destroying one of my potted plants or throwing his toys out the window."

Marta looks at all of us, even Person, like we should be shocked. Like we should feel sorry for her. But this is the part we do remember. Being sad. Being bad. Being so scared we didn't even know what we were doing.

"And Flora . . . Flora wouldn't . . . she couldn't . . . She only watched television. She would for hours a day. I tried and tried to coach her on how to be more lovable."

"Lovable?" Person says. "All children are lovable. Flora is incredibly lovable."

"She—" Marta starts, but Person interrupts her. She leans across the table to grab my hand and looks in my eyes. "I love you, Flora," she says.

I'm startled by it almost. Not by the fact that Person loves me, but by how important it is that she loves me. How important it is to *her*.

Julian grabs my other hand. "I love you too, Florey," he mumbles.

Person lets go and sits down. Julian holds tighter.

"Well, anyway," Marta says, "she didn't . . . she couldn't . . . Well, you see, I didn't realize I would be adopting a disabled child. In fact, I specifically requested healthy children."

"Flora's not disabled," Julian says.

"*Requested healthy children?*" Person says, too angry.

"I'm afraid . . . ," Marta says. "I mean, she didn't speak . . . it was only the television . . . she made noises, but . . . I'm afraid . . ."

"Flora is not disabled," Julian says, loudly this time.

"You did always claim she spoke to you," Marta says. "But I wasn't so sure . . ."

Of course now I can't speak. My words are stuck.

Finally, Person takes a deep breath and speaks more calmly. "Marta, Flora is not disabled. She has some side effects of trauma, as all foster kids do, and some of hers are very pronounced. But she doesn't have a disability. But that's not actually important. I think the main point here is that when you become a parent you do not get to design your kids like you designed this house. We all have strengths and weaknesses. You cannot pick your child's abilities and disabilities. You commit to—"

"I was committed. I had committed to . . . healthy . . . children. I was . . . I did my best . . . they had everything—"

Person cuts her off again.

"Are you telling me that you pushed kids back into foster care because you thought one of them needed extra help? Is foster care where you thought they would get it?"

"No, I . . . I tried . . . I . . ."

"Stop," Person says. "Later tonight you can sit in this big empty house and tell yourself how you did the best you could, but I won't let you say it in front of my kids. They needed better than you gave them. They cannot be made to feel guilty in any way for what happened under your roof. I need to point out the ways you failed them. And giving up on an adoption without planning for the children's future—"

"I didn't give up," Marta says. "I wanted to adopt Julian but—"

"And NOT FLORA?" Julian shouts.

"I gave you everything," Marta says to him. "I gave you everything you could want and you just never seemed . . . grateful."

I'm shaking. Julian's face is red. I'm 100 percent positive that Marta's potted plants are about to end up on the floor again.

"Flora was such a . . . different child . . . and I'm afraid I couldn't handle her. I thought Julian would be better off—"

"ELEPHANT!" The word is huge and loud and it comes from Person.

Julian and I both jump.

"I'm sorry," Person says. She's fake-polite now, like Marta was before. "My children and I need to go see about an elephant."

"What?" Marta says. "What are you talking about?"

But Person gets out of her seat and walks behind Marta to grab Julian and me by the wrists. She's holding my wrist a little too hard but it still feels like love.

"I didn't mean to—" Marta is saying.

"I told you," Person says. "We need to go see an elephant.

Thank you for emailing me the pictures. Please know that I'll be back here if you don't."

Marta says, "I don't see—"

"There's an elephant," Person says, and then we're out the door.

We collapse into the car, breathless. Person turns to look at us as we buckle ourselves into the backseat.

"You guys OK?"

"Yeah," Julian says, but he's smiling so I don't know what to believe.

I shrug. My words are gone. Marta stole them when she said she tried to steal Julian.

We still have the presents in our hands. I push the paper together on mine. I try to make it explode with my brain.

Person sees me looking at the pink paper.

"I have an idea," she says. She backs out of the driveway and a few minutes later pulls into a grocery store parking lot, but she stays at the back of it, away from the grocery store. She rolls down the car window. "There," she says, pointing at the big blue garbage Dumpster. "That should be big enough, right?"

"Yes!" Julian says. He's not smiling anymore.

We jump out of the car and throw the presents on the ground. We jump on them. We kick them. We pound and break and trample them. We throw them into the Dumpster.

* * *

The next day Person says we get to spend the whole day on the beach, no visits, no tough stuff except what's already inside our heads. That's good. But my words are still gone, which is bad. I'm tired. Bone tired. The way I used to be when we first came to live with Person.

I lie in the sand at the place where the ocean laps at my ankles and stare at the clouds.

I listen behind me as Person texts and texts and texts. When her phone rings, she jumps up and runs a little bit away from us to answer it so we can't hear her. But I know what's happening. I know what she's doing.

Part of me wants to see where we lived before Marta. Part of me wants to know everything about what happened to us.

And part of me is afraid that if every house keeps getting worse and worse like that, my words will leave for good and never come back. That version of Forever is too easy for me to believe in.

Julian splashes in the water a few feet away from me. He's upset that I'm not talking.

But he's smiling crazy.

Nineteen
FAMILIES PRETEND

IT'S THE NEXT MORNING AND PERSON'S hand is stroking my head. *Part-ear-neck*.

I'm awake. Her hand woke me up. But I don't open my eyes right away so that she'll think I'm still sleeping and keep stroking me and for as long as her hand is on my head so soft and I'm in that strange space between asleep and awake I can think that she's still my person, my only person, all mine, forever.

I can pretend that there was no way I was ever going to get left in Maryland far away from her and with someone who loved Julian but couldn't *handle* me.

I can pretend not to worry that she wishes we still lived there so that she could focus on this new, real, almost born-baby.

She whispers, "Good morning, my sleepyhead."

I open my eyes. I open my mouth to say "good morning." But nothing comes out.

My words are still stuck.

I haven't even been able to remind Person that we got another point at Marta's house. The television point. Maybe Julian and I came out of the television and the way I stared at it the whole time I was at Marta's was me trying to climb back in.

But I don't care so much about points anymore.

The past two days were hard. I want to tell her that they were the hardest days of my life. Except that I used to live with that woman, Marta. I used to call her *Mom*. So they couldn't be the hardest days. Only the hardest days I remember.

And I can't tell Person that anyway because I have no words.

"You're so brave," she says.

I shrug. I think she's mostly wishing I was brave, which is another thing I can't do for her. How can I be brave if my words are too afraid to leave my lungs?

"I wish we could do this differently," Person says. "I wish we could go more slowly. I wish we could go home for a few days or months before we take this next step into your past." Person pats her tummy. "But we're up against a deadline here. And I found your foster mothers from before Marta. Do you want to keep going? Do you want to learn more? They sound incredibly nice, but we can stop anytime."

Person kisses me on the top of the head.

I can't answer any of her questions. I can tell she wants me to say stop. She wants me to ask her to take us home. But I can't yet. I have to know more. I have to find the white house. So I sit up in bed and think about what I'll wear for this one, for this other home, this next place.

I hope it's the white house even though both of our first memories are sad. Then we'll find out where we come from, and then we'll be all done.

Julian comes out of the bathroom. Person pats my head one more time and goes in to shower.

Julian comes to the foot of the bed and looks at me.

"Person wants to stop," I say. My words come unstuck, but only for Julian, I think.

"Person?" he says.

I feel my face get hot. "Mom wants us to stop."

"Because it's hard," he says. "I don't want to stop, do you?" He looks worried. He looks worried about whatever answer I give.

"I don't think so," I say.

The cell phone rings and Julian pastes on that lying smile before answering.

Person said to get ready but she also keeps saying we're on vacation and we can have little luxuries, so I rest my head back on the pillow and listen to Julian's half of the conversation.

"Hi, Dad! . . . Yeah, the beach is so fun! . . . I wish you were too . . . I don't know, some other house . . . no, I'm happy we found it! That was the end of the files. Mom is so happy . . . I want to see them all . . ."

I glare at him. I don't understand how he lies like that.

"She's not really talking today . . . OK . . . OK," he says.

Then he hits the phone so it's on speaker and hands it to me.

"Just wanted to say good morning and I love you," Dad's voice comes, tinny, through the phone. "I wish Elena and I could be with you today," he says.

I hand the phone back to Julian to say good-bye, feeling guilty. They could be here. The only reason they aren't is because I punched her.

Julian hangs up. I make a face at him.

"I don't know why you think pretending happy is so much worse than just not talking," he says.

I want to say, *I can't help it.*

I want to say, *I can't lie if I'm not talking.*

Julian doesn't even wait for me to respond because he knows I won't.

Person comes out of the bathroom.

Julian says, "Good morning, Mom! Guess what? Dad just called! Where are we going today?"

And I hate him. I'm so mad at him.

I'm sure I've never been this mad at him in the state of Maryland.

Turns out Julian and I are coming apart anyway. Just like Marta wanted.

The three of us are in the car on the way to the next ex-home when Person's phone buzzes again.

She presses something on the dashboard and calls out "Hey, honey! We're all in the car together this morning."

Dad's voice spills in between the seats. "Hi, everybody!" he says. "Hey, Flora?"

My eyebrows jump.

"She's nodding," Julian says. "She's still not talking yet."

He's said this a million times to a million people in the years and years we've been Onlys. This is the first time he sounded annoyed.

"OK," Dad says. "Well, hey, Flora. I have some good news. Maybe this will help. Guess what came in the mail?"

Person pulls the car over. It's sudden and jerky and my head whips back and forth before we're stopped on the shoulder.

"Oh my gosh. Oh my gosh," she's saying over and over again.

My heart is sinking. It can't be true. If it is, I can't hear it today.

Dad singsongs, "Guess who's going to the fifth grade?"

Immediately there are tears in my eyes.

Julian is squinting at me like he wants to smile but he's too mad at me to be proud of me. Person is weeping in the front seat and also saying over and over again, "I'm so happy. I'm so proud of you, Florey. I'm so proud of you. I'm so happy."

I'm finally making her happy but it feels so weird. Why did I have to lose Ms. K in order to make my person happy?

Dad is saying, "I so wish I could hug you, Flora. You worked so hard. You've come so far."

It's like no one notices that my words are still stuck and actually I'm right back where I came from.

I can't lose Ms. K today. Today when I don't even have Julian.

Person turns around with the happy tears dancing in her eyes.

"Still no words?" she says.

I shrug.

"Well," she says. "I couldn't be any prouder of you."

I don't know what else to do. I have to make her happy. I have to.

Julian nudges me.

I smile.

I smile even though I'm sad and confused.

I'm as bad as Julian after all.

THEORY #8

We come from the gray spot, my brother and me. That part in your day when you aren't quite you and you aren't quite anyone. That part when you don't know what worried you yesterday or who you love or where you live.

The space between awake and asleep.

We were only the air at the beginning and end of each day. Until someone heard voice, and then we were words. Until someone thought about hands, and then we were hands.

With more thoughts, with more days, we became more solid. Days passed and days passed and we became closer and closer to real.

We were your thoughts. . . . And then we were kids that no one knew what to do with.

That's where we come from, my brother and me.

We come from you.

Twenty
FAMILIES GET SEPARATED

AN HOUR LATER, WE PULL UP outside a brick house with blue shutters. My blood slows down. My breath comes more smoothly. I feel a headache I didn't even know was there dissolve out of my skull through my hair.

"Now, we're heading pretty far back in time at this one," Person says from the front seat. "You were with Marta over a year. You were with Gloria for eleven months. And you've been with me for about two years now. So when you left this home you were seven and eight. I just want you guys to know that if you don't remember that would be totally normal and not mean anything about . . ."

But I'm already shaking my head.

And Julian says, "This is . . . familiar."

And we get out of the car without Person even telling us to.

It's not that there's anything specific I remember yet. It's only good feelings and a certainty that I've been on the other side of the door.

It bursts open and two women rush out of it, calling our names. "Julian!" "Flora!" "Flora!" "Julian!"

One is white and one is black. They are the same height but the black one is skinny and the white one is not. They have smiles that look like someone drew a smile on a pancake in maple syrup.

They're rushing at us.

Within seconds we're in their arms. I don't remember this woman's name but I remember her smell. I remember the soft folds of her body making a perfect cushion for my head. I remember in a way that doesn't have words or facts, just feelings.

I remember riding on her shoulders.

At the same time, they pull back and look at us and then they switch and the other mom is holding me.

They switch again.

Again.

They're crying and smiling at the same time.

After about four hugs, I wonder what's happened to Person and when I turn I see she's standing a few feet away, smiling and crying too. She sort of looks like she's watching something touching and emotional on television. She looks separate.

I want to pull her into this hug but I don't know how.

When the women stop hugging us, they rush at Person. Julian and I watch three women smiling and crying over us, their arms tight around each other. "Thank you, thank you," the women say to Person. "Thank you."

Finally, one of the women pulls back and takes Person's face in her hands. "Honey," she says. "We were afraid we'd never get to see them again."

I realize that I'm smiling. And when I look hard at these women, side by side, I realize that I do remember them in some sort of real way. I'm not sure what their names are. I called them each "Mommy."

A little while later they lead us into the brick house.

The smell is instantly familiar. It's honey and cinnamon and something else that says "home." A million memories rush back at me in a way that makes me dizzy and confused, but I somehow manage to hold on to some of the happy. It's not like entirely new memories. More like the other half of half memories. I remembered cooking with someone in a kitchen sometimes. Now I remember the someone and the kitchen. "Weren't there more . . . colors? Toys?"

Julian and Person gasp quietly and I realize that I said that out loud. My words are back. Of course they are. I'm transported here—far away from fifth grade and Marta and ever being separate from Julian.

The black mom chuckles. "Well," she says, "I don't have any kids living here anymore so there aren't toys and artwork and all of that around."

"You don't?" Person says.

"How long did we live here?" I ask.

"Flora!" the white mom says. "Listen to you. Your voice is just beautiful!"

"It still gets stuck sometimes," I say. And the mom nods at me like she knows what I mean. She looks right at me without bending down or squatting or making me feel like she's looking down at me even though she's a lot taller than me. I don't know how she does that, it seems like magic and it makes me feel good and grown and important.

"You and your brother lived here three years," she says. "And we loved you every single day and we've loved you every day since." She smiles. "You call me Margie now, OK?"

"And you'll call me Vanessa," the other mom says. "Because praise the Lord you've got a forever mommy now!" She pats Person on the hand. Person looks nervous even though the rest of us look happy. "Now come in!" Vanessa says. "I've got a spread laid out for you."

We follow her into the dining room. It's covered in all of our favorite foods. And hanging above it is a homemade construction paper banner that says, "Welcome back, Flora and Julian!"

"Score!" Julian says, and immediately runs toward the pizza. Then he freezes and looks back at the moms. "Sorry, I mean, may I please have some pizza?"

Vanessa laughs big and bold. "You may! It's for you, isn't it?"

We all make plates and sit around the table, Vanessa and Margie talking the whole time.

"We took these children to swimming lessons," Margie is

saying. "And Julian was just terrified of the water. But Flora, she jumped right in. We thought it'd be the other way around but no. Flora would have swum right across the pool if she were able. And Julian. He stood on the side saying 'sister, sister' the whole time that first lesson."

Vanessa and Margie laugh.

"But he got in the water eventually," Vanessa says. "We got this little one swimming."

"So you're who taught them to swim," Person whispers, almost like a prayer.

"Sure did!" Margie says.

"We still know how!" Julian chirps, and I hope hope hope he's as happy as I am right now and not faking happy. I would have been happier every day of fourth grade if I only remembered that this house existed the whole time.

"What else?" I say. "What else did you teach us?"

I pick up a piece of fried broccoli and take the tiniest bite. I forgot all about fried broccoli and how I love it. I'm eating it as slowly as possible. I want this meal to last all day and into tomorrow.

"Well, let's see," Vanessa says. "We got you set up with speech lessons, Flora. When you first came to us you were four years old and barely talking. By the time you left you were a regular old chatterbox!"

"Speech?" I say. A vague memory comes over me of a person helping me learn how to shape my mouth for certain words and letters.

"Thank you," Person says. "Wow. Thank you for that."

"I'm not a chatterbox, though," I say. I think about everything that happened between these two moms and Person. I wonder if all of those in-between people stole my lung filters.

"We can get you speech therapy if it'll help, Flora," Person says. She's talking too fast. "That's a good idea. We can get you back to chatterbox. Or you don't have to be a chatterbox. Whatever you want."

"What else?" Julian says.

"Well, you guys were preschoolers," Margie says. "So of course we worked on the basics. You learned your colors and your animals and the alphabet and how to count."

I look around the room. I can see the living room through one of the dining room doors and I can see the little kitchen through the other one. I learned the beginning of math here. Right here.

"And we played a lot. Julian, we potty trained you," Vanessa says.

"Thank you," Person says. She keeps saying *thank you*. Like Vanessa and Margie were a training ground for Person the way Ms. K was a training ground for fifth grade.

I don't think I like the *thank yous*.

"We dressed you up for Halloween. Julian, when you were five you were just dying to be a tortoise. You kept saying 'I don't want to be a turtle, Mommy, I want to be a tortoise.'"

Margie stops talking and looks at Person. "Sorry . . . I mean, they . . . they were with us a while. They called us Mom then."

Person's eyes get big. They look wet. "I know," she says. She isn't smiling.

But I can't think about it too much because I'm so hungry. Not for food. I finished my pizza and fried broccoli. I'm hungry for these stories.

Margie pats Person on the hand.

"Anyway," Vanessa says. "We kept asking you what the difference was between a tortoise and a turtle so we could figure out the right costume for you. And you kept answering 'no ribbons.' We had no idea what you meant. Do you?"

Julian shakes his head. I shake mine too even though she's talking to Julian. I want to know what little Julian thought ribbons had to do with turtles. I want to remember little Julian more than I do. More than just that he was there.

"You were talking about Ninja Turtles!"

"Oh!" Julian says.

"Oh!" I say.

We all laugh.

"I wanted to be the animal. I thought all turtles were cartoons!" Julian says, and I wonder if he's remembering or just filling in the blanks.

"That's right," Margie says. She drums her fingers on the table. "Let's see. What else can we tell you?"

"Normal," I say. And everyone looks at me.

"What, Flora?" Vanessa says.

"I want to hear the normal."

Person says, "Explain, sweetie."

So I take a second. I put my words together. I say, "Can you tell me about a normal day?"

"Oh," Vanessa says. She closes her eyes and takes a deep breath, almost like *she's* resetting.

"We can do that," Margie says.

And they talk. What they're saying is the most important stuff ever, but I only half listen. I don't pay attention to particular words or to which mom is talking at any given moment. Instead, I let the meaning of it wash over me.

As they speak, I'm able to remember it, the living here, the normal-ness.

Vanessa waking me up every morning and helping me get into the clothes we'd laid out the day before. Vanessa cooking us breakfast and taking us to school. Margie picking us up at the end of the day and asking us about the day's highlights on the car ride home. She always used that word: *highlights*. Afternoons with Margie always looked different—the park, or baking cookies, or playing with toys in the living room, or making a craft—but somehow they were always a little the same. Dinner around this table when Vanessa came home from work and how it was always warm food in the winter. Learning to use a knife and fork and stay at the table until everyone was finished. Bedtime routine with either mom that involved stories and being tucked into the top bunk while Julian was tucked into the bottom.

The feelings of it all come back.

Security. Love. Family.

Having two parents who work together.

Having two parents who love my brother like they love me.

Having two parents who love each other like they love us.

"We're making it sound pretty idyllic, I'm afraid," Vanessa says. "We had our rough moments."

"Of course," Margie says. "We had regression and behaviors and tantrums and all of that. It wasn't all easy. But . . . we've been missing them so much for so long."

"So the good parts are what we remember," Vanessa says.

And then I feel lucky. For the first time in my life, I feel lucky. Lucky to have found people who choose to remember only the good parts of me and not how angry I am and how hard it is for me to talk and how I'm someone from nowhere.

Margie goes into the kitchen and comes back with a yellow cake. "I brought dessert," she says.

She places it right in front of me and the smell of lemon crawls up my nostrils and wiggles into my brain and somehow gets to my memory.

"Lemon cake!" I say. "I wanted a lemon cake!"

Vanessa laughs. "That's right. When you were—"

"No!" I shout, making Person and Julian and both the moms jump.

"Sorry," I say. "I want to tell it. I think I can remember."

"OK," Margie says. She sits without slicing the cake and I think-think-think-think-think harder than I ever have.

"It was my birthday, right?" I say.

Both the moms nod.

"How old?" I ask.

"Seven," Vanessa says quietly. "It was only a few weeks before you left."

I nod and think and think.

"I saw a lemon cake on television. With lemons on it."

"Yup," Margie says.

"I said 'I want that kind' or something, and then someone said she didn't know how to make a lemon cake."

"That would be me!" Margie says.

"We watched a video about it?"

"That's right," Margie says. "We looked up how to do it on the internet."

"We went to the store and bought the lemons," I say.

"And everything else," Margie says.

"And then we made the cake together," I say.

"Wow," Person says. "Wow. Flora. That was amazing." She looks impressed and sad at the same time.

I feel like I won a trophy. I feel like I won the whole world. I feel so exhausted from all the remembering and all the words that I could fall asleep in the lemon cake in front of me. The lemons are shiny on the top of it. I remember that's from letting them sit in sugar syrup.

Margie slices the cake and we eat.

Person sighs.

Vanessa pats her hand. "Are you OK, Mommy?" she asks.

"It's just they had this whole life," Person says. "You guys were amazing and . . ."

"And what happened?" Margie says.

"Yeah," Julian says. "What happened?"

Person nods but it looks like she wanted to say something else. "I hate to have to ask the tough questions," she says.

"I know," Vanessa says. "If we all loved each other so much, why did they leave? Right?"

"Right," Person says.

I stop eating. My fork crashes into the plate. I suddenly think this lemon cake is the grossest thing in the world.

I don't want to hear about the awful thing I did to make these two sugary wonderful women give us up.

"You guys are nine and eleven now," Margie says. "So it's truth time." She turns to Person. "That's what this is about, huh?"

"Yes," Person says. "Their therapist says by the time they're twelve, they should know everything I know. But I don't know too much. No one knows that much about these kids, my kids. And they're asking now so . . ."

"Good for you. Doing that hard work," Margie says. "Well . . . the official story from the state is that they left to find more permanent placements."

"Permanent?" Julian cries.

"I know," Vanessa says. "I gather it didn't turn out that way."

"Why couldn't you permanent?" The words fall out of me like usual. I don't want the answer.

But of course I need it. I need the whole truth. I need to

know about all the awful things that meant we had to move and move and move.

Margie reaches out and pats my cheek. "You know we wanted to, Flora. More than anything we wanted to be your moms."

Vanessa pats Julian's cheeks. "And yours."

And once again I'm reminded how great it was: two moms for two kids.

"So what happened?" Person asks.

Even though it doesn't matter anymore. I didn't mess it up. She wanted me. They wanted us. That's the part that counts.

"Flora and Julian came to us when they were three and four years old. At the time, their goal was still Return to Parent," Vanessa says.

"What does that mean?" I ask.

Vanessa looks at me. "It means your caseworkers and the judge and everyone was still hoping you could go back to your first family."

My eyebrows go up. All of these people thought we had a first family. A bio family. All of them were wrong.

Because they have to be wrong. Because we couldn't have had a first mother. Because if we did . . . where did she go?

"You were coming from an emergency placement, meaning you were supposed to be there just a short while. They decided they needed to get you settled somewhere because it was taking a long time to find a relative."

"Did they ever find anyone?" Julian asks.

Margie sighs. "We don't think so, but to be honest, we don't know. Since we were never the legal parents and we never got a chance to adopt you, we weren't ever allowed to read your whole file."

"But . . . ," Person says. "Why didn't you adopt them?"

"The official story from the state is that our house was deemed inappropriate," Vanessa says.

Julian and I look around. "Why?" he asks.

"Well, we only had two bedrooms. We had you guys sharing a room. And once children are seven, it's considered inappropriate to have them share a room unless they're the same sex."

"So we had to leave because Julian's not a girl?" I ask.

That's the stupidest thing I've ever heard. And I know I worded it weirdly. I'm afraid for a second that they're going to giggle like I'm being cute even though this is way too important for giggling.

They don't.

"No," Margie says. "We'd never blame Julian!" She pats his hand and I nod and I want to tell him that's not what I meant but I think he knows already. "And anyway, we told them we'd move before he turned seven. We said we'd give one of the kids our room and we'd sleep in the living room if necessary. But they took the kids anyway."

"What?" Julian says. "Why?"

I can see Person's sad heart right through her eyes. "No," she says. "It wasn't . . ."

Margie nods. "We'll never know. We can't prove it. But it felt . . ."

"Discriminatory," Vanessa finishes.

"Discriminatory?" I say.

Person takes my hand and looks right at me. "Because they're both moms," she says.

My eyes go big. That's the dumbest thing I've ever heard. Having two moms was part of what made this home work so well.

No one says anything for a minute. Julian and I were ripped out of this place where they wanted us and put into a home that only wanted perfect kids. And that happened because the world is stupid.

It's stupider than me and I barely passed the fourth grade.

"I can see why you stopped taking kids. That sounds so painful," Person says.

"Well, actually . . . ," Vanessa starts, then she looks at us and trails off. She glances at Margie. "We have to give them the whole truth, don't we?"

Margie sighs. "I still have a foster child from time to time," she says. "I do emergency placements now. The kids still need homes and . . . well . . . having my heart broken when Julian and Flora left . . . it was sort of a reminder of how much pain these kids must be in every day."

"Wait," Person says. She looks at Margie. "You still foster kids"—she pauses and looks at Vanessa—"and you don't?"

The moms nod. They keep their eyes on the lemon cake

crumbs left on their plates. They look guilty.

"You're separated?" Person says. "Oh my God, I'm so sorry."

They nod again.

"Separated?" I cry. "Like divorced?"

It feels like a part of my heart just got stitched back together only to have one of the stitches fall back out right away.

"Well, we never got married, officially," Vanessa says. "But yes, it's like we're divorced."

"No!" I say. I feel tears building in my throat. How could I go from so happy to so sad so quickly?

"But I wanted to invite you both to my birthday party!" Julian says.

It's such a stupid thing to say. I want to kick him under the table.

But the three moms all laugh.

"You can still do that," Margie says. "If it's alright with your mom. We are obviously capable of having a meal together, still."

"Consider yourselves invited," Person says. She's still not being her normal smiley self, but I don't think Margie and Vanessa can tell.

And I'm not supposed to worry about that. I'm not supposed to worry.

"If you can make it all the way to Jersey City," Person adds.

"Of course we can!" Margie says.

"We'll carpool," Vanessa says.

Suddenly it's all smiles around the table again while I still have the tears building.

"But the kids you take care of now," I say to Margie. "They only get one of you."

"Well, yes, but that's OK. I mean, you only have one mom, one parent, now, right?"

"We used to," I say. I feel a little better. Person was enough all on her own. But that's different because there was always only one. Right now it feels like Margie-without-Vanessa wouldn't be a whole Margie. Or Vanessa-without-Margie wouldn't be a whole Vanessa.

"We have a dad too," Julian says. "Now."

"Really?" Margie and Vanessa yelp. "Well, congratulations!" they say to Person. "That's fantastic news. Tell us about your daddy."

Julian and I spout off a few Dad facts and everyone gets happy again and it seems like the divorce doesn't matter and maybe it doesn't because we don't even live here anymore and anyway, both of these moms are coming to Julian's birthday party so maybe it doesn't matter at all that they don't live together and that they don't mom kids together. But even if it doesn't matter in any sort of practical way and even if everyone can still be happy . . . it matters to me.

We move into the living room. We talk and laugh and tell stories. We hunt through the hallways and the living and dining rooms and count the pictures of us left on the wall in Vanessa's house. Twelve total. Four of me. Four of Julian. Four of both of us together or with Vanessa or both moms.

We don't start to say good-bye until the sun is setting.

At the door, Vanessa holds me close. "I'm so happy I got to see you guys again," she says. "I feel like there was a Flora-shaped hole in my heart for the past years and hugging you filled it in."

I feel the same way except maybe there are more holes with a lot more names in my heart and I don't even know the names.

Then I hug Margie, who says, "We'll see you next month! This isn't good-bye this time. Isn't that exciting!"

At the last minute, before we leave, Margie hands two white rectangular books to Person. "You have these, right? We passed a copy of them along to Kelly to give to the next parents so that—"

And then Person starts crying. Big huge tears. "Are these Lifebooks?" she says.

Margie rubs her back. "I take it you didn't have them?"

"You have no idea how much we need these," she says. She turns to Julian and me. "Kiddos, these books are your right. They're your history. They're the answer."

We smile back at her, but I feel like I have the most important answers already.

Born or not born, Margie and Vanessa wanted us.

Twenty-One
FAMILIES DO NOT ALWAYS LIVE TOGETHER

WE ARE QUIET IN THE CAR on the way back to our hotel.

I watch the sunset paint the sky pink and purple out the window. I think about what it was like having two moms. I marvel that I remember, that a lot of it has come back to me.

Person pulls into the parking lot but once the car stops moving, she doesn't unbuckle her seat belt. She takes a deep breath and then speaks toward the windshield, without looking at us. "What do you say, kids? Is that enough for now?"

Julian and I look at each other. He scrunches his eyebrows. "Huh?" he says.

"Should we enjoy some days at the beach and stop looking backward?" Person says.

My heart speeds up.

"Should we stop here for now? Should we let Margie and Vanessa be the last house we visit instead of looking for the one that came before? Should we end on a high note?"

"Not really, right?" I say.

"What?" Person says. She turns to look at me now. It's like my question snapped something in her face and put her back in mom-mode. "That wasn't really a high note? You guys both seemed so happy."

"No, I mean, that's it, actually, isn't it?"

"That's really the last house?" Julian translates. "That's the beginning?"

"You guys were three and four when you came to live with Margie and Vanessa."

Julian and I shrug. We nod. Maybe that was the beginning. It makes sense.

"Guys," Person says, turning around in the parked car to look at us. "You were babies. You were born. If we keep going, we're going to find proof of that."

Julian and I shake our heads.

"Well, I guess that's the answer," Person says. "I guess we better keep going. We'll look at your Lifebooks over dinner. I bet there's more in there; I bet they found some things from previous homes. Maybe there's baby pictures."

"OK," I say.

"OK," Julian says.

But he's wearing a fake-crazy smile. He knows as well as I do there aren't any baby pictures in these books. Or anywhere.

As we get out of the car, I notice Person rubbing her belly.

And I remember the baby. I think about that baby so rarely here in Maryland that whenever I remember it, it's like it's shoving itself into my brain like an intruder.

It's too late to go out for crabs again, Person says, so we go to a little shop down the street from our hotel where you order at the counter and then bring the food to a picnic table. Julian and I get burgers and fries and Person gets a crab cake, which makes Julian and me both laugh because we never knew she was obsessed with crabs.

Maybe we never thought too much about what Person liked. Besides us.

Person puts our Lifebooks in front of us. They look like white photo albums, the kind you send away to an online photo place to make the way Dad and Person did after their wedding. We have one at home full of me and Elena in our purple dresses and Julian holding the rings and Person and Dad kissing.

This looks like the same thing, except it's going to be full of pictures of me and Julian and Vanessa or me and Julian and Margie. It's going to be me in another family.

The front covers are different. Mine has a picture of a little girl plastered in sand and holding a shovel. She's in a pink bathing suit, crouching over what looks like it used to be a sandcastle, and she's smiling huge but she's missing her two front teeth. It's me.

The other one has a picture of a little boy. He's got a puppy in his lap.

We haven't even opened them yet and I say, "Hey, two more points for us." I point to mine. "The sand theory." I point to Julian's. "The dog theory."

"That's like five to zero!" Julian says, fake-happy.

Person smiles at him. She's never been able to tell when he's lying the way that I can.

"Alright, well, I only need one point. The first baby picture in there and I win, right?" Person says.

"Sure, Mom!" Julian happy-lies.

I shrug. There aren't going to be any baby pictures in here but I almost wish there were. I almost wish Person was right so that she would win so that she had to keep loving us the same as the baby.

Except if Person is right, that means we had another person before Person. A person who was a mother. A mother who is now gone. It's a weird thing to wish for. I'm not sure if I can wish for that.

"OK," Person says. "Open on the count of three. Ready? One, two, three!"

I put my hand on the front cover and I think about the Jesus from Ms. K's religion book. *Baby picture, baby picture, baby picture,* I pray. Person says that's it. One picture would prove it. If Jesus is as powerful as Ms. K's religion books said, surely he could put one baby picture in there.

I flip open the cover. Nope. It's a picture of Julian and me looking tiny and scared, but standing on two feet with our hands out in front of us. Small, but not babies. Julian's book starts with the same picture.

"No baby picture," I say.

Person's eyes are big. She looks surprised. "I thought for sure they would have . . ." Then she trails off.

"Well, let's look," she says.

We flip through the books side by side and the story of our life with Vanessa and Margie blooms around us for the second time today. Some of the pictures are things I remember, and other pictures make me remember, and some of them are things I just forget. There are tons of pictures of us, together and apart, with the two moms or without them, with other kids, in huge groups of kids all lined up and with a teacher, or with packs of kids at the beach or in the yard. There are pictures of the house the way it used to look, covered in toys and artwork and schoolwork. There are pictures of Christmas time and Easter time and Halloween time and Thanksgiving time. There are pictures of us taking swimming lessons and music lessons and Julian taking karate lessons and me taking dance lessons. There are pictures of babies, but they aren't us. I remember the babies that Margie and Vanessa had every once in a while. Foster babies, but born ones.

Then there are things that aren't even pictures. There's my first-grade report card and the beginning of my second-grade one. There's notes from my kindergarten and first-grade teachers. There's evaluations from my speech therapist.

There's silly valentines I received from my classmates and birthday cards I got from Vanessa's and Margie's parents. There's so much.

I'm not even to the end when I pause. I can feel the warmth of living there, feel what it was like to be surrounded by so many people, by two moms.

"Are you OK, Florey?" Person asks.

"Yeah . . . ," I say. "It's just . . . I . . . I remember it."

Person smiles. "That's so great, Flora. I'm so proud of you."

"No, I mean like. Not just the big stuff. Not just moments. I remember . . . I remember what it was like to be there. I remember being."

Julian stops and looks up from his book. "Me too," he says.

Person lowers her eyebrows at me. "That's a good thing, right? You wanted to remember?" She looks sad when she says it though.

"Yeah," I say. "But . . . it's so sad they got divorced."

Julian shrugs beside me. "They're still coming to my birthday party together," he says.

"Yeah, but . . . if they're divorced, are they still family?" I ask.

"Oh," Person says. "Well, that's sort of complicated, isn't it? But they certainly still look like family to me."

I nod.

"And either way, both Margie and Vanessa still love you, Flora. I really have to think about that and learn to accept it.

We have to invite them to birthday parties. I have to let them in."

I bite my lip and keep my eyes on the book. It's almost like she's convincing herself she has to love them back, even though they're the most wonderful people ever.

"They're still each *your* family," Person concludes.

I look up at Person. "No," I say. "They aren't."

"Sweetie, they still love you so much. I'm your forever mother but they loved you like only a mother can."

"But I don't live with them anymore."

Person's eyebrows lower. "You're telling me that you don't think those two women are your family just because they don't live in our house?"

I shrug.

"So am I your family?" Person asks.

I giggle. Beside me, Julian is listening with a lying smile. I decide to ignore him. I have both words and the truth for this conversation. I'm doing the best I can. "Of course you're my family," I say.

"Why?" Person asks.

I think and think. I try to come up with an answer. Images pop into my brain. Person rubbing my head *part-ear-neck* in the dark. Person patting my back in the middle of the night when I was bent over the toilet with the stomach flu. Person checking my homework even after she's had her glasses on for hours so I know she's so tired. But these pictures don't have words. I say the only words I can come up with. "Because I live in your house."

Person looks so startled she leans back from the table before leaning forward toward my face. "Excuse me, dear," she says. "It's our house."

"I know," I say.

"I don't want all of these other houses to confuse you. This is part of what I'm worried about. Your house used to be Gloria's house. So you called it yours and now you call it Gloria's. But I am not Gloria or Marta or Margie or Vanessa. I'm Mom."

My cheeks get red. I'm really good at the truth, most of the time. But Person doesn't know that I don't call her *Mom.*

"I know," I say.

She almost looks a little angry. I'm not sure what I did wrong. Could it just be because I said *your house*? Or could it be this whole trip? Maybe she's angry that we're so complicated.

Person shakes her head and seems to snap back into mom-mode again. "So that's really your definition of family, Flora?" Person says. "Just people who live in the same house?"

I nod.

"So are you telling me that when you grow up and get married and have your own kids, if that's what you choose to do, that you won't be my family anymore, just because you have your own house?"

I shrug.

"And are you telling me that if Marta had succeeded in

keeping Julian, you two would no longer be a family?"

I look at my brother. That's impossible.

"And what if Julian went and lived somewhere else for a while—" Person says, then she must see the look of alarm on our faces because she interrupts herself. "That's not happening, don't worry. We are together forever. But if that did happen, wouldn't you still be family?"

I shrug. Of course we would. But then how do I explain it? What makes a family?

"Family isn't just who you live with, Flora," Person says.

"Who is it then?" I ask.

Person thinks for a minute. She takes a slow bite of crab cake. "I'd guess there's a lot of ways to define it, and if you wanted to use your live-together definition you could. You could say that family is people who live together. But that doesn't sound like my family. I'd say my family is the small group of people who are bonded to me, who I'm choosing to love forever. My parents, my sisters, Cate, you guys, Dad, Elena, and the baby. And now, because of you guys, Margie and Vanessa."

It feels weird. Ms. K is left out: she can't be my family even though she loved me more than Marta ever did. And Marta and Gloria were my family but aren't anymore?

There's no room for levels, which means it doesn't quite work. Julian is more my family than even Person is. He's my other Only.

Julian nods. "OK," he says. "That's my family too." His fake smile is gone. I honest-ed him right out of it.

Person pats his hand. "Sounds good, J. Because whoever is my family is also your family. Right?"

"But this is supposed to be a family vacation," I say.

"Hm. The vacation parts are but all of this visiting and hard stuff isn't exactly vacation," Person says. "Next year we'll take a real family vacation where we don't have to worry about anything."

I look at her. She didn't understand me, which is normal. But this time she doesn't realize that she didn't understand me.

"Can I borrow your phone?" I ask. "I have to make a call."

Person lowers her eyebrows and seems like she's about to laugh and call me cute again. But then she gives me her phone and I take it to the side of the restaurant where Person can still see me but she won't be able to hear me, and where I can hear the waves from the beach echoing between the houses.

"Hi, babe," Dad says when he answers the phone.

"It's me," I say.

"Oh!" he says. "Hi, Flora. It's so nice to hear your voice!"

I don't know what to say so I don't say anything.

After a moment, Dad says, "How are you guys? How is the beach? What did you do today?"

"We didn't go to the beach. We saw Margie and Vanessa."

"Tell me about them," Dad says.

I'm filled up with wanting to tell him. All the bits—the Lifebook, the remembering, the divorce—bubble around my lung filters.

But I know there's something else I have to do. Something I'm scared to do. So I skip to the important words, but in a good way this time.

When I don't say anything he keeps talking, but I don't hear his words.

I think about the ones I want to say. I make myself speak them. "Dad . . . can I talk to Elena?"

He stops talking suddenly like I startled him.

"I . . . I'll go get her," he says.

While I'm waiting for her to come to the phone, I watch Person and Julian eating their food. They're talking and pointing at things in Julian's Lifebook.

Family, I think. *Person and Julian, family. Dad, family. Elena, family. Margie and Vanessa, family.*

I watch Person rub her belly.

And the baby, family.

I can do this.

"Flora?" Elena says after a minute. She sounds quiet and small.

"Hi, Elena," I say.

Silence.

Say it, Flora. Say it.

"Did you call to tell me something?" Elena says. It's not exactly mean the way she says it. More like desperate.

"No," I say.

"No?" she says.

"I . . . I want to ask you something."

Elena sighs so loudly into the phone it sounds like a wave from the ocean. "You're supposed to say you're sorry," she says. "You punched me."

I know I'm supposed to say sorry. I thought I had the word ready. But now it's sinking back into my stomach and rotting there.

I know I won't be able to say everything, so I say the part I think will matter. "Some of our old parents are divorced, too . . ."

"Oh," Elena says.

"I . . . it's stupid . . . I mean, I'm not even living with them . . . anymore . . . but they used to be . . . well, I just . . . it stinks," I say.

"Yeah," Elena says. "It does."

"Yeah," I say. "Divorce stinks."

"Remember . . . it's not your fault," Elena says.

"OK." I wonder if Elena thinks that Dad and Meredith's divorce is her fault sometimes the way I sometimes think it's my fault that we had to move so much.

"Do you and Dad want to come to the beach tomorrow?" I blurt. "I mean, for the next few days? We're supposed to be on a family vacation and . . . you . . . you're not . . . here."

It's quiet for a minute. I wonder if she's still too mad at me. I wonder if anyone ever says yes to going on a vacation when the person asking punched her in the face.

"Let me go ask Dad if we can come," Elena says finally.

While she's gone I make a list of all the stuff I wasn't able to say. The words that were too heavy to come to my tongue:

You are my family. My sister. I get it now.

It turns out you aren't so lucky.

It actually stinks worse for you because in all this listing of family we haven't mentioned your mom once.

I'm sorry for punching you.

When Dad comes back to the phone, he turns on speaker so I can talk to both of them. He sounds happier than anyone has ever sounded and I have to interrupt him to say, "Did I make you sound like that?"

"Like what?" Dad says.

"Happy," I say.

He laughs. "Yes, Flora. You made me very happy."

"So we can go?" Elena says, in the background, also sounding happy. "You're going to ask my mom?"

"I don't have to ask her," Dad says. "She might not like it but this is my time with you so it's my decision and I say we're going."

"Hooray," Elena says. I smile.

"Listen," he says. "Let's make this a surprise for your mother, yeah?"

"OK," I say. He sounds so happy and excited that I push how difficult that conversation with Elena was out of my head.

"You guys have a brunch tomorrow with someone. We'll be at your hotel when you get back," he says. "Tell Julian if you want, but let's surprise Mom. She deserves it!"

When we hang up, I feel as happy as he sounded.

* * *

That night, while Julian is in the shower with the water running, and I'm bent over our suitcase looking for pajamas, Person says, "What a day, huh, Florey?"

"Yeah," I mumble.

"So much has happened . . . and we found out you passed the fourth grade!"

I look up at her, but she's pulling the blankets down on her bed so she can climb in and get comfy. She's not searching my eyes too deeply. It's like she doesn't realize how important this conversation is.

"I'm really proud of you," Person says. "You worked so hard to get to the fifth grade. We're going to have a proper celebration for you as soon as we see Dad again."

I shrug, but she doesn't see. Then, Person looks up.

"Flora, are you OK?"

I shrug again.

Person rushes to my side. She kneels on the hotel floor beside me.

"What's going on, sweetheart?"

Express yourself, express yourself. That's what Person asked me to do. Express myself. Don't worry. Be born.

There's only one of those three I can do at the moment.

"I guess . . . Ms. K. I . . . I wanted her to be family too."

"Oh!" Person's face breaks open. She wraps her arms around me. "You're going to miss Ms. K, I know. She was such a good teacher."

Now I'm crying but Person is good enough to ignore it. I fit myself over her belly and give in to the hug.

"She's the best teacher I ever had," I say.

"I know," Person says. "I'll miss her too."

I pull back from the hug so I can see her face. "You will?" I say.

Person nods. "She was so good to us," she says. "I can see why you'd want her in your life a little longer. And it's OK to miss her, it is."

"Ms. K loved me," I say.

"She did," Person says.

"I loved her too," I say. Then, since I can tell she's a little bothered about all the love at Margie and Vanessa's, I add, "I'm sorry if that bothers you."

"Bothers me?" Person says, surprised. "Of course it doesn't. I love Ms. K too, for everything she did for you."

"You do?" I say.

"Of course," Person says. "But you know what? You'll be OK. Missing people is a part of life for everyone."

"Not just foster kids, you mean?" I say.

"Flora," Person says, "everyone misses people. It hurts and then it gets better. I promise."

Person tucks me into a hug again and then she whispers, "But I'm here forever, right? Any time you're missing a teacher or an old foster mom, you come to me and we'll remember her together."

Believe in Forever.

It's the other thing Person asked me to do. And if I can just do it, if I can just believe in Person-Forever, it'll make it easier to love all of the non-forever people who come into my life but who I know I'll have to miss one day.

Twenty-Two

FAMILIES ARE FULL OF SURPRISES

THE NEXT MORNING, JULIAN PULLS A bathing suit out of our shared suitcase and I realize I haven't told him about our surprise of the day. Person is in the bathroom so now is my chance.

"We're not going to the beach," I say. "We're going to brunch."

"Brunch?" Julian says. He turns to look at me. I'm looking at him so I can't see the bathroom door but I listen for the click of it opening behind my head while I whisper. "Yeah, brunch."

"How do you know that?" Julian says.

"Yeah, Flora, how do you know that?" Person calls from the bathroom.

I turn around quickly, my cheeks burning. The door to the bathroom is wide open. Person is leaning across the sink putting mascara on her eyelashes.

I start breathing too quickly. I almost ruined the whole thing.

"How do you know about brunch?" Person says.

"Um," I say. "Dad told me." I don't know how to lie. Person's right about that.

She comes out of the bathroom and sits on the bottom of our bed. She's wearing shorts but she's still in her silky button-down pajama top. Julian is still holding on to his bathing suit.

Person has the sad look again. "Do you guys want to go to the beach?" she asks. "I could cancel the brunch, if you want."

"Brunch?" Julian asks. "Like breakfast and lunch at the same time?" He smiles. "I've never been to brunch."

"Ah," Person says. "But we can always go to brunch. We can only go to the beach when we're here."

"Nah, that's OK," Julian says. He tosses his bathing suit back into our suitcase and starts rummaging through it for shorts or something. I tilt my head at him. I watch Person watch him with that sad look on her face.

I know what's happening here. I'm so surprised that I'm the one who knows, but I know. It's not about food or the beach.

"Who are we going to brunch with?" I ask Person.

She turns the sad look from Julian to me. "I'm not sure if you'll remember her, but her name is Kelly."

Julian looks up so quickly. "Kelly?" he says. The smile on his face is real.

"We remember Kelly," I say.

I have cloudy memories of being in a car with her as she

talked in a soothing voice and I got the impression that what she was saying was really important but I couldn't make myself focus on the words. I remember her coming to visit me at my house, but I don't know where she was visiting me. I remember thinking she was sort of my friend when I didn't have enough words to make any friends.

"And you want to see her?" Person says.

Julian and I nod. I don't want to nod. I want to tell Person we can skip it and go to the beach. But Dr. Fredrick says it's OK to want things, to ask for things. I have to remember that.

At the restaurant we order weird combinations of breakfast and lunch. I get a turkey sandwich but on a bagel. Julian gets spaghetti with a side of bacon which Person says is just fine but not very typical. Kelly is shorter and rounder than I remember her but her smile is just as bright as she orders her yogurt and granola with a side salad.

"I don't get it," Person says to Kelly as soon as the food comes. "I don't get how all of this happened to my children."

Julian looks as happy to see Kelly as I am, but Person is not. Person is angry at her.

"I know," Kelly says. "It's . . . enraging. It's so frustrating. And I—"

But Person cuts her off. "Explain it," she says. "You were their caseworker. You were in charge of placing them. Explain how they ended up with a woman who wanted to separate them. Explain how their files were lost, making it so I was informed that they had no significant attachments when clearly they did. Explain—"

"Emily," Kelly says quietly. "I was trying my best."

I've only ever seen Person like this once. The time with Meredith and Elena. But that was different because I was angry also. And I was in trouble.

This time we're just finding out. We're talking about things that already happened. And I don't want Person to be angry that we aren't with Margie and Vanessa. I want her to be happy that we're with her.

I want them all to love me. Easily.

I wonder for a second if that's how Elena felt when Meredith and Person were fighting.

"Mom," I squeak.

"I'm sorry, Flora," Person says. She takes a deep breath like she's trying to calm herself. "The last thing I want to do is upset you. But I don't understand it, and one day you're going to have these questions for Kelly too. I'd like to get you the answers sooner than later."

Answers. We're here for the answers. I don't even know the questions but I know I want the answers.

"OK," I say.

Person asks Kelly, "Why were my children taken away from a couple who truly loved them and put in a home in which they weren't fully accepted? Where they were almost separated?"

Oh yeah, that. I do want that answer. But I don't want

Person to want the answer. I want Person to be happy she has us now.

"I understand," Kelly says. "You should do whatever you can to learn everything about their life before you. And you should share everything you know with your children. You, as a parent, need to embrace their past. You can't run away from it or be threatened by it. Even if it wasn't perfect."

"I'm here, aren't I?" Person says. "Does it look like I'm running away?"

"Postcards," I say, before I can think to keep the word in my brain.

I look at Julian to explain for me, but he's smiling so I know he'll lie. "It's OK about the postcards now," he says. "We found Gloria anyway."

It's not OK, though. If Person had let us see the first postcard, we maybe could have known all of this a while ago. We maybe could have found Margie and Vanessa in time for them to come to *my* birthday party.

"Megan B.," I say, because we still haven't found her. "The white house."

"We're here looking for these things, Flora. That's why we're here. I'm here, embracing your past," Person says.

I think about how she didn't even want to come to brunch today but I manage not to say it out loud.

The restaurant around us is busy. Waiters are constantly clunking things onto the red-and-white checked tables. They call out to each other over the heads of the customers. The

other diners are loud with their voices and their clinking
utensils. And Kelly speaks quietly which makes us all look
at her and listen when she opens her mouth. "I'm not saying
you're doing anything wrong. I'm so glad to see you guys in a
family who loves you and is willing to do this for you. I'm just
saying that—"

"I know," Person says. "I know we should have done this
more slowly. More gradually." She rubs her stomach. "I was . . .
I should have started earlier but now . . . we're running out of
time."

"I was wondering," Kelly says. "Congratulations."

Person nods and we're all quiet for a minute. I wonder if
this was Kelly's job with us. She came and made the moms
less mad. It was something like that. Something that made her
seem like a savior, with limits.

"We need a baby picture," Person says.

I shake my head. I wait for Julian to say something. We
don't need that because there isn't one. And even if there
were, we'd need more. We need all of the days in between.

"We saw our Lifebooks yesterday," Julian says. "And there
weren't any baby pictures."

Say it, I think. *Tell Person we need more than just to be born.
We need to know what happened to us.*

But he doesn't say anything.

Kelly looks at Person. "You didn't show them their Lifebooks until yesterday?"

"We didn't even have them until yesterday," I say.

At that Kelly looks at me so quickly, I almost jump. "What do you mean didn't have them?" She looks at Person. "Where were they?"

"Margie and Vanessa had them," Julian says.

"No," Kelly says. "No. I know for sure I gave them to your adoptive placement coordinator. Before I separated from the agency. Before they stopped telling me anything. I passed those Lifebooks on."

"You did," Person says. "Marta said she lost track of them when Julian and Flora left. They got lost in the shuffle with the rest of their things."

"You're kidding me!" Kelly says. "They're supposed to follow you guys. So is everything else, by the way. She should have given you everything she had of yours. But those Lifebooks— they're important."

Person is biting her lip.

Kelly says, "They were the one thing I thought I could do for you guys. They were the one way I told myself I really helped."

"You helped," Julian lies. Maybe it's not a lie that Kelly helped. Just being nice to us as little kids probably did help. But the happy way he says it is a lie.

Person says, "The Lifebooks only went back as far as when they were three or four years old."

Kelly nods. "I know," she says. "Vanessa and Margie did

the Lifebooks. I only met Julian and Flora right before they were moved in with Vanessa and Margie so I don't have any baby pictures."

"Why did they have to leave Margie and Vanessa?" Person asks.

I'm shrinking. Every time she asks this, I shrink. Why does it matter when we're with Person now?

I remember how she hugged me last night. I was so close to really believing in Forever. And now it's like she wished she never met us.

Across the table from me, Julian shrinks too. He's not even faking happy anymore. It's like Person doesn't notice.

"I don't know," Kelly says. "They were excellent foster parents. The best we had."

"They were?" Person asks, even though we saw how great they were yesterday.

"All I can tell you is that when Julian and Flora became free for adoption, the judge determined that their house was not appropriate for these two in a permanent capacity. We were stunned. We were all so upset."

"Some judge who didn't know them? That's why they were removed from a loving home?"

I'm getting angry. Or sad. It's hard to tell the difference.

Across from me, Julian's face is turning red behind his smile. Mine must look the same.

I wish Person would stop asking this question.

"Some judge who barely knew Margie and Vanessa and

didn't know Julian and Flora at all," Kelly says.

"But it's your job to advocate for them," Person says. "Why didn't you?"

Why won't she stop talking like this?

"I did. I tried," Kelly says in that quiet, calm voice. "I didn't have too much more power than Margie and Vanessa."

"Then why didn't you find them better homes? I don't understand. These children could have had permanency in a loving home at three and four. Instead they came to me at eight and nine. Instead they had years more trauma."

I'm so small I can barely see over the table. I'm so hot I'm sure if I touched the tablecloth it would explode into flames.

Person used to say that was the best thing that ever happened to her: us arriving at nine and eight years old. Now it's like she's angry about it. Now that there's a real baby, she's upset we didn't stay where we were.

Person is still talking. "Why didn't you try to find them a better home, then? Some place they could stay together? Some place they could get the help they needed and be free to mess up and be who they are?"

"I was the foster care caseworker," Kelly said. "I did what I could. I was working on finding the children a connection to their first family. When I failed at that, the judge freed them for adoption and I was no longer their worker. I talked with the adoption caseworker about getting Margie and Vanessa certified for adoption and that looked possible for a while but . . . she was . . . she was . . . and it's procedure to give all

of our freed children a photo-listing just in case something
happens . . . and the adoption case worker . . . she was . . . she
put a lot of value on . . . material wealth, so when Marta came
forward—I did . . ."

"Sounds like you didn't do anything to help them stay
where they were loved," Person says.

Julian is not smiling anymore. Instead I hear him squeak.

I feel like squeaking too. And crying.

"I mean, I made a lot of noise about it. And then I was
gone. Social workers and foster parents . . . we can't make too
much noise."

Julian's face is so red it looks like his head will fly to the
ceiling. I'm breathing hard I'm so scared. What does Person
want? Does she want a time machine so that she can go back
to when we were three and four and have us stay with Margie
and Vanessa? Now that she knows someone else loved us,
does she not want to love us anymore?

"Listen," Person says. "There has to be someone to blame
for what happened to Flora and Julian when—"

At the sound of his name Julian erupts. A glass still full
of water flies across the table and splashes me and Kelly. It
explodes on the floor between us, glass everywhere.

I morph back to my regular size and regular temperature
as I stare at my tiny, red-hot brother. It's like he had the tan-
trum for me.

"I don't want to live with Margie and Vanessa!" he shouts.
"I want to live with MOM!"

I nod at him. "Me too," I say. "I want to live with Pers—Mom. I'm not . . . Julian and me need . . . no time machine."

"You said forever," he yells at Person.

Then he turns. He runs through the restaurant so fast he looks like nothing but a streak of colors. On the way to the door he bumps into tables, he knocks plates of strangers' food onto the ground, he upends an empty high chair.

He sort of makes these things look like an accident but I know better. The more he throws and shoves and knocks over, the harder it'll be for Person to keep loving us. This is what happens when you're faking all the reasons for her to love you.

You show her how to change her mind in an instant.

Person promised us that we will always live with her. She promised she'd be our mom forever, no matter what.

But that doesn't mean she always has to love us, right? No one can promise what they're going to feel tomorrow, can they?

Person looks at Kelly. "I didn't realize what I was . . . ," she says. But before she finishes her sentence, she gets up and goes after Julian.

Julian was always my voice. When my words got stuck, he always found them. But he didn't always say things at the right time or the right volume. Julian was getting better too, before we found out about the baby. All the fake-happy was a symptom of things going bad again.

"He hasn't done that in a long, long time," I say to Kelly.

Kelly shrugs. "Then maybe it won't happen again for a long

time. That's how it goes. Things get better for a while, then
tough for a while."

"Things for people like us?" I say. The not-real kids. The
unreal kids. The foster kids.

Kelly shakes her head. "No," she says. "Things go up and
down for everyone everywhere. That's a way you guys are
completely average."

I smile.

"You know that your mom wants you guys more than anything, right?"

I shrug.

Not more than the new baby. The born baby.

I want to ask a question but it's full of so many important
words I don't think I can get them all out. Still, I don't want
to ask it the way Julian did: with an explosion.

I want to use my words the way Person said I should. To
express myself. To save myself.

I put them together carefully. "But," I say. I take a second.
"But she's going to have a baby."

"Oh," Kelly says. "You're worried about that?"

I nod.

"Well, it's OK to be worried. Most kids would be. Biological or adopted or foster or whatever—most kids are worried
when there's a new baby."

"They are?" I say.

Kelly nods. "Sometimes kids are upset once the new baby is
born too. They might get jealous when it gets a lot of attention

and all the adults around talk about how cute it is or something like that. They might get sad when the baby gets praise for stuff the big kids know how to do really well."

"Like what?" I ask.

Kelly smiles. "Like going on the toilet."

I laugh with her. I don't need any praise for going to the bathroom, thank you. I don't think I'll get jealous of that. But I can see what she means.

"But the good news is that I already know you'll be great at it, Flora. You'll be an above average big sister," Kelly says.

"Why?" I ask.

"Well, think about right now. Are you upset your mom isn't with you right now?"

"No," I say. "Julian needs her."

"Exactly," Kelly says. "You're already a great sister to Julian. And now there will be three of you. It'll be hard sometimes but ultimately love grows if you try even a little bit."

Love divides. That's what Elena said. Now we'll be down to 33.3 percent of Person's love, or less if you count Elena.

But what if love grew instead? What if the baby made us more real instead of less real?

I think about that for a second. I take a bite of my french fry.

I look across the table and see that Julian only ate half of his food. At that moment, the waiter comes over to the table and says, "The other lady took care of you guys already. You're good to go."

But I know Julian will want the rest of his food. And I also know this restaurant is not going to let him back in here after he messed up the whole place.

"I'd like a doggy bag, please," I say. My own plate only has three fries and the edge of my bagel. But I stare at the waiter until he shrugs and brings me the doggy bag.

"I have a sister too, now," I tell Kelly as I'm packing up Julian's food. "I'm not as good to her as I am to Julian. It's not . . . easy. Julian is my family."

"Hm," Kelly says. "I'd say your sister is your family too," she says.

"I know," I say. But I think she knows what I mean. She knew me when Julian was all I had. It's hard to give that up. It's hard to give other people like Person and Dad and Elena the same title I give Julian. It's hard to trust them the way I trust him.

We gather our things and walk outside. Person and Julian are leaning on the car, watching the clouds. I remember now that this was her trick to calm him down when he used to freak out like that when we first moved into her house. On the day he killed Person's goldfish, I think we spent four straight hours in the park watching the clouds, even though it was November and chilly.

"We watch the clouds, we all calm down. And we do it together, because we're a family." That's what Person said.

It always amazed me that she wanted to spend time by our sides, even when we'd just messed up. Will that keep going? Even with a baby crying?

Now they lean against Person's car with their noses in the sky. I see where the tears made dark lines on Julian's cheeks but he's not crying anymore.

I walk up to them. "I brought you the rest of your lunch," I say.

He lets out a breath so long it's like he wasn't breathing the whole time he was looking at the clouds. "Thank you," he says.

Then he drops to the parking lot, crisscross-applesauce, and starts eating the food from the bag. And I realize that we're sharing a suitcase and I haven't found any sandwich crusts or leftover french fries or even so much as a ketchup packet. He hasn't been hiding food in his clothes here. He's been putting it all in his stomach.

He's been keeping that promise to Person.

He must have been so scared when he realized he left without his lunch.

"Seems like things are better out here," Kelly says. "You OK, Julian?"

Julian looks up but his mouth is stuffed so he just nods.

"Things always get better once they get worse again, right, J?" Person says. "But no matter what, we stay together. No matter what, I'm your mom."

Person is acting like she's talking to Julian. She rubs the top of his head. But she's looking right at me.

"We love Margie and Vanessa but I'm your mom. That's

the way it is forever now. And if that gets confusing, it's OK. But you just come and talk to me about it."

I nod. Julian keeps eating.

He seems to be thinking only about his bacon but I know it's more than that. Food is what reminds him he's alive. It's what reminds him he'll be here tomorrow. It's what makes him know he counts.

"So, tomorrow . . . ," Kelly says to Person. "It's going to be rough. I became the caseworker when the kids were at this placement . . . and . . . there's a reason I moved them from her. Remember . . . just because remembering something is painful doesn't mean it's damaging."

Person nods.

"Trauma is weird like that. It's worse for your brain and your future if you don't remember it."

"I think I've proven that I understand that," Person says. Then she shakes her head. "I'm sorry. I'm so sorry. I'm having so much trouble not being mad at you even though I know you're just . . . part of it."

"Part of what?" Kelly asks.

"The system," Person says. "Part of the system that screwed over my kids."

Kelly shakes her head. "The system hurt me too," she says. "I loved these kids. I tried to do any small thing for them. I thought I did one. One thing. And they didn't even get their Lifebooks, they didn't even let me do that one thing . . . but look, Emily. You got them. They're your kids now. No more system." Then Kelly leans in so close to Person I'm sure I'm not supposed to hear the last part. "Don't forget to tell them how happy you are about that."

Person looks startled. Kelly turns to leave and I almost expect Julian to call out and ask her to come to his birthday party, but he's worn-out and focused on his food.

So instead it's me. I'm my own voice. "Kelly?" I say. She turns back to face me. "Did you know us since the beginning?"

I didn't put my words together. I'm not sure she's going to understand. But she shakes her head. "I'm sorry, Flora. I met you when you were three and Julian was two. I don't know what happened before that. I don't know anything about your bios. Maybe Jeannie can help with that? I hope so."

We don't have bios.

"Jeannie?" I say.

Kelly nods. "That's who you're going to see tomorrow."

"Jeannie," I say again. There's something familiar about the word on my tongue. Even just the name scares me.

"That's another point for us," I say on the ride back to the hotel. "Even Kelly doesn't know that we were babies."

"Yes," Person says. "She knows you were babies because you're people. All people were babies."

"Not us," Julian says.

Person turns to look at us. She's at a stoplight.

"Well, I don't mind," she says. "You can have all the points you want because I already won."

"Huh?" I say. "No you didn't. We didn't see one baby picture. We didn't meet one person who knew us when we were born, which is because we weren't."

Person smiles. "Look, guys, I'm sorry. I owe you an apology."

"No you don't," I say. Because I feel like we're the ones who owe Person the apology. We're the ones who dragged her on this trip.

"I do," she says. "I've been messing up a big thing."

"No you haven't," I say quickly. Because Person doesn't mess up.

"I have," Person says. "I've been trying to be your mother so well that I mother you right out of everything else that happened to you. I've been trying to erase everything that happened before you had a mother. And I realize now that was never going to work, and it wasn't fair to you. It's just, I love you so much. I didn't want to have to share it."

"Share it?" Julian says.

"I've been so confused about Margie and Vanessa because they loved you so much too. It seems like they loved you like I did. And most moms don't have to share that bond." Person takes a breath. "But this isn't about me. It's about me loving you exactly the way you are, all of your days before and all of your days in the future."

We don't say anything for a minute. Person looks at the windshield, then turns back and looks at us again. "It doesn't matter how many points you get about any of your theories because I already won. I get to be your mom.

That's the best kind of winning."

Julian looks at me with his eyebrows raised. And I know what he's thinking because I'm thinking it too.

The best kind of winning is when you get to be a mom to a little boy who throws water glasses across a restaurant? To a little girl whose words get stuck all the time? Who punches her sister? Who hides all the food in his closet? Who barely passes fourth grade and is sad when she does? Who kills your goldfish?

But Person looks like she means it.

"You're a weird mom," Julian says.

"The weirdest," I agree.

And Person laughs.

Then I remember what's about to happen. If she loves us when we're not talking and throwing things and punching people, she is definitely going to love us when we get back to the hotel.

Person stands frozen in the doorway. Dad and Elena are already in there, smiling like they have the most delicious secret in the world.

"Surprise," Elena says simply.

"How did you . . . what did . . . what?" I've never heard Person's words get stuck before. I pat her on the back and it's enough to wake her up. She goes rushing at Dad and Julian and I rush in right behind her. We're all hugging Dad.

Elena stands a few feet away, watching. Then Julian breaks

the hug to wave her over. "Come on, Elena," he says.

"What happened?" Person asks. Her voice is almost stuck in the hug with her mouth pressed into Dad's chest. But her words aren't stuck anymore.

Dad says, "Flora. She called us."

Person pulls out of the hug and puts a hand on my right shoulder and Elena's left shoulder.

"Flora?" she says. "You apologized?"

My face turns pink as soon as she asks. I realize that no, I didn't.

I should do it now, I know. I punched Elena and no matter what you have to apologize when you hit someone unless that someone also hit you and then it was self-defense. I know I need to apologize. But that word, *sorry*, is so huge and sticky it'll never get out of my lungs.

And maybe I'm still not exactly sorry. Maybe punching Elena felt a little like self-defense because at that moment she was hurting Julian with all that laughing and laughing sometimes hurts worse than hitting.

And I sometimes forget where Julian ends and where I begin.

And maybe that's why it's so scary when I can't tell whether Julian is happy or whether he's faking happy. Maybe it's not because faking happy always ends in explosions. I can handle the explosions. I've been living with them my whole life. Maybe the fake-happy is scary because I can't tell. Because that means we're separate.

Twenty-Three
FAMILIES TEACH THE MOST IMPORTANT LESSONS

WE QUICK-QUICK CHANGE INTO OUR BATHING suits and slather on the sunblock that Person always makes us wear even though she's the only one who gets sunburned. Then we all spend the day on the beach. Julian and I build a sandcastle. Elena and I jump waves. Person and Elena and I go for a walk. Dad and Julian and Elena play catch. We all go swimming.

I let it happen in all the groups. Five. Four. Three. Two. One. Sometimes Julian and I are together, and sometimes we're not. But we're still family even with all these other people between us.

I think that's what I needed to do to make Person happy. I needed to let her between us sometimes.

I notice strangers on the beach looking at us with these faint half smiles.

I feel a weird sense of something.

Of normal-ness.

But we are separate. I want to grow up and be like Person with my own family where Julian is just an uncle. I want to go to high school in a few years and leave Julian back at St. Peter's. I want to be my own person with a brother instead of someone who can't find her edges.

And all of these reasons are why *sorry* gets stuck in my throat. Or maybe somewhere far away. All of these reasons are why *sorry* gets stuck and I can't find it.

But Elena says, "She did better."

Person smiles at her. "What does that mean?" Person asks.

"She didn't say I'm sorry," Elena says. "She . . . She said 'divorce stinks.'"

And then Elena is in Person's arms, folded over her belly so that she can be squeezed in the tightest hug ever. And I'm not even jealous because that's my sister. If my mother can share me with Margie and Vanessa and Gloria and Ms. K and Dad and Kelly, I should be able to share my mother with my sister. And the new baby.

Normal family.

People look at us and think: family.

And they're right.

After the beach we go out for crabs again. Elena and Dad have never eaten them, so Julian and I help Person teach them how. Once everyone has the hang of it, the crabs do their magic again and the words start flowing out of Julian and me like someone turned a faucet.

We tell Elena and Dad about Gloria who loved us but loved too many children at once. We tell them about Marta who wanted to love us but only if we were perfect, and tried to separate us when we weren't. And we tell them about Margie and Vanessa and Kelly who loved us completely.

"There's a theory about people," Person says. "In order to be healthy, we need to live with each other, you know? We need to live in community."

"Or else we get lonely," Julian says.

"Yup," Person says. "And did you know that being lonely can actually affect your body? Your health?"

"It can?" Elena asks.

"It can," Person says. "And that's why it's so dangerous for babies and little kids who don't have parents. If no one teaches them how to attach, they can grow up to be very unhealthy."

"But it's not like tying a shoe," I say.

"Yeah," says Elena. "It's not like someone had to teach me how to hang out with other people. How to like them."

I look at Elena. Is it possible that she just interpreted for me like Julian always does?

"Actually," Person says. "Your dad and mom did a great job teaching you how to attach. All of that time they spent with you that you don't remember, that's how you learned. When they fed you from a bottle, they looked into your eyes. When you cried, they came to see what you wanted. When you hurt yourself, they hugged you and kissed your boo-boo."

"That's what parents do," Elena says, shrugging.

And I think: but I was never a baby and I had no first parents. Person didn't do those things for me.

"You're right," Person says. "It's the most important job in the universe and yet everyone can do it: look in someone's eyes, kiss a boo-boo. It's not easy, but it's doable. Isn't that amazing?"

If Person had done those things for me, would I believe in Forever?

I'm sure she wants to have done those things for me. I've never been so sure of anything else in my life.

"So I am who I am just because of my parents?" Elena asks.

Person shakes her head. "No, no," she says. "You're Elena because you're you. All the way. I'm saying . . . well, think for a second about the people you love, OK?"

Elena closes her eyes. I realize I've never heard her talk to Person like this. This is the way Person talks to Julian and me, sometimes. Or a lot. But I don't think I've ever heard Person talk to Elena like this.

I hope Person is on the list she's thinking of.

I hope I am too.

"OK," Elena says.

"What I'm saying is that your ability to love them isn't instinct. It's a skill. It's the first skill you learn, when you are tiny, before you can talk or walk or anything. And for you, Elena, it's your parents who taught you."

She nods. "That makes sense."

Person turns from her to Julian and me.

"We all love you guys so much. I think Margie and Vanessa did some of that work for you. But I want to know who did it when you were smaller. That's why we are down here. You guys love each other; you love me; you love Dad and Elena."

We nod.

I do love Person. I do believe in her. Maybe I can learn to believe in forever just by being around her more and more.

"I had to work really hard at this. Because sometimes it makes me sad that I wasn't the person who looked in your eyes when you got a bottle and kissed your boo-boos. Sometimes I'm sad I wasn't there to potty train you and teach you how to swim. But I see you guys now and you're the best people I know. So, I want to shake the hand of all the people who gave you those skills. Tomorrow is the next piece of the puzzle. Even if it is rough, like Kelly said it might be. And I'm hoping Jeannie can tell us who came before her. Maybe she can finally lead us back to your bio mom."

"I want to go!" Elena says. She looks at Dad. "Please?"

Person looks nervous but Dad speaks firmly, more firmly
than I've ever heard. "Absolutely. We're a family. We'll all go."

After dinner, I take a deep breath and ask Person if we can go
for a walk on the beach, just my mom and me. I have something big to ask her. I'm nervous. And she can tell.

But we're having this Serious Talk the way I want to. With
our eyes on the waves. With the air moving around our faces.
So I don't have to look at her when I say it. "You said Margie
and Vanessa loved me like only a mother can," I say.

"I think they did," Person says.

"And you said sometimes that makes you sad. That we had
all these mothers. Not just Margie and Vanessa but Gloria
and Marta and I guess Jeannie too."

"It shouldn't make me sad, Flora," Person says. "I don't
want you to worry about that, OK?"

I dig my toe into the sand and Person stops next to me. We
both watch my toe.

"I wanted to tell you that . . . to me . . . you're different."

Person laughs but I'm not making a joke or being cute.

"I might not always believe you all the way. But I know
you're different from the other mommies. I've known from
the start. Do you want to know how I know that I know?"

I risk it and look in her face.

"Sure," she says.

"Inside my head I don't even call you 'Mom.' I've just . . .
I've used that word too much."

Person's eyebrows lower and I see her hand twitch. I'm afraid right now. Afraid she won't see this as a good thing. But also I believe in her. I believe in Person. And I believe in me.

"What do you call me?" she asks.

I smile. "I call you my person."

And then tears come to her eyes and she leans over and hugs me.

"You got that right, Flora," Person says. "*Mom* is just a word. I don't mind what you call me. But you got it right. I'm your person. One hundred percent."

That night, Person and Dad sleep in the hotel room that Dad booked when he came this afternoon. It's connected to our original hotel room by a door, which they leave open so I can hear Dad snoring. Elena sleeps in the bed Person had been in. Julian and I stay put.

It's late at night and I don't think I've closed my eyes once. We had such a good day. I feel so proud of myself for doing something nice for Person and for forgiving Elena and for being forgiven by Elena and for being a part of such a normal family that people gave us half smiles on the beach.

But tomorrow is coming.

"Hey," I whisper as quietly as I can.

Julian turns over and looks at me. It turns out he's lying there awake too.

"Are you nervous about tomorrow?" he asks.

I nod.

"Me too," he says.

"Do you remember Jeannie?" I ask.

Julian shakes his head against his pillow. "I don't remember her . . . but . . . it has to be the white house."

"Yeah," I say. "It's the end."

What is Person going to do when she really finds out we were never born? Or . . . what am I going to feel if it turns out Person is right, there was some first mom, and then she left us and disappeared?

"Team?" Julian says.

"Team," I say.

I think that's the end of the conversation, but after a minute he says, "Hey, Florey?"

"Yeah?" I say.

"Let's try to believe in forever tomorrow. Even if it's really bad."

It's exactly what I've been thinking. "OK," I say.

"Remember Mom said just two weeks? We've been trying, trusting her for two weeks, haven't we?" Julian says.

"Mostly," I say. "I . . . I've messed up a little. I've . . . wondered."

"Me too," Julian says. "But tomorrow, it'll only be a few hours. Let's trust. Let's believe."

"Yeah," I say.

"That means I won't pretend I'm happy if Mom is making me worried or sad. I'll tell her my real feelings. Or I'll do my best."

"OK," I say.

"And that means you can't lose your words," Julian says. "You have to trust Mom and me and Dad enough to keep talking."

I take a deep breath. "I'll try," I say. "I'll really, really try."

Twenty-Four
FAMILIES GET ANGRY

JULIAN AND I HOLD HANDS IN the back of the car while Person drives toward this next house. I'm sitting in the middle of the backseat and Elena is leaning just a little bit into my shoulder. We're all too quiet.

The house is tan and on the corner of the street. It has a little yard like Gloria's house but there aren't any toys in it. It's the biggest house we've seen, besides Marta's mansion, but it's also quiet. Almost creepy quiet.

"Oh, OK, come in," Jeannie says when she opens the door. "They told me you'd be coming, but you'll have to understand that we're in the middle of lunchtime here and I'm going to have to go about my day. I have seven at the moment."

Jeannie is tiny, white with graying black hair. She's a foot shorter than Person and looks a little older but not too old. When she talks her voice clips off each word almost before she's finished saying it.

The house smells like floor polish and Windex. The smell makes my heart race in a way that's not quite remembering but almost. Dad, Elena, and Person take off following Jeannie down the dark hallway but Julian and I stay frozen, until Person turns around and takes our hands.

We're in a white hallway. In front of us we see a white kitchen with a tiny table.

Don't lose your voice, Flora.

"This is it," I whisper to Person and Julian.

"This is the white house," Julian says.

My hand shakes in Person's. She says, "Remember the elephant, right?" We nod. Then we walk down the hallway, walk into our past, armed by our mother.

"Seven?" Dad is saying in the kitchen. "You have seven right now? Children?"

"Yes," Jeannie says.

"You must be busy," Dad says with a smile that's fake like Julian's. But I don't really mind it because the smell and the quiet make this house seem like one where it's not safe to be honest.

There's a kid-sized table with plastic chairs in all different colors in the corner. Julian points at it with huge eyes. This is it. This is so it.

It's like being a dream, except having your family with you and they're really here so they're all going to remember it.

Five kids sit around the mini-table. Two smaller ones sit in high chairs. No one makes a sound. The five kids have their hands folded together and they stare at the tops of their fingers like they're praying. The two in the high chairs are slumped over and staring straight ahead, into space. They drool a little.

They're babies.

Someone should be looking them in the eyes, I think. Looking babies in the eyes is the most important work that isn't easy but that everyone can do.

"Clean hands!" Jeannie says. It's not a shout but it is a command. All the little kids around the table raise their hands in the air and Jeannie circles them, inspecting each one. She says "Um-hmm" ten times, one for each hand.

"Alright, lunchtime," Jeannie says. She picks up a Tupperware from the counter and each of the five children holds out two cupped hands. As Jeannie comes behind each child, he or she separates his or her hands, so that a dollop of cooked carrots falls onto his or her plate.

"Measure," Jeannie says once she's gotten to all five plates.

One of the babies starts to cry. Person and Dad look at him. Jeannie does not.

The five children place their cupped hands over their carrots. Each pile fits perfectly into their two hands.

"Eat," Jeannie says.

They pick up forks and start to eat. They're painfully silent. The only noise in the room is the crying baby.

My family is standing in a clump in the doorway, watching.

This is not what I remember. I remember chaos. I remember noise. I remember crowds.

This is worse.

As the kids eat the carrots, Jeannie goes to the sink and starts mixing powder into water in baby bottles. I breathe a sigh of relief. The crying baby will get to eat.

The other baby starts to cry.

Jeannie is careful as she measures just the right amount of formula. She's not saying anything to any of the kids or babies. The kids are not saying anything to each other.

"Is carrots their whole lunch?" Person asks.

Elena is tugging on our father's arm and whispering "Dad." He's trying to shush her.

Jeannie turns and almost seems startled to see us still standing there in the doorway. "Of course not," she says.

And that's it. She stops talking.

I wonder if her words get stuck. She looks too strong, too in control for stuck-words like mine.

Jeannie fastens the two bottles into something that almost looks like a wire coat hanger. Then she shoves it up between the two babies.

"They can hold their bottles now, but they choose not to," Jeannie says to us. One of the babies takes his bottle. He puts his hands and mouth on it where it hangs in the wire-thing. The other begins to cry.

"Dad. Dad! Why isn't anyone looking into their eyes?"

Elena says, being my voice again. Julian can't be my voice because he's shaking like I am. He's in this weird dream with me.

His smile is crazy. My voice is gone. We both broke our promises but I know we'll forgive each other.

"Sixty seconds to finish your carrots if you'd like mac and cheese," Jeannie says to the kids at the table.

I watch as the oldest-looking boy takes his last bite of carrots and then holds his two hands in the air. Slowly the other kids follow. They look too young to know what "sixty seconds" means. Jeannie must have taught them that. Somehow. For some reason.

Every single kid eats all of his or her cooked carrots. There's something scary about that too. Cooked carrots are slimy and mushy and gross. Most kids hate them. Definitely at least one of these kids doesn't like them. But they're all gone.

We watch as Jeannie does the same thing with the mac and cheese, measuring each dollop to the size of the kid's two cupped hands.

The other baby has figured out how to drink from the bottle.

I want to step out from behind Person's leg and stand in front of the baby while she sucks at it. I want to look her in the eyes.

Jeannie finally looks at us. "I thought Kelly said there were two children?"

"Oh!" Person says. She sounds surprised to be addressed.

"Yes. Of course. Flora and Julian. Castillo was their name."

She shoves us forward and Jeannie looks us up and down. "Well, they've found a family. That's nice."

"I'm their sister," Elena offers.

Jeannie nods.

"Do you have any pictures of them? Or any information?" Person asks the question it seems like she came to ask each mom.

Mom. This person was my mom. It's hard to believe. She seems more like a doctor. More like a bus driver.

"Yes," Jeannie says. And we all look at each other, surprised. It doesn't even seem like she remembers us. How would she have pictures? "I'll get them for you after the kids' lunch."

"OK," Person says. Then it seems like her lung filters fail. "What happens after lunch?" She looks concerned and happy at once. I didn't know that was possible.

"Quiet time," Jeannie says. "The younger ones nap. The older ones read books or play quietly in their rooms."

"Oh," Person says. Then, "What happens after quiet time?"

"Dinner," Jeannie says, her voice thin. She's losing patience with Person.

"And then bedtime?" Person asks. Her voice is also thin. I look at her. I agree with her. It's bad for kids to be quiet all day all through lunch and dinner and bedtime and in-between. But I want her to stop asking. I don't want Jeannie to get too impatient with her and kick us out before we see the pictures. I don't want to see Person's face when she realizes this is it, this is the end. But I do want to see the oldest picture of the smallest me.

I think I'll be naked in it. I won't have any clothes because where would I get them? Maybe I'll be covered in sand or water or maybe I'll be just covered in dirt. I'll look sad and lonely. I won't know how to look at the camera because no one will have taught me how to love yet. Person will be sad when she see this, when she realizes this white house really is our beginning.

But I need to see it anyway.

The biggest kid holds his hands up. Jeannie takes his plate.

One dollop of cooked carrots. One dollop of mac and cheese. That doesn't seem like enough lunch for that kid. He looks around six years old.

"That's it?" Person says. "That's his lunch?"

Jeannie looks right at her. "I'm an emergency home," she says. "I keep children when the state cannot find anywhere else. I must maintain a clear structure or else I would not be able to handle it."

"OK . . . ," Person says. "But . . . was that enough food?"

No. It wasn't. I only barely passed the fourth grade and even I know that. But Person is asking it like a question because she doesn't want Jeannie to be mad at us and then to not show us our baby pictures. That's how much Person believes we were born.

I see the boy lace his hands together in front of his chest and stare at them like he's praying again. I wonder if he's praying for Jeannie to listen to Person, if he's praying for more food.

Jeannie looks right at Person from where she's in the middle of clearing a girl's plate. "It's exactly the correct amount of food. I follow all of the state's guidelines to a tee, including nutrition plans, and I'll have you know that the state and the caseworkers love me. I rarely have children for more than thirty days. I'm an emergency placement," she repeats, as if that's the important part and not the fact that this little boy has to exist on a tiny bit of carrots and mac and cheese until dinner. "It's important that I keep to a structure. It's good for the children to learn there are limits."

"Limits?" Dad says. "*These* kids? You think they don't understand limits? Everything in their life is limited. Their *family* is limited."

"My kids were not with you for thirty days," Person says. "They were with you for a long time, we think."

But then one of the children at the table makes a squeak and Person looks at Dad like she just remembered that they aren't carrot-and-mac-and-cheese-eating robots and they can hear her.

Elena doesn't realize that. "He's hungry!" she says. "They're still hungry!"

The oldest boy looks scared enough to hide under the table. I look at Dad to try to make him make Elena be quiet.

Elena doesn't understand that this isn't a safe house.

Elena has never been in a not-safe house.

"My brother. He's still hungry. He was here when he was like three and now he's almost ten and still! He's still hungry because of you."

She's crying a little. For Julian.

Her voice is quiet. I hope it doesn't get these kids in trouble, the way our sister cried for us. I hope the next time I want to punch her, I can look at her and remember that she cried for us.

"And Flora, my sister . . . she's still lonely. It was years ago and they're still lonely and tired and hungry . . . all you had to do was look them in the eyes . . ."

She doesn't think we're lucky anymore.

Jeannie barely reacts. She says, "If you all would like to take a seat on the couch in the next room, I will get you the pictures in a few minutes."

Person looks at us. "I think maybe Elena should go see the elephant. Does anyone else need to see an elephant?"

Julian and I shake our heads. I've never been so uncomfortable, but I know I need to be here. I need to be here when Person finds out this is really the end. I need to see the look in her eyes at that moment. I need to know if it's love.

Dad must know what "elephant" means because he tucks Elena under his arm and goes out the front door while we follow Jeannie into the living room. It's also white. We sit on the white couch: me, Person, Julian.

Jeannie disappears to finish up lunch and Julian and I shake under Person's arms. We don't say anything.

"This is not a family," Jeannie says as she comes through the door after a few minutes. "This is a foster house. I do things differently. I give children warm meals and a warm bed and that's what the state has asked me to do."

Person says, "We'll just take the pictures and the information and get out of your hair."

Jeannie goes to a set of white binders she has on a shelf on the wall. "Castillo you said, correct?"

"Yes," Person says through gritted teeth.

Jeannie pulls one of the binders down. "I take a picture the day a child arrives and the day they leave," she explains. "I keep track of any information they came in with. First names again?" she asks.

This was our mom for a while. We don't even know how long. But she doesn't remember our names.

"Flora and Julian," Person says. I can tell her lung filters are working overtime keeping everything else she wants to say down.

Jeannie flips open to a page and I see my brother as a toddler. I totally remember him like this: round and roly-poly with dimples in his cheeks and elbows. He's not naked or covered in sand or anything like I pictured. He's in a blue T-shirt. He's looking at the camera.

How?

Person snaps a picture of the picture with her phone and Jeannie turns the page.

"You're right," she says. "He was with me for quite some

time. Eleven months."

The picture on the next page is still a toddler, but he's skinny. His arms hang like ropes. His dimples are gone. His hair is even thinner. He doesn't smile.

How can Jeannie look at these pictures and not see how she broke him? She broke my brother.

I hate her as much as Person does. I wish we could kick her and then leave.

I wish we didn't need stuff from her.

Person takes a picture of the picture. She puts her arm around Julian and pulls him close. But she doesn't say anything.

And then I see it, in the fist of that littler toddler, the picture from when we first came to Jeannie's, is a ball.

"Did you give him that ball?" I ask.

It's red. Rubber. The kind that bounces.

"I'm not in the practice of handing out toys when children arrive. He must have come in with it."

He came with a ball? Then he came from somewhere. From someone. From someone who had a ball and a blue T-shirt.

"Do you know where they were before here?" Person asks Jeannie.

Jeannie flips pages. "Let me see," she says. "Ah!"

My heart speeds up. I can almost feel Person's heart and Julian's heart through my shoulders. We all lean a little forward on the couch.

"Well, it says here that they were dropped off in the middle

of the night. Neglect."

Jeannie looks up at Person like that's the answer.

"And?" Person says.

"I don't know anything else. It was a case of neglect, which means wherever they were before, they were not getting proper care in terms of food or supervision or some such."

"I know what neglect means," Person says. I can feel her trying not to shout.

Don't get us kicked out before we see my pictures, Person. Please.

"But didn't they come with a history? Didn't you have any details on the case?"

Jeannie shakes her head at Person. "It was seven years ago," she says. "All I have written is that the state failed to ever find the previous caretakers."

I know what that means. It's simple. It means no first mother.

I look at Person. Now is the moment. Does she need us to be born? Will she be OK now that she knows we aren't?

But she still seems unconvinced.

"You didn't document anything?" Person asks. She sounds close to tears. I reach up. I just want to see my picture. It's the oldest picture of the youngest me I'll ever see.

"I document everything." Jeannie says. "I cannot document what I am not told."

"Who took them here? Where did they come from?"

"All it says here," Jeannie says, getting louder, "is that a government official dropped them off on August second, at three a.m. The next day I was told I would receive details via a phone call. The call said that there was no information on the previous caretaker and I would be informed when there was. I was not informed of anything for eleven months. Then the children were re-homed. At this time, I was told that the caseworkers had been looking for a birth family, but that they were missing. You can see that I took the children to all of their dental and doctor appointments as scheduled."

Person shoves those pages of the binder away from her face.

She's angry. She's angry there was no first family.

But if there was no first family, how did Julian get that ball?

"That's it?" Person says. "That's *it?*"

"But we didn't *start* here?" Julian says.

Jeannie looks at him like he's insane. "What?" she asks. "You weren't born here. I'm not your mother, of course."

"I didn't say born," Julian says. "I said we didn't—"

Jeannie cuts him off. "You came in the middle of the night because the state needed someone to take care of you. Since it was the middle of the night, I assume you came from your birth mother, but I don't know."

You can't assume birth if you don't know.

I look at Julian. He's not smiling. I make myself talk.

"Do you have that ball still? The red rubber one?" I ask.

Jeannie shakes her head like I'm ridiculous.

"The next foster family would have gotten more information because they would be a long-term placement. I'm just an emergency placement."

"The next parents didn't know anything," Person says.

Jeannie shrugs. "People disappear. Happens more than you realize." She says this a little more gently though.

Then she hands me the binder.

Before I look at the picture, I list what I know: someone dropped me off here in the middle of the night. I was with Julian.

The only question is what happened before. Was it the sea or the TV or the horizon or the dogs or the crabs? The picture has to tell me. It's the only way I'll ever know.

Then I see myself at three years old. I'm in a pink dress and white shoes. Someone dressed me nicely. I even have white lacy socks on. I'm hugging the neck of a doll someone gave me. I'm smiling and looking right at the camera, like looking right into someone's eyes.

Someone gave me a pink dress and white socks and a doll. Someone gave Julian a ball.

There was a someone. A someone who cared enough about us to give us a doll and a ball.

Someone taught us to hug and to look at cameras.

Person was right. There was something before. The white house was not the beginning.

I decide not to look at the next picture, the one after eleven

months in this awful white house. I decide to keep that picture of myself in a pink dress with a baby doll in my brain
forever.

There was someone before. There was someone at the
beginning.

When we get back to the car, Elena has calmed down. Julian
looks at me and says, "I told you there was a mom who only
let us eat what fit into our hands."

I stare at him. He did tell me that. But I can't confirm it
because my words are so stuck. My words are more stuck
than they've ever been since I was wearing that pink dress,
maybe.

I shrug.

He gives me a crazy smile and shrugs back.

I'm sad and happy. I'm angry for the new kids there and
for little Julian and little Flora. I'm lucky that Person found
us eventually. I'm sad that she didn't find us here while we
were in a pink dress and a blue shirt before any of the bad
stuff happened. I'm happy that someone taught me to look at
cameras and someone gave me lacy socks and a doll. I'm sad
that I don't have the doll anymore. I'm sad that I might never
find it or the person who gave it to me.

I can't talk with all of this other stuff going on in my lungs.

My words are stuck. I failed Julian. But he's smiling like a
crazy person even though we're both sad and I'm not mad at
him about that this time.

We have different reactions to bad news. We're different.

Person turns to us. She has tears in her eyes. She's sadder than Julian and me. She's learning and we're remembering what we already knew, somewhere deep inside ourselves. Elena seems sadder than us. Dad seems sadder than us.

"We can keep going," Person says.

"Huh?" Julian says. "No. This was the white house."

Person sighs. "I know," she says. "But it wasn't the beginning. We can keep searching for your birth family. We can look at birth records. Hospital records. Police records. We can go to the police tomorrow and see if a detective—"

Person cuts herself off when she sees me shaking my head.

"We're done," Julian says.

I nod.

"I want to give you all of the information you need," Person says. "I so wanted to find you guys your beginning."

I try to say it's OK. Julian says, "It's OK, Mom."

"But listen," Person says. "You were born. You had a birth mom. You had someone who loved you. I know you did because that's the only way you came through eleven months with that awful woman still loving each other at the end of it. Someone taught you how to do that before you were dropped off here. You were born. You were babies. You didn't come from the sky or the sea or the sand. You came from a mom who loved you but who couldn't take care of you like you deserve, like I'm trying to. Because the world wasn't fair to you guys and it probably wasn't fair to her either. I thought we'd find out who she was, where she was. I thought we'd find a baby picture or an old address but . . . I don't know what to do. I . . . I don't know what to do except ask you to trust me. To believe me. About this."

I look at Person. And I nod.

She shakes her head like she can't believe me. "Really?" she asks.

I nod again.

I was born. We were born. We had a first family.

"Really?" she asks again.

Julian says, "Yeah . . ." He looks at me. "You think so, Flora? We were born after all."

I nod. I think so.

Person thinks I needed to see a baby picture to believe that. But I think a pink dress and white lacy socks and a doll might be enough proof.

Julian puts his head on my shoulder and I realize I have even better proof than a pink dress: a brother who has always loved me, a brother who I've always loved. A brother who learned to love and the love inside of me for him that I must have learned from someone.

"It's OK your words are stuck, Florey," Julian says through the crazy, wrinkly smile. "They'll come back eventually. We have until forever, I guess."

I hug him. I nod.

Person starts weeping like she did when I passed the fourth grade and Elena puts her arms around Julian and me and we freeze like that until Person is done.

"Let's go home," Julian says. "All the way home. That's enough, for now. Right, Flora?"

I nod. It's enough.

Person chuckles. "Sounds good to me," she says. Dad reaches out and holds her hand. And the five of us leave the white house for the last, last time.

Oops.

I mean six.

The six of us leave the white house for the last, last time.

My words will come back, I know it. They'll come back smoother and faster now that I have Person and Dad and Elena and baby and Margie and Vanessa and Kelly and Ms. K and Dr. Fredrick and all the other people.

Now that I've let Julian be just my brother, outside my edges, I have more edges to share with other people and other people love my words.

My words will come back and get stuck again and come back and get stuck again. They'll get stuck when the baby comes. They'll get stuck when Meredith calls us dysfunctional again or when Elena gets jealous again. They'll get stuck when I have to go to fifth grade without Ms. K or when I finally get invited to my first birthday party.

But they'll come back.

With my family, my words will always come back.

THEORY #0

I come from the place where the words get stuck.

My brother comes from the hiding spots in his closet.

We were maybe born like the rest of you. Born to a woman who gave us things like red rubber balls and pink dresses.

But we come from the hidden corners. The dark spots in lungs or closets where secrets get lodged, the kind of secrets that take years to wiggle loose.

We come from the places where things get stuck and hidden and lost.

But Person, and people, love us anyway.

ACKNOWLEDGMENTS

Thanks from the bottom of my heart goes out to:

Karen Chaplin, for your brilliant insights, unbridled encouragement, and startling confidence in both me and Flora.

Kate McKean, for your advocating, your last-minute pep-talks, and your last-minute readings on this one.

Erin Fitzsimmons, for this beautiful, breathtaking cover that I know Flora would stare at for hours if she could.

Everyone at Harper—school and library, publicity and marketing, and everyone else—for your continued commitment and enthusiasm!

Jessica Verdi, Corey Ann Haydu, Alyson Gerber, and Amy Ewing, for your support, brilliant thoughts . . . and friendship.

Beth Carter, Bill Carter, Dan Carter, all the Larssons, the Carter-fam, and the Keating-fam, for your love and support.

All of my friends. I keep trying to list you but there're too many, which makes me especially blessed. Know that I appreciate your support more than I could ever say.

My writing communities—The New School, The Lucky

13s, The Class of 2K13, Binders—and the wonderful friends, teachers, and mentors I've met through them, especially David Levithan, Patricia McCormick, Leila Sales, Mary G. Thompson, Kathryn Holms, Alison Cherry, Lindsay Ribar, Mindy Raff, Dahlia Adler, Caron Levis . . . I could go on. . . .

Greg. For everything.